TROPICAL DARKNESS

TROPICAL DARKNESS

David McLaurin

For Brett,

who hates sharks,

with every best wish,

Alexander David McLaurin

Chelsea 27. 12. 96.

Duckworth

To Cristina Odone,
sometime Editor of the
Catholic Herald
with fondest love

First published in 1996 by
Gerald Duckworth & Co. Ltd.
The Old Piano Factory
48 Hoxton Square, London N1 6PB
Tel: 0171 729 5986
Fax: 0171 729 0015

A catalogue record for this book is available
from the British Library

ISBN 0 7156 2735 X

Typeset by Ray Davies
Printed in Great Britain by
Redwood Books Ltd, Trowbridge

I

'Not a pleasure boat,' said Caroline.

They had had a pleasure boat in Tobago, when he had been a child; he remembered being dragged on to it, kicking and screaming in the strong brown arms of his nurse, while his mother watched. And off they would row, the frail craft taking them further away from the beach and surely providing no protection from sharks, while his mother diminished in the distance, an indifferent figure, dressed in white, her face obscured by cigarette smoke. That pleasure boat – it was odd how phrases jumped generations and jogged the memory – that horrid little boat had never given him a moment's enjoyment.

'There are sharks in the Anegada Passage,' he said, remembering his oldest fear once more.

'There are sharks everywhere,' said Artemis, his younger daughter.

'It has got nothing to do with sharks,' said Caroline. 'Nothing at all,' she repeated, wishing she could get her father and sister to stick to the point, something they hardly ever seemed to want to do or even to be capable of doing. 'It's just that the *Warspite* isn't a pleasure boat. There isn't an inch of shade on deck, and there are no loos.'

'You're always thinking of things like loos,' said Artemis.

'Well, someone has to,' replied Caroline. 'Loos are necessary. It takes six hours there and the same back. And when you get there there is nothing much to see – just a rock. Judy Blomberg told me all about it; the Canon has actually been there; it is simply a rock. The lighthouse keepers hate it. It is in the middle of nowhere: there are cliffs all round and the sharks gather there – '

'I love the sound of it,' said Artemis.

'But it is desolate,' insisted Caroline. 'They've mined the place for phosphates and it looks like the surface of the moon. Craters everywhere.'

'I want to go to Sombrero Island,' said Artemis in the voice her sister recognised as signifying inflexibility. In such circumstances there was no dissuading her. Long experience told Caroline that further remonstrance would be futile. Artemis wanted to go to Sombrero Island; that meant that she would have to go too; Artemis was like that.

Their father stared into his soup and smiled. He, too, was thinking of Sombrero Island. He had not the slightest intention of going with his daughters. He hated the direct light of the sun, and saw no reason to sit on a boiling deck alone in shark-infested waters. Such things were against nature, clean contrary to common sense. He hadn't been brought up to do these things; he was a native West Indian, not a tourist; yet it amused him to think how English Caroline and Artemis were; it was almost as if they were not his daughters at all. And indeed they were not; they were their mother's. They had nothing to do with him; of course, he was, technically, their father; they bore his name; they even looked like him. But he often thought that these were merely coincidental resemblances, and these two strangers were accidental accretions, like the burrs that clung to your clothes when you came back from a country walk in England.

'I suppose the Canon will drop by tonight,' he said, looking up from his soup, which was made out of pig's tail and was remarkably good. 'Will the Canon go with you to Sombrero Island?'

'Oh, I shouldn't think so,' said Caroline quickly, jumping in with her reply before Artemis howled with laughter. She did not know quite why, but it upset her to hear her father and Artemis making the Canon into a shared joke.

'The Canon couldn't possibly come,' said Artemis. 'When you get there, they put you into a little boat, and you are rowed to this ladder and you have to climb up it, this steel ladder embedded in the cliff. You have to be quite agile to do that; when there's a swell the sailors don't allow you even to try.'

'Why not?' asked her father, in sudden curiosity.

'Because if there's a swell, and you can't quite leap from the heaving boat on to the ladder, you'll fall in and that will be that. The sharks gather there to eat the rubbish that the lighthouse men throw into the sea. And just think how many sharks the Canon would feed.'

But her father didn't laugh. It was perfectly true that the Canon was large and ungainly, which made him ridiculous, and a clergyman as well, which made him still more into a joke figure, but sharks were never to be laughed at.

'I can't think why you are always so unkind about the Canon,' said Caroline, taking advantage of her father's silence and hoping to cure Artemis of the nasty habit of making fun of people as a way of passing the time. 'It's not his fault that he's fat.'

'Nor is it my fault that I find him amusing,' said Artemis.

They had finished their soup. Dutifully, Caroline began to stack the plates. Artemis pushed her chair away from the table with a long sigh. It was an ugly table and an ugly chair – speckled plastic and chrome. Their verandah, on which they always sat to eat, was also ugly, a place where concrete and greyness predominated. Wood never lasted in this climate. Everything now was hurricane-proof and termite-proof, designed to outlast the humans who used them by centuries. But at least the verandah was cool; underneath them was the water cistern: they were sitting above water during the very hottest hours of the day.

Artemis stood up, while her sister took the soup plates through to the kitchen. She lit a cigarette and looked at the view. Of all the views they had ever had sight of, this was probably the finest. At the bottom of their garden was a patch of idle scrub, then a narrow white sandy beach, then the sea, and a mile distant St Martin. In that direction lay civilisation. St Martin was the next island in the Leeward chain. There were other islands beyond it. You could island-hop in a little plane, once you got to St Martin.

7

There were even regular scheduled flights to St Kitts, Antigua, Barbados, and from there on to London. Of course, there was an airfield in Anguilla too, but apart from Sombrero, which you could hardly count, this was the last of the Leewards. When you arrived at Anguilla, your island-hopping stopped. It was the last of the islands, this place in which her father had chosen to live.

Artemis smoked her cigarette and contemplated St Martin, which seemed such a pretty island, at least from this distance. On the French side even the place-names were poetic, names such as Marigot, Grand Case. But out of sight, on the other side, the Dutch part of the island, brash tourists bought things they did not want but surely deserved, flexing the muscle of the mighty dollar. Only five miles away from where she was now there were shops and casinos, a duty-free paradise. But here, at Blowing Point, Anguilla, that sort of civilisation had yet to arrive. It remained, to use the usual phrase, unspoilt. There were hotels, but as yet no guests; they had been to see the new hotels, which were still concrete shells, awaiting windows, furniture and tourists. It had been odd going round the empty buildings; it had reminded her of trips to Pompeii, and other echoing cities of the dead.

Her elder sister was standing next to her. Caroline had cut her hair short, and it made her more of an elder sister than ever. Six years and a mental distance as wide as the shark-infested Anegada Passage separated them. Their minds so often failed to meet. Artemis could not imagine why Caroline might object to her making fun of the Canon. The Canon was so very ridiculous. Unless of course, poor Caroline, stuck on this flat island, had been reduced to finding the Canon an object of interest. Could that be true?

'I'd like to learn scuba diving,' said Artemis suddenly. 'It would be so odd, being able to float around under water, and be able to breathe. You'd feel like a spaceman.'

'I feel like a spaceman already,' said Caroline.

'Do you? Why?'

Caroline considered.

'I feel weightless,' she said at last. 'As if I was floating and needed to be weighed down. I don't feel real. I suppose it is this place ...'

'You ought to go to London and get some sort of job,' said Artemis sensibly. 'I can't think why you haven't done so already.'

'Perhaps I'd feel like a spaceman in London too, floating around Camden Town or South Ken, getting the tube, sitting in an office, insulated from the atmosphere, and breathing in my own bottled air.'

'But if you had to get a job, you'd feel differently,' said Artemis. 'You'd feel normal. You don't have to stay here and live like this.'

This was true. She did not have to live with her father. It was her choice: she had followed him around the world. Artemis had her job in London: she did something in an office in Regent Street – just what was never quite clear. Did she 'sell space'? That was a phrase that was used. But who bought space? And what did they use it for once they had bought it? Whatever Artemis's job was, it was hardly exacting, for no one in Regent Street seemed to mind when she took six weeks' leave to come out to Anguilla. But of course, Artemis did not need to work. Neither of them needed to work. They were rich. They could both well afford to live in expensive little flats in London, do trifling jobs and spend the evenings drinking champagne. But only one of them had chosen to do so.

'I was going to say,' said Caroline, 'that I feel responsible for him. But that isn't the word. That is only half of it.'

'Responsible for him?' said Artemis, a little incredulously, turning her head slightly towards the interior of the house that lay behind them. 'What on earth could you stop him doing, if he had a mind to do it?'

This was true, thought Caroline. Artemis knew their father well.

'I mean,' continued Artemis, 'you lived with him in Rome the entire time, and did that make a difference to him? And if he does decide to leave his money to someone or another, it won't make much difference to us, will it?'

Caroline felt the injustice of this remark. She hadn't taken up the burden of living with their father on this inhospitable island merely to safeguard their inheritance. That was not the point, not the point at all.

'I feel I can't leave him,' said Caroline. 'Or at least that I ought not to.'

She realised that this sounded inadequate. Her father did not need her; but there was this bond that held them together, or at least held her to him.

'You are one for bogging yourself down,' said Artemis. 'I am not. And what on earth does he do here all day?'

'You know what he does.'

'I suppose I do. I meant ... I am not sure what I meant. Perhaps I am just surprised by the way he seems content with this aimless sort of life. You can't read Aristotle all your life, can you, even in the Greek original?'

'Some people can,' said Caroline defensively. The accusation that they were wasting their time on this island hurt her, because it was, she realised, true.

'And what shall we do this afternoon?' said Artemis, determined not to fall into aimlessness, intent on making plans.

'Swim,' said Caroline. 'Let's go and swim at Road Bay.'

Road Bay was picturesque. Between the salt pan and the sea lay the village, which unaccountably seemed to have escaped the mania for hurricane-proof concrete. There was a jetty and there were boats too: boats drawn up under the trees, awaiting repair, and others afloat in the bay itself. One such was the *Warspite*, a schooner of a certain age, which once a month made the trip to Sombrero Island.

They walked to the far end of the beach and swam from there. Artemis had brought *The Charterhouse of Parma* to read: she liked the idea of long books which had a certain dullness about them, so that you felt a virtue in reading them. Such improving literature had to be brought all the way from England. The house at Blowing Point was full of books that she had brought out in previous years, most of which she had never finished, and which she had left behind for Caroline to read in her stead.

The beach, despite the proximity of human habitation, was deserted. All the beaches on this island were. Artemis wore a bikini, and had her long blonde hair tied up in a bun. She was beautiful. Caroline knew it, everyone knew it, even Artemis herself. By contrast, Caroline felt a certain modesty as she slipped out of her beach-dress and stood there on the sand in her one-piece. She wasn't jealous, only a little numbed by her sister's beauty, her clear green eyes, the rich gold of her hair and the slimness of her figure – this only made her feel the more her own failure to shine. Under her sensible costume, she could feel her bosom, flat and heavy, like a pair of soup plates. But Artemis's figure – how did the people who appreciate these things describe it? Her breasts were like champagne glasses; or was it ice-cream cones? How ridiculous to think of men idolising these rather elusive protuberances which defied sensible description. And Artemis, one could tell by the way she stood there at the water's edge, she too was indifferent to public opinion, to what men might think. She was beautiful, but it was beauty for its own sake; she was indifferent to praise or blame.

'There's a yacht out there,' she said, after her swim, whilst she lay on the sand, staring out to sea, failing to read her book.

'I noticed it,' conceded Caroline.

'Who does it belong to?'

'Judy will know. When you have had enough of the sun we can go into Judy's. She'll tell us.'

Judy, Mrs Blomberg, kept a bar in the village; if the group of houses under the trees could be called a village, and if Judy's hut could be called a bar.

'Yes,' said Artemis, 'we'll go and see Judy. Did I tell you,' she added suddenly, 'that a man wanted to marry me?'

'Who?'

'No one you would know. Terribly good-looking he was. I think you would have liked him; you would have thought him nice, if

11

that is the word. He was some sort of lawyer in the Inner Temple, I think.'

'You think?'

'Men bore me when they talk about their work. I suppose he must have told me what he did exactly, but I can't have been listening at the time. He did something in a wig and a gown; at least I think he did. I imagined him, in the few moments he caught my imagination, dressed in a wig and gown. But you haven't asked me what I said to him when he asked me to marry him.'

'I hardly need to,' said Caroline, not looking up from her book.

'How well you know me, dear,' said Artemis. 'Of course I sent him packing. He was most upset. He asked why and I told him. I said to him that I couldn't have anything to do with a man whose mind was set on marriage. I couldn't stand the look in his eyes when he looked at me. It was as if he was sizing me up, imagining my future, seeing me at his dinner parties, sitting next to him in the Volvo, driving his children to school. No thank you, I said.'

'But if you had refused him – '

'That was what he said. He had the idea that we wouldn't get married and just go on as before. What do you mean, I asked. You know, he said, our present arrangement. That was the fatal error on his part. I told him that I was not going to be party to any arrangements with anyone. From now on I think I'll stick with married men; they seem to know what is what.'

'You're an anarchist,' said Caroline. 'Like our father: no one could ever tie him down either.'

'Heredity,' said Artemis, returning to her book.

Caroline closed her eyes and abandoned herself to the warm embrace of the comforting sand. Tourists paid thousands to do just this, to laze on a tropical beach with a good book. But her father hadn't come here to find an island in the sun. He wasn't a tourist, but a native West Indian, born in Trinidad of Trinidadian parents. But his daughters, they were English, just as their mother had been. And if their poor mother had not been run over attempting to cross the High in Oxford whilst under the influence of alcohol (she could still remember the Coroner's words) then perhaps Artemis would have turned out differently. She herself might have too. But Artemis had been sixteen when their mother had died. Poor mother, thought Caroline, and poor Artemis; though if the truth were told, the person most affected by her mother's untimely death had been herself. Both father and sister had taken the tragedy remarkably calmly.

'I think I am about to fall asleep,' she heard Artemis say. 'And one shouldn't do so in the sun. It's dangerous. And I've only been here four days.'

'Judy's,' said Caroline decisively, opening her eyes.

'What was his name?' asked Caroline, as they trudged through the hot white sand.

'Whose name?' asked Artemis, from under her sun-hat, from beneath her dark glasses.

'The man in the wig and gown,' said her sister, wondering why she should feel it necessary to use this absurd circumlocution.

'Oh, him. I suppose he must have had a name, but I can't for the life of me remember it. He might well have been called something like Sebastian, something decorative and upper-class like that.'

'And was he?'

'What?'

'Decorative and upper-class?'

'With a name like Sebastian he would have to be, wouldn't he?'

'I can't believe you are so vague,' said Caroline. 'If I'd had an affair with someone called Sebastian, I'd have some basic grasp of detail. I'd be able to remember things about him, things like his name.'

'Yes, I am sure you would. You are so methodical. But it wasn't an affair, as you so charmingly call it. I haven't heard that term in years. Do people still have affairs?'

'I am beginning to feel quite sorry for your Sebastian.'

13

'He was in no sense mine. You might want a brother-in-law,' said Artemis. 'But I don't want a husband.'

'You mean you don't want one now,' said Caroline.

'I don't want one ever,' said Artemis. 'I've known that since I was sixteen. What on earth would I do with a husband? I've got everything that I want already. And where would I put him? The flat's full enough as it is, what with all the stuff I am storing for Jamie.'

Jamie was their father; Artemis was the only person who ever called him by this name; most people called him by his surname, Duxbury; Caroline usually called him nothing at all.

'Husbands don't take up much room,' said Caroline. 'It is children that take up room.'

'Husbands fill all available space,' said Artemis, firmly. 'They take over your entire life.'

'Having your life taken over might be quite a pleasant experience.'

'I don't think so. And please don't tell me that I will change my mind, because I honestly don't think I will.'

They walked on in silence. Caroline said nothing, but still did not believe her.

Presently they arrived at Judy's. Judy's was open. It was rather a ramshackle building, set back from the beach, and its opening times were vague, depending as they did on the whim of the owner rather than anything more predictable.

'The beer is cold,' said Judy, as soon as they came into the welcoming shade. 'The man came and looked at the fridge this morning.'

'Thank God for that,' said Caroline, glad to be out of the searing heat.

'Talking of God,' said Judy, 'the Canon was in here the other day. He makes me feel quite respectable.'

'But you are respectable,' said Artemis, looking at her.

Judy was about fifty years old. She had greying hair tied up in a bun, and was barefoot. The frock she wore had little shape and no real colour in it, thanks to repeated laundering.

14

'How's your father?' she asked, getting some beers out of the fridge. It was the question she always asked.

'Fine,' said Caroline, giving the answer she always gave.

'He's impossible,' said Artemis.

'I wish he would come round here,' said Judy, lighting a cigarette. 'He is such a good-looking man. Instead I have to make do with the Canon. We had a long talk about women priests. I asked him to explain his position to me.'

'And did he?'

'In a manner of speaking,' said Judy gravely. 'Anglicans make things so complicated for themselves.'

'He's discussed it with my father too,' said Caroline.

The Canon had in fact come to the West Indies to get away from women priests. He was a clerical refugee. They hadn't as yet ordained women in the Church of the West Indies, or whatever this particular patch of the Anglican world was called. They were still discussing it. But in Basingstoke, where the Canon had previously had the cure of souls, women priests had already arrived. He had come to the other side of the world to avoid them.

'You see,' said Judy, 'it is all to do with the flying bishops. The Canon objects to the idea of the flying bishops. It seems that they have no precedent in either Scripture or tradition. He says that your father agrees with him on that one.'

'But my father is an atheist,' said Artemis. 'It really is too bad of him to get stuck into arguments about Scripture and tradition with the poor old Canon. It's cruel.'

'The Canon is only a few years past forty,' said Judy. 'Not old at all.'

'Religion is just another hobby,' said Artemis severely. 'It's like stamp-collecting. But if you were to spend every day of your life being a philatelist, you would go mad. Or rather, you would have to be mad in the first place to do so.'

'The Canon isn't mad,' said Caroline. 'It is just that you think he's ridiculous.'

'And so he is,' said Artemis.

15

'Well, Judy and I don't think so, do we, Judy?'

Judy considered this appeal, and then said: 'The Canon is a domestic animal. I call him George now. That is his name: George Cartwright. It has weight to it. You would imagine him as a Domestic Chaplain, whatever that is. But I'm not an Anglican – Anglicans are a little tame, and they belong in the Home Counties. You don't expect to find Canons so far from civilisation.'

Even Artemis seemed to see the justice in this evaluation.

'Do you think he'll come with us on the *Warspite* when we go to Sombrero Island?' she asked.

'Not if he has any sense,' replied Judy. 'He's too sensible to play the part of international gypsy. Have you seen the yacht out there?'

'Yes,' said Caroline. 'We were meaning to ask you about it.'

'It belongs to the idle rich. Just the sort of person you wouldn't approve of, Artemis my dear.'

'She doesn't need encouragement,' said Caroline.

'Oh, she does,' said Judy. 'If I weren't to warn her, there's no telling what might happen. The yacht is under the charge of two young men, both of them improbably handsome. You know the type I mean. They seem at first sight to be a little too fresh-faced to be true. And Artemis is here for six weeks, and there is so little to do she might fall in love with one or both of them.'

'Only five weeks to go actually,' said Artemis. 'But who are they?'

'The boat belongs to an Englishman. The other man with him seems to sail the boat. He's thinking of buying a hotel here.'

'Where?'

'One at Shoal Bay, I think. Or was it Rendezvous Bay? One or the other. The place has gone bankrupt and he thought he could pick it up cheap.'

'But none of the hotels have even opened,' said Artemis. 'We have seen them.'

'That's why they haven't been finished,' explained Judy, with

16

the pleasure of someone who has just mastered a mystery. 'They can't put in the windows and things like that because the company has gone bankrupt before the thing is finished. They have run out of cash, and this young man is thinking of buying the shell from the liquidating company, I think that was the terms.'

'And what is his name?' asked Caroline, who always wanted things to be clear.

Judy pointed at her beer bottle.

'That's his name,' she said. 'He's a brewer.'

'I don't believe you,' said Artemis. 'Brewers stay in England and live in country houses.'

'Not this one,' said Judy. 'He's different.'

'There is something about a yacht,' conceded Caroline. 'But you said there were two of them,' she added, turning her mind back to practicalities. 'Is the brewer attached in some way?'

'No. The other is a man, I told you.'

'That means nothing,' said Artemis.

'An Italian,' said Judy.

'Oh God,' said Caroline. 'I suppose you're now going to tell me that the yachting brewer went to Oxford.'

'Actually I think he did tell me that,' said Judy.

'You're neurotic,' said Artemis, as they drove back home. 'Just because someone turns up on this island who happens to have been at Oxford, which happens to be the city where our mother got killed trying to cross the road, you go all pale, knock back your drink, and drive off in a cloud of dust. What will Judy think?'

'I don't like Oxford,' said Caroline, shouting over the noise of the engine.

'And you don't seem to like Italians either,' retorted Artemis.

'I lived in Rome, you didn't. You were having a good time at university then.'

'Anyone would think these two yacht people were the Eumenides,' said Artemis, a classicist's daughter. 'That they had come to track you down. And there are so few people on this island, so few white people, I mean, that you are bound to meet them sooner or later. You'll just have to get used to the idea.'

Caroline knew she was right.

II

As it turned out, she met the brewer the very next day. He was in the supermarket, examining some oranges, which were on sale for a dollar each. She knew at once it was him. It wasn't that he looked like a brewer, but rather, bearing in mind Judy's description, he couldn't have been anyone else. There were, as Artemis had pointed out, very few Englishmen on the island. There was the Commissioner, Mr Demmer, the Chief Secretary and the Attorney General; there was the rather dull man who ran Cable and Wireless, and the man who taught General Science in the secondary school. (Her father and the Canon, being over-familiar to her, she did not count.) Clearly the man examining the oranges was not one of the aforementioned whites. He was for a start younger than any of them. He seemed to be about thirty, which was her own age, but whilst she no longer considered herself quite young, nevertheless thirty was young in a man. He was wearing shorts, which showed off tanned legs; and he was holding a wire supermarket basket. His arms seemed strong, and the lower parts of them were covered in fine blond hair.

There was nothing particularly romantic about the supermarket setting; it wasn't even a coincidence seeing him there. There was only one real supermarket on the island, and he had to do his shopping somewhere. You met everyone in the Galaxy Supermarket eventually. But she liked the idea of men doing shopping. Shopping was domestic and so was she. (Her father, needless to say, had never actually bought anything, except perhaps over the telephone, in his life.) She now felt a sudden desire to examine the oranges herself.

'Hello,' he said, with a smile. 'Do they mean American dollars?' he asked, referring to the price.

'Oh no, EC dollars,' she said.

'Ah,' he replied.

There was a pause. He looked at the oranges, and then into the wire basket. If he were to pick up some oranges, place them in the basket, there would be no further excuse for conversation. But why should he need an excuse? This wasn't England. Outside England you could speak to strangers without being introduced, and not incur a stare of withering scorn.

'Are you Miss Duxbury?' he asked.

'Yes, I am,' she said. 'Caroline Duxbury. No one has called me Miss Duxbury in years.'

'I wondered whether you were Caroline or Artemis,' he said. 'Judy Blomberg mentioned you to me.'

As he said this, he realised that it was Artemis, the other one, who had to be the pretty sister, of whom Judy had made such mention. Caroline, though not ugly, could hardly be called pretty. Her expression was a little forbidding. Her face was round and not unpleasant; her hair was unexpectedly short. She was not smiling, but rather looking at him as if he was some sort of intruder into her tropical paradise.

'I am Charles Broughton, by the way,' he said with a tentative smile, designed to disarm suspicion.

As he said that, he wondered where on earth the pretty sister could be. Did she ever go shopping? Or was she sitting on some shady verandah somewhere, gazing out to sea, and doing whatever pretty women did at eleven o'clock in the morning?

'Are you here for long?' asked Caroline, feeling she ought to make conversation, and that this was the most obvious question to ask. He did seem a pleasant enough man, and yes, he was certainly good-looking in that improbable manner that Judy had described. She kept her eyes on the oranges, not wanting to look into his face, or at his bare legs. The fact was that one didn't, or couldn't, look at English people. They weren't like Italians. Rome, Italy, these were different places, different customs. When dealing with the English you had to learn all these strange customs all over again. It was now eight years since she had been in England.

He, too, looked at the oranges, wondering what their fascination could be.

'At least a few days,' he said, in answer to her question. 'I've got a boat. Perhaps you would like to come out for a drink? Tonight?'

'Yes, I'd love to,' said Caroline, much against her will. But there were no excuses to hand. You could hardly claim you were already booked up on an island this small. You could not invent a fictitious dinner party, or cocktail party or trip to the ballet. Such things simply did not happen on this island: there were no dinner parties, or cocktail parties, and no ballet.

'Good,' said Charles Broughton. 'Just stand at the end of the jetty and shout, and one of us will row over to get you.'

He assumed she knew where his boat would be; but there again, she did know. Of course there was no way in which he could force her to bring her sister with her, and he was far too polite to hint that the sister's attendance would be considered essential to the evening's enjoyment. He had no particular desire to spend the evening confined to his yacht with the reincarnation of George Eliot. To him she seemed to be a typical don's daughter, North Oxford born and bred, bicycling strict, the type who got up early to row on the river every morning. Perhaps her sister would be typical don's daughter too – but typical of the other sort.

'What time shall we come?' she asked him, with her usual mania for detail. (Living with her father, she had developed a passion for making domestic arrangements, in reaction to his own anarchical streak.) 'Before or after dinner?'

'After dinner would be nice,' he said, glad she had used the plural, wishing that his vocabulary did not contain words as tame as 'nice', words which rose irresistibly to the tongue whenever he spoke to women.

'So that was the local talent,' said Gianni, who was waiting in the car outside the supermarket. 'I saw her as she came out. Good grief.'

'Her sister is supposed to be the pretty one,' said Charles, starting the engine. 'I think that was what Judy said. At least I hope I've got it right.'

'If that is the beautiful one, we should find another island,' said Gianni. 'Why did you buy all these oranges? Were they going cheap? You never eat oranges.'

'They were actually very expensive. Have one,' said Charles. 'They're good for you. I didn't really mean to buy them, they were just there.'

'You are always buying things you don't need or want,' said Gianni. 'Yachts, hotels ...'

Charles laughed a little ruefully. It was true. He had bought the yacht, without quite meaning to, in Barbados. After that there had been a cruise around the Grenadines, then to Antigua, Nevis, St Kitts, St Barts, and now finally to Anguilla, which, of all the islands he had seen, was easily the least interesting. It was true that it had the most superb sandy beaches, ripe for touristic development, but there was little else. The island was long, flat and featureless, a coral lump covered with scrub and six thousand people, the majority of whom seemed to be children. Of greater interest were the hotels; he had half convinced himself that the reason he was here was to buy a hotel. Charles had lots of money; he had plenty of relations too – but Broughton's was a huge company. He did not have to work; he did not have to do anything. He had in the past toyed with the idea of getting some sort of job. After university he had wanted to be an Egyptologist. Egyptology was not at all remunerative, and there was a tradition of very rich Englishmen pouring their wealth away in the sands of the Near East. He had in fact advanced in his ambition far enough to go out to Egypt and look at hieroglyphics and tablets covered with cuneiform script, but his heart had sunk as he had done so. Looking at old stones had not satisfied him. There had to be something else, beyond this present existence, that would make him happy; but what it was, he did not know; he continued to stare at stones, wondering whether he would find it.

On one such expedition he had met Gianni. It had been in the Gaza strip, where, bored by some inscriptions, he had had half a mind to buy a ruinous hotel, which, he was assured by a man he met in a bar, would become a gold-mine, once the Arabs and the Israelis sorted out their differences. The fact that he did not need a gold-mine, that he had enough money, more than he knew what to do with, made the prospect of a good investment seem something of a poisoned chalice. He had not bought the money-spinning hotel; instead he had taken Gianni on board.

Gianni was, if the truth were to be told – and Charles did not particularly like the truth – something of a financial liability; in other words he was a parasite; but as Charles had so much money, Gianni's company was one way of spending it. What Gianni had been doing in Gaza of all places was never clear. But it had been Gianni who had rescued him in the bar and steered him away from the prospect of becoming a Middle Eastern hotel owner; later Gianni told him about the delights of yachting, and with Italian subtlety introduced Charles to the idea of the freedom of the seas, never expecting that Charles would suggest that they go to Barbados, buy a yacht there, and tour the West Indies. In Gianni's world, such dreams did not come true; in Charles's world, where money was no object, such dreams had largely lost their charm. And here they were, a year later, on the very edge of the Leeward Islands.

It had been Judy Blomberg who had told Charles about Duxbury and his daughters. She had dropped the name casually.

'Duxbury of *Ancient Attica*?' he had asked.

'Where?'

'It's a book,' he had said. '*Ancient Attica*. There was someone called Duxbury in Oxford about eight years ago, who had written a book called *Ancient Attica*.'

'Then that's him,' said Judy. 'He has two daughters, one plainish and the other beautiful.'

'And his wife is dead, isn't she?'

23

'Yes, about eight years ago.'

'I remember it,' he said.

He did remember it. Mrs Duxbury had been killed crossing the road, run over by a truck in the High. She had not been looking when she had stepped off the pavement; in fact, it had emerged that the reason for her inattention was that she was a little drunk, having just emerged from the Wheatsheaf pub, where she had been drinking with some of her female friends. That had been something of a scandal at the time. Dons' wives were not supposed to get drunk in pubs at lunchtime, even in those days. The fact that she was no ordinary don's wife, but the spouse of Jamie Duxbury, author of *Ancient Attica*, added spice to the incident. Why had she found it necessary to get drunk at lunchtime in a not very pleasant pub? Charles knew that the late Mrs Duxbury had been a very rich woman; being very rich oneself meant that one tended to know who else was very rich. Mrs Duxbury's family had made their fortunes in sugar; everyone had always supposed that Duxbury had married her for her money. It was taken for granted that she was unhappy in her marriage. The friends she had been lunching with in the Wheatsheaf on that fatal day soon took care to spread the tale of the late Mrs Duxbury's marital woes from Senior Common Room to Senior Common Room. It had always been known that Duxbury had never been a model husband: but who in Oxford was? Gradually a story emerged, and it ran like this.

Mrs Duxbury had been drinking at lunchtime, something she normally never did, in order to give herself the strength to confront her husband. She was going to go home and tell him that she was leaving him; that she could put up with his appalling behaviour no longer. To her friends she outlined past infidelities, to which she had turned a blind eye; but now, she hinted, she had made a new discovery – something so really serious and shameful that she had to leave him at once. She had, to use the common phrase, discovered the straw that had broken the camel's back.

Her sudden extinction before she could confront her husband with his mysterious crime had been an enormous stroke of luck for Jamie Duxbury. If she had succeeded in leaving him, and taking all her money with her, his life might well have changed for the worse. But as it was, he inherited half her fortune, and was left in the happy position of being able to get on with the rest of his life, no longer shackled to a wife he had long since come to despise. At least, that was what should have happened, had it not been for one of those strange fits of morality to which the collective conscience of Oxford is sometimes subject.

This storm of moral indignation started with a cloud no bigger than a man's hand. Duxbury had always been unpopular amongst his colleagues, but had always been too arrogant to mind it. He despised them and could not have cared less about their opinions of him. He was the sort of man whose habit it was to sit in his beautiful college rooms, surrounded by the fruits of several pillaging expeditions to Greece – beautiful things bought with his wife's money – giving tutorials to undergraduates about Greek vase painting and the more recondite aspects of Ancient History. Like every great don, he affected to despise undergraduates; like every great don, he disdained the scorn of the rest of the university. Consequently he ignored the gossip that was circulating about him, and the various stories about just what he had done which had provoked his long-suffering wife into deciding to leave him. He took no notice until it was far too late. In fact, so long did he ignore the danger of the situation he was in, that, by the time he became sensible to the peril, not even the cleverest of lawyers would have been able to help him. Cursing the ingratitude of Oxford, Jamie Duxbury was left with no choice but to resign his fellowship. In a fit of pique, he had gone to live in Rome, taking his elder daughter with him; the younger was left behind in England, being a schoolgirl of sixteen at the time.

That was the story; and Charles reviewed it in his mind over lunch.

'Caroline Duxbury is ugly,' said Gianni, when the prospect of drinks that evening was raised.

'No, not ugly,' said Charles. 'She could be described as plain.

Or perhaps she's just someone who doesn't make the most of her attractions.'

'Plain,' said Gianni, 'is as good as ugly.'

'She must have had a hard life,' said Charles. 'I knew her father by sight some years ago. I must have been to some lectures he gave, or something like that. Living with a man like him might make any woman plain. They used to live in Rome, after they left Oxford, I know that much.'

'Oh,' said Gianni, who was himself Roman, consuming an orange, having dealt with a not particularly satisfying main course.

'It is all rather sad,' said Charles, more to himself than to Gianni. 'I don't suppose they could ever go back to England now. Probably wouldn't want to either.'

'Why not?'

'He got into trouble with the police,' said Charles shortly. 'Or at least he was threatened with trouble with the police. He was supposed to be a terrible womaniser.'

'Is that a crime in England?' asked Gianni.

'You see,' explained Charles, 'he was supposed to have sexually harassed a student; because he was so unpopular with his colleagues and because the student's parents took umbrage, there was a real chance the thing might have come to court. That's why he left Oxford. He was driven out. But the real reason is because people thought that he was cruel to his wife. It was the women who ganged up against him first, I seem to remember. All the talk of being charged with sexual harassment was merely an excuse to get at Duxbury. Things started to get hot for him, so he threw it all up and went to Rome.'

'And was he guilty?'

'Of being cruel to his wife? Undoubtedly. But as for what else he was supposed to have done, as it never came out into the open, who knows?'

'But what was he supposed to have done?'

'He's supposed to have pestered a student. Everyone knew that he had done that in the past. He had that reputation. But this

26

time the student is supposed to have objected. How his wife is supposed to have got to hear of it, I can't imagine. They said at the time that she decided to leave him because the student in question was male, and that was the straw that broke the camel's back. He'd always chased girls, but when he started chasing boys, she thought enough was enough. But I really never could quite believe that. I think that was spiteful gossip.'

'The English are very odd. Does this Duxbury like men or women?'

'Women,' said Charles. 'At least he used to.'

'In Italy sexual harassment isn't illegal,' said Gianni. 'So he lived happily ever after.'

'But he can't be a very pleasant character,' said Charles, whose family had been brewing beer on evangelical lines to sell to the Catholic Irish for centuries, and who lacked Gianni's more tolerant southern attitude.

The unpleasant character in question was at that moment having lunch with his daughters.

'I went around the Galaxy this morning,' Caroline was saying. 'You know, the supermarket. I met the yacht man there.'

'What's he like?' enquired Artemis.

'He's invited us to come and have drinks with him on his yacht after dinner tonight.'

'We might as well go,' said Artemis a little wearily. She had spent the morning indoors, feeling yesterday's sunburn, and failing to make much headway with *The Charterhouse of Parma*.

'The Canon, who is a wondrous source of parish gossip, I suppose you'd call it, says that he is very rich,' said their father suddenly. 'Rich and good-looking. We talked about it over chess last night. The Canon had his information straight from your friend Mrs Blomberg. She's what is called a reliable source. At least she is here. Anywhere else in the world and she wouldn't be. But here all sorts of things change. It's the genius of the place to transform people.'

27

'He is good-looking, but only in an English sort of way,' said Caroline.

'Ah,' said Duxbury. 'That is what has made Mrs Blomberg so excited. She has hopes.'

'What is Judy hoping for?' asked Artemis a little coldly.

'Of course, my dears, Mrs Blomberg is your friend and not mine,' said Duxbury with the ghost of a smile. 'I suppose I would recognise her if I bumped into her; there can't be too many people of her age and appearance and habits on this island. Indeed Anguilla can only support one of her species. Here she sits, in her beach bar, sipping beer and smoking cigarettes, on the look-out for customers, a bit like a praying mantis. And her mind, in so far as it does anything, turns to thought. Deep down I suspect Mrs B is very conventional indeed. Her husband's cousin was a High Court judge. (The Canon told me that.) Mrs Blomberg may have left her husband all those years ago to live a Bohemian life – but the old-fashioned love story remains her firm favourite. According to the Canon, Mrs Blomberg has already said to him, "I bet you that Charles falls in love with Artemis and vice versa." It seems,' he concluded, 'that this young man is called Charles.'

'Charles will do no such thing if he's got any sense,' said Caroline, suddenly feeling an irrational dislike of the way Duxbury was trivialising the idea of love.

'Do you mean that she's actually made a bet with the Canon, a bet with money?' asked Artemis gravely, fearing that a price had been put on her, but knowing that she ought not to care about it. For if she didn't value love, why should she object?

'That I didn't establish. But I think that her main idea is that this is bound to happen. The woman is a romantic. She thinks that these things are inevitable, that there are higher powers at work. Of course, she is right – to a small extent. The man from the yacht is bound to admire you, my dear, but not because a higher power is at work, but because a lower one is.'

'You are completely right,' said Artemis, carefully. 'Romance is just a word people use to cover up the lower instincts. Not that I have any objections to the lower instincts. I enjoy the lower

28

instincts; I don't enjoy being paired off by Judy. I'd prefer to make my own choices.'

'If you were to fall in love,' said Caroline, 'I think that it would be a terrible shock to you.'

'It would,' she said. 'And I won't.'

Caroline noticed that her father was smiling his secret smile of satisfaction. He did not believe in love, and neither did Artemis. Caroline herself was her mother's daughter; and she felt that it would do her sister the world of good to fall in love; it would pierce her armour of self-sufficiency. She was always so remote, so withdrawn. But if anyone were to shake her self-possession this summer, it would have to be Charles Broughton. There were no other candidates on the island.

'You are a romantic,' said Artemis to Caroline, as if reading her thoughts.

'Like your mother,' added her father.

'I suppose so,' she said.

She was like her mother; but it was a cruel comparison. Romance had killed her mother. She had died of being romantic too long; at least that was what her maternal uncles had told her, and she had believed them. They had tried to persuade her against marrying Duxbury; she had refused to listen; their attempts had hardened her resolve. She had been in love; she had ended up marrying a man who did not love her, and who, as soon as the flattery of her devotion wore off, rapidly found her an embarrassment. Caroline wondered whether she ought to remind her father that, however much he now despised it, he had once been flattered by a romantic attachment. And it was to her mother's romantic passion that he owed the money that allowed him to live in his present idleness. The same was true of Artemis: her flat, her money, all the things that enabled her to turn her nose up at love, came from the fact that her mother had married her father against all advice. But she could not say it. Instead she stared at her food, which only that morning had been on display in the Galaxy, and now looked far less alluring on her plate, and contented herself with saying:

'Love isn't all that bad.'

'You're softening,' said Artemis, who liked to think of men as The Enemy. 'I hope the Canon has not been working on you.'

'He's called George, you know,' said Caroline.

'That's how my parents married,' said Duxbury. 'My mother married my father because he was the only man she could find. Her father was the Surgeon General of British Guiana at the time, you see, and he was very cross, as my mother married his best friend, a man old enough to be her father. And the old man, my grandfather, had counted on keeping her at his side forever. Of course, she had to become a Catholic, quite a thing when you consider she had been brought up as a strict Presbyterian. But people will do anything to get married, once they have set their minds on it.'

'You don't honestly think I'd marry the Canon, do you?' asked Caroline in exasperation. 'Or that he'd even ask me?'

'You'd have to become an Anglican,' said Artemis in all seriousness, warming to the theme. 'Of course, it isn't hard. Anglicans don't really believe anything; I'm sure that Judy has told you that.'

'Anglicans believe the greatest lie of all,' said Duxbury. 'They believe that left to themselves people will behave well. Not even the Catholics are stupid enough to believe that, and they believe some pretty silly things. The truth of the matter is that left to themselves people will revert to the law of the jungle. It's such nonsense to pretend anything else. And once you realise that there is no God and that man isn't in God's image, then you realise that man simply isn't lovable.'

'Quite,' said Artemis. 'Men are ghastly.'

'I converted you to blasphemy,' said Duxbury with grave pleasure.

Artemis said nothing.

'The Canon isn't ghastly,' said Caroline, feeling the need to defend humanity, but not knowing where to start. Of course, Oxford was a very small tank inhabited by piranha fish, but the whole world was not like that.

'I wonder whether the Canon is queer,' said Artemis in a spirit of scientific curiosity, suddenly changing the subject, another habit that she had inherited from her father.

'No,' said Duxbury. 'He comes from Basingstoke.'

Caroline wished they would eat up, so she could clear away the plates. Lunch was becoming an agony for her. She felt a residual guilt about the inadequacy of the food: the hamburgers had actually looked quite nice when on display in the Galaxy, all pink and ruddy. They had only gone grey when she had got the maid to cook them. She did hope they were not now going to launch into a discussion about homosexuality: it was the subject she hated more than any other. It embarrassed her. Perhaps her father could sense her discomfort; he had an acute sense of what made her uncomfortable. She could feel his eyes on her now, and dared not look at him, in case she should see his amused little smile. Her poor mother: had she been treated like this as well? For her it would have been worse; she had been married to Duxbury; Caroline was only his daughter. The scandal with which he was tainted was not so close to her; it would have touched her mother more painfully. If indeed there had been a scandal; but there had never been anything said openly about Duxbury's behaviour – only things whispered in quadrangles and SCRs. Her mother had put up with it, hidden her pain, because she had loved Duxbury. Caroline loved him too. She was in the same unhappy position as her mother, who had needed several stiff drinks before even being able to face the possibility of leaving him; the person she most loved was the person who most made her unhappy.

'The Canon is most wonderfully informative,' Duxbury now said, much to Caroline's relief. 'I need never go to Blomberg's bar, for the simple reason that he tells me everything she says. I have no need to meet Mrs Blomberg. I gather she often entertains the Government. She's a political hostess.'

'Who in particular?' asked Artemis.

'The Chief Minister, I gather. Now that is a useful contact.'

The Chief Minister was their landlord. He was a polite, rather shy man, with a moustache. The table and chairs they were now using were his.

'But apparently she has never had the Commissioner round for a drink,' said Duxbury. 'That social triumph has escaped her. I think she's nutty, frankly.'

The Commissioner was a Mr Demmer, a rather dull-looking man with a youngish wife whose invitations to drinks Duxbury had always refused. Without ever meeting Mrs Demmer, he had decided she was a ghastly woman.

'I don't think Judy's a snob,' said Caroline.

'Yes she is,' said Artemis. 'She wants to pair me off with the yacht man. I'll tell her what I think of that.'

'If you protest too much,' said Caroline, 'she will jump to the wrong conclusion. I think that with the Canon: you're always being so dismissive about him, but I think he's just the sort of man you like – older and dependable. And you haven't even seen the yacht man yet – he's called Charles Broughton, in case you have forgotten.'

'Nor have I seen his Italian friend,' said Artemis, stung by what Caroline had said about the Canon, and thinking the Italian was the last thing her sister would like to hear mentioned.

(For Artemis, who usually ascribed low motives to everyone, had always assumed that her father had gone to live in Rome, not to study the classics, but for immoral purposes which could be more comfortably pursued there than in Oxford; she herself had been to Rome but once or twice, and thought that her sister's extreme discomfort with the idea of Italy stemmed from her shame over what her father had done there. Artemis was convinced Caroline was swayed by middle-class morality.)

A little gleam seemed to come into Duxbury's eyes at the mention of an Italian; he had reasonably pleasant memories of his four years' residence in Rome, though not quite for the reasons Artemis surmised. Caroline had been with him all that time; it had not been happy for her: Artemis did not know it, but Rome had been the tragedy of her sister's life.

III

Charles had opened an account at Blomberg's. The accounts book was a rather battered jotter, the sort of thing that schoolboys used. He was given a page to himself, just after the Chief Minister's. Gianni had shown no particular desire to open an account, and Judy had assumed, correctly as it turned out, that his drinks would be put down to Charles's.

'So you see, he's rich,' explained Judy. 'He doesn't mind paying for the Italian chap as well. In fact, he seemed to expect it. I'm going to make him pay ten dollars a drink.'

'But I thought you liked him,' said Caroline.

'I do,' said Judy. 'But from each according to his means. Some people pay fifteen. There's one chap who's actually paying twenty.'

'Oh,' said Caroline, who knew that she only paid seven.

The Canon, who got away with five, said nothing.

It was four in the afternoon. They often gathered like this in the shade of the bar at one of the hottest times of the day. Caroline enjoyed these encounters, where beer took the place of tea.

'It's all imported, you know,' said Judy, still on the subject of prices. 'People expect it to be expensive. And the Chief Minister fixes the taxes,' she added defensively, for it was the Chief Minister who paid twenty. 'Where's your sister?' she asked.

'At home. Sunburned. She wants to avoid the sun. We're going to go out tonight, to the yacht. She's resting in anticipation. Perhaps later we will have a swim from Blowing Point, before supper.'

'What's she going to wear?' asked Judy.

This sudden interest in clothes struck Caroline as unusual.

'I really have no idea. She certainly brought enough clothes out with her from England. I expect she's bound to have something suitable.'

'Ah,' said Judy.

The Canon coughed meaningfully.

'You don't honestly think, do you,' said Caroline in the resultant pause, 'that Artemis is making elaborate preparations for drinks with Mr Broughton, and that is why she isn't here? I mean ...'

'First impressions are crucial,' said Judy.

'It would be nice if she did settle down with a good-looking, good-natured brewing millionaire,' said Caroline. 'But I don't think she will. She's certainly said often enough that she never will.'

'She says that,' said the Canon, 'and I am sure she is sincere. It is a mistake to assume that people always mean the opposite of what they say. She means it – but I can't help feeling it's because she hasn't met anyone yet.'

'She's met hundreds of people,' said Caroline crisply, blending social with sexual promiscuity.

'But not the right one,' said Judy. 'Just you wait.'

'It is good of you to take so much interest in her,' said Caroline, wondering if she was becoming embittered. People did take such an interest in Artemis. The more withdrawn she became, the more people became fascinated by her. It was enough to make one jealous.

The other two could think of no reply to this. They felt a little guilty. Neither of them particularly liked Artemis, and thus they had both independently come to the conclusion that it would be best for Caroline if some hapless man were to come along and take on the burden of entertaining Artemis for the rest of her life. It would give Caroline a break. They were thinking of her; she seemed to think that they were thinking only of Artemis, yet the opposite was true. What a muddle; they only wanted to help – but Caroline was so sensitive, always getting the wrong end of the stick, always imagining slights that were never intended. It still embarrassed the Canon to remember how he had once likened Duxbury to Socrates; he had thought it an amusing idea, Duxbury as the Socrates of the Caribbean. He had quite failed to understand Caroline's taking offence at it. Later Judy had explained it to him: Socrates, sentenced by his peers to drink hemlock for ridiculing the gods and corrupting the youth of Athens, simply wasn't a tactful subject where Duxbury was concerned. But those were points of comparison that he had never intended, only Caroline had seen them at once, she who could see what no one else could.

'I think Artemis ought to get married,' said Judy, breaking the silence. 'I was married, in fact I still am, and I don't regret it too much. There's something rather odd about people deciding never to marry, don't you think?'

'Only the other day you were saying how you couldn't stand wives, I seem to remember,' said Caroline a touch accusingly. 'I think you meant Mrs Demmer. And you know, not every woman can get married. I know it sounds dreadfully Victorian of me to say so, but I am not married and neither is George. I don't feel like a spare part all the time.'

'Men are different,' said Judy, by way of reply. 'Aren't they, George?'

'Yes,' said the Canon, without quite seeing how this followed from what Caroline had said; but Judy had this way of cutting through swathes of conversation, of getting to the conclusions without having to wade through the arguments first.

The Canon's voice was deep and liturgical. He was wearing an open-necked shirt and shorts, but despite this relatively casual attire was still every inch a clergyman of the Church of England. One could tell by looking at him that he had deep-seated objections to women priests.

'If you mean that men are different and that they don't have to get married in the same way as women do,' said Caroline, 'that isn't as true as it was.' She became aware that she was rehashing an argument she had first heard Artemis use. 'Women can get

35

jobs and they don't have to be supported by a man. And they don't have to get married to have sex any more. They can do what men have always done.'

'I suppose they can,' said Judy. 'I suppose they do. But if you spend your life having sex with a series of relative strangers, how on earth are you ever going to get to know anyone? Love is what is important and that means permanency and that means getting married – or becoming a nun.'

'Yes,' said Caroline. 'I like the idea of permanence. Permanence anchors you to reality. A husband would be someone you could rely on. But I'm not sure …' She was about to doubt whether any man would ever want to stay with her permanently, but she changed her mind and said: 'I am not sure that Artemis would want that. She likes being free. She's comfortable with her job, her flat, her freedom. There's no reason for her to get married.'

'There's never any reason to get married,' said Judy. 'If I had used my reason I would never have married Mr Blomberg.'

'Then why did you marry him?' asked the Canon, suddenly interested.

'I was in love with him,' she said.

'Judy,' said Caroline, 'what on earth happened to Mr Blomberg?'

'Nothing happened to Mr Blomberg. He is still there, I suppose. In London, doing what he always did.'

'London,' said Caroline. 'Another planet.'

'Yes,' agreed the Canon, thinking of Evensong at the Abbey, Bishops lunching at the Athenaeum, and his own more modest trips up from Basingstoke, which would end with sandwiches and a half-pint at a pub near Waterloo. London was another world.

'No one is immune to it,' said Judy, still on the topic of love. 'Not even Artemis. Not even I was, though I wish I had been. Artemis may seem cold and remote and simply not interested, but somewhere in her there has to be a heart. She can't be purely rational.'

'I doubt whether she's rational at all sometimes,' said Caroline.

'She has decided that she wants to go to Sombrero Island on the *Warspite*. I've tried to persuade her against it, but she won't listen to reason.'

'Perhaps she finds Anguilla too small,' said Judy. 'She'll find Sombrero tiny.'

'You should get Mr Broughton to take you to Saba, or to St Barts, on his yacht instead,' suggested the Canon. 'I wouldn't mind going to Saba myself,' he added, hopefully.

'Poor Mr Broughton,' said Caroline, compassionately. 'People have such high expectations of him. We may be all terribly disappointed. And now I must be getting back to Blowing Point. Artemis will be waking up soon; I said that I'd go for a swim with her in front of the house at about six.'

'Perhaps I'll go to Sombrero too,' said Canon Cartwright, once Caroline had gone. 'Do you think Artemis will bite?'

'Yes, I do,' said Judy suddenly. 'I think that she's just dying for someone to take pity on her. She wants to be loved, and no one has ever been able to get through to her up to now. The only thing that I'm worried about is him. She's such an odd girl that if he has any sense he wouldn't touch her with a bargepole. But most men only look at pretty faces, not at characters, I suppose.'

'And she is a beautiful girl.'

'Quite. But Caroline is a much nicer person. A sensible man would choose Caroline.'

'Yes,' said the Canon, meditatively.

'And yet here she is stuck with that dreadful father of hers,' said Judy. 'I am sure he is cruel to her.'

'If he was, she'd leave him, surely.'

'One day,' said Judy, 'you really must get me to tell you the entire story about Mr Blomberg.'

And she got up to pour some more drinks.

Despite her well-publicised scorn for the opposite sex, Artemis took considerable pains over her appearance that evening, keeping her sister waiting for the bathroom for some time. When she emerged, her fragrance fought with that of the curry. She had even put on make-up. After the vindaloo, she delicately retouched her lipstick.

'He's a sailor, you know,' said her father. 'Such precautions are quite unnecessary. Usually sailors are content with any port in a storm. If you find them amusing, make sure you invite them here to dinner tomorrow evening.'

'I put on lipstick for my own amusement, not for his,' said Artemis.

By contrast with her sister, Caroline felt very plain. It was as if she were a chaperon.

'You want to torture men,' she said, when they were in the car.

'Hardly. I don't need to. They torture themselves.'

'They do it to us,' said Caroline, feelingly.

'Only if you let them,' said Artemis, without the slightest hint of passion in her voice.

On they drove in silence, through the scattered darkened houses that made up the village of Blowing Point, up towards the main road that ran along the spine of the long thin island. Every tragedy, thought Caroline, was caused by love. But Artemis was immune to it, no matter what Judy said to the contrary; she was beautiful, but cold; Caroline pictured Artemis's heart as something small, knobbly and hard, rather like a walnut. The seat of her own affections was by contrast more like a peach – one of those rather awful peaches that you used to buy in England years ago: sweet, bruised and far too soft. This was what came of being her mother's daughter and not her father's.

Presently they arrived. The yacht was there, out in the bay, an expensive little oasis of privacy. They went to the end of the jetty and shouted. A small boat, with Charles in it, appeared. It was still light, but by the time the boat arrived at the beach, darkness had fallen.

'I hope you don't mind getting your feet a little wet,' he said, jumping out on to the sand. 'You must be Artemis,' he said to the smaller of the two figures in the darkness. 'I am Charles Broughton.'

Artemis took his extended hand, but said nothing.

'We don't mind wet feet, and neither of us are wearing stockings,' said Caroline, as she always did, filling in the silence.

They were soon aboard, and he rowed them away from the shore.

'Well,' said Judy, who had been observing the scene from the door of her bar, while ostensibly pretending to scratch her foot. 'You say there is a chiropodist in St Martin?'

'Yes,' said the Canon. 'On the Dutch side. My sister found out about it when she was over here last summer. She has trouble with her feet.'

'Does she?' said Judy with sudden interest, for she remembered the Canon's sister, who had had a grim fascination about her. 'What sort of trouble?'

'Oh, I don't quite know. Didn't like to ask.'

'Ah,' said Judy. She could imagine that the Canon's sister was just the sort of woman one wouldn't like to ask anything of, being of large frame and silent disposition.

'Of course, if it hadn't been for Maude, I might never have come here,' said the Canon in a rather confidential tone. (He had been drinking in the bar with Judy since four that afternoon: drink was making him reckless.)

'Maude?' asked Judy, not quite recognising the name. She wondered if she should switch on the lights, but, on balance, preferred to hear about Maude. The darkness might encourage revelations about the Canon's secret life and loves. She pictured vicarage tea parties in far-off England, understandings being reached amidst the cupcakes, and the flowering of quiet clerical loves.

'My sister,' said the Canon. 'She's called Maude. We shared a house, you know – only we had theological disagreements. Maude is evangelical.'

'Is she?' said Judy, with sympathy. (Being an old-fashioned Catholic, she didn't like Protestants, and really felt little reason why she should, no matter how much people tried to convince her to the contrary.)

'Yes. And in favour of women's ordination. She was a leading light in the Movement for the Ordination of Women. It made life very difficult.'

'I can well imagine,' said Judy.

And she could: she hadn't taken to Miss Maude Cartwright; her sympathy was entirely with the Canon. How he must have suffered being hectored by his sister over Scripture, Tradition and the rights of women. Maude would have hectored: the strong silent types always did, once they actually opened their mouths. She shuddered. And even when Maude hadn't been hectoring the poor Canon, her silences must have been equally terrifying and pregnant with menace.

'You've only got to look at all the people who support the ordination of women to see that they must be wrong,' said Judy. 'It's like fox-hunting. Give me the dear old Holy Father any day.'

'I took this job to get away from Maude,' said the Canon, not wanting to enter into another discussion on Papal Infallibility. (Being a creature of compromise he found any discussion of belief painful.)

Judy lit a cigarette in the darkness, and then said: 'We all seem to be here because we want to get away from something. And I suppose that when all the hotels are opened, and this poor island is filled with ghastly tourists who will make it just like everywhere else in the Caribbean, we'll all have to go somewhere else. All of us, you, me and Duxbury. I hope there are still some desert islands left.'

'You'd like Duxbury,' said the Canon. 'If you met him, that is.'

'I've seen him,' she said. 'It was in the public library. He was asking the lady at the desk for a copy of Aristotle's *Metaphysics*. She told him that it would have to be flown in from Antigua, that being the next library along, so to speak. It does make you feel a little cut off, doesn't it, knowing that the nearest copy of Aristotle is so far away?'

'Duxbury was supposed to have been the most brilliant classicist of his generation,' said the Canon.

'That may be so. But it can't be much fun for that poor girl living with him.'

'Artemis?'

'No, Caroline. Clever men frequently do a lot of harm. And clever good-looking men are the very worst, I fear. They have an air of effortless superiority about them, just as Duxbury has. He has always had everything he's ever wanted.'

'But he's hardly had a happy life, has he?' said the Canon. 'I mean, here he is, hiding away, when he could have been Warden of All Souls, or whatever the cleverest men of their generation are supposed to do.'

'I bet you that the present Warden of All Souls,' said Judy, 'is just some dedicated old soul who got to the top by hard work and politeness, by publishing timely little articles and remembering people's names at cocktail parties. Now Duxbury would never stoop to that, would he?'

'Of course, he's not conventionally polite, by any means,' said the Canon, who had spent one evening a week at Duxbury's ever since arriving in Anguilla, ostensibly to play chess. 'No, he's not eager to please at all,' he said, with an air of concession. And it was true: there was an undercurrent of mockery in Duxbury's conversation which made one perpetually uncomfortable in his presence. One couldn't help but feel that Duxbury simply didn't like people, although one hoped that in one's own case, an exception was being made.

'But you know,' said the Canon, putting aside these disturbing thoughts, 'there is one thing that you have forgotten. Caroline stays with him. That is something of a mystery. I mean, why does she live here? He must inspire some sort of devotion. Of course, Duxbury is fond of her, but he could fairly well do without her. He has the maid to see to his needs; he doesn't seem to depend on her company. And Caroline has money of her own: she doesn't need to live here, in a concrete bungalow, without decent furniture, without even a comfortable chair to sit on. And she doesn't even particularly like it here either. There's nothing for her to do here. She could quite easily go and do what Artemis does – go to London, live in a flat, do a job to fill in her time, and start to enjoy herself. But she doesn't? Why not?'

'I think it is because she feels she wants to be wanted,' said Judy. 'That's why she stays here with him.'

'She wants to be wanted by her father?'

'Yes. He has the gift of captivating women,' said Judy. 'Isn't that how he married his wife in the first place? And now, I don't suppose you happen to remember the chiropodist's name or where he lived, do you?'

The sound of high clear laughter floated across the water; it was Artemis laughing. Someone had told a joke. She was a don's daughter, born in Norham Road, and generally she liked to give the impression that jokes, especially silly ones – and this had been a very silly one – did not amuse her. But it was Gianni who had told the joke, and it had entered her mind that if she were to flirt with Gianni it would not only confound all expectations, but probably annoy her sister too, as well as being rather fun.

'And have you found a hotel you want to buy yet?' Caroline was asking, getting on with the spadework of conversation, her face pale and round and serious.

'Yes,' said Charles, 'and no at the same time. I've seen one that would be a good buy, but just as I have seen it my interest in hotel buying has started to wane.'

'Then why are you still here?' she asked.

'You don't have to have a reason to be here,' said Artemis. 'Not a real reason. That is why so few people do come here.'

'The opposite is true,' said Caroline. 'This place is so out of the way that only people with very serious reasons for doing so make the effort to come here in the first place.'

'I am afraid I am not the sort of man who spends his time doing anything for serious reasons,' said Charles, feeling a little shamed in front of her earnestness.

'But I am sure you do do serious things, don't you?' said Caroline, hoping that he did, because she wanted to like him. Indeed, she liked him already; and already she had the disquieting feeling that she was frightening him away.

'He used to look at hieroglyphics,' said Gianni with a trace of mockery in his voice.

'That is so serious it sounds deadly dull,' said Artemis. 'Did you really look at hieroglyphics? Like Lord Thing?'

'Carnarvon,' said Caroline, tidying away this loose end.

'Yes,' said Charles. 'A little like him, I suppose, except without all the excitement. It *was* deadly dull, now you come to mention it, and Egypt is something of a hell-hole. These places you read about so often are.'

'Then why on earth did you do it?' asked Artemis. 'I never do anything I don't want to do,' she added with refreshing honesty. 'Perhaps you felt you had to atone for something? How very Victorian. You do hear about these people from time to time who either go and live in deserts or work in leper colonies because of something awful they have done, such as shooting someone in a duel. Are you one of those? It might make you rather interesting if you were.'

'I am afraid I am not very interesting at all,' said Charles. 'It's simply that I have too much money and nothing to spend it on. Except possibly hotels.'

'Have you never done anything remotely wicked?' asked Artemis.

'No,' he admitted.

'Then you are too nice,' said Artemis. 'I suppose no one is really wicked, or unconventional these days. Life is too tame, don't you think?'

'And what would you do to escape the tameness of it all?' asked Gianni.

'If I had had the fate to be born a hundred years ago, perhaps I would have gone to Africa to teach children. I don't really know.'

'You would have been a nun?' said Gianni, smiling.

'Yes,' said Artemis. 'That would have been quite fun. I wouldn't have lived in a world where men would have told me what to do all day. It would have been better than being a boring old wife. I think I would have liked being a nun. It would have been an adventure.'

Gianni looked appalled at the thought of a woman, especially a pretty one, renouncing the company of men such as himself.

'We're atheists, you know,' said Caroline, realising that Gianni was a Catholic and needed explanations, just as his co-religionist Judy did. 'At least we have been brought up that way. Our father thought that non-belief was better.'

'Atheists?' said Gianni, almost scandalised.

'I would have been a sort of atheist nun,' said Artemis.

'But why did your father want you to be atheists?' asked Gianni.

'He's a bit odd in that sort of way,' admitted Artemis, rather regretting the serious turn to the conversation.

'He's a follower of Aristotle, not Plato,' explained Caroline, painfully conscious now that she was being a bore. What would these young men think? But how was she to turn back now, once the philosophical digression was begun? 'It's all to do with the Unmoved Mover of all things,' she concluded lamely.

'But the Unmoved Mover of all things proves that God exists,' said Gianni. 'Aristotle believed in God.'

'Yes,' said Caroline, hurriedly, remembering that Italians did have this penchant for pseudo-intellectual conversations. 'But my father takes Russell's view that if Aristotle had lived after Newton he would have used the same argument to prove the very opposite.'

'But Aristotle didn't live after Newton, did he?' said Gianni.

'Despite your unbelief,' said Charles, cutting in, realising that Gianni didn't understand the basic rule of social chitchat, namely, avoid sincerity at all costs, 'despite your unbelief, you're all very friendly with the Canon.'

'Absolutely,' said Artemis, spotting her favourite joke on the horizon. 'Caroline will be the Canon's first convert.'

Charles felt another stab of discomfort. Artemis was being unkind. This wasn't typical after-dinner conversation, which was not altogether surprising; these were daughters of Duxbury, blue-stockings, brought up to discuss Plato and Aristotle at dinner parties in North Oxford, educated in the tradition of high seriousness, spiced with irony directed at anything they had been taught to despise. Even though he was one of the few men alive who could read hieroglyphics, Charles still felt a little foolish. For here they were, seemingly eager not to be charmed and not to enjoy themselves, their minds critical, serious, questioning. But why he should make the effort to try and charm them was not entirely clear in his own mind. Was it because he took his duties as host seriously, no matter how insignificant the party, and was determined that they should leave feeling they had been entertained? Or was it simply that he was a rich and idle man with a yacht, and this sort of thing was expected of him? He was meant to be charming to beautiful girls, even when he didn't particularly like them. For why else should a man cruise the West Indies at great trouble and expense, enduring the cramped conditions of yacht life, if not to make himself generally agreeable to everyone he met?

'You were at Oxford, weren't you?' Caroline was now saying to him.

'Yes,' he replied, and told her which college.

'I was at Somerville,' she said. 'I suppose we were up at about the same time,' she added, alluding to the parity of their ages.

'Yes, I suppose so,' he said, swallowing the thought that she looked much older than thirty. But they were the same age, and they had both been at Oxford at the same time.

The subject of her father's disgrace hung between them.

'Can I show you the yacht?' asked Gianni, leaning forward to Artemis, oblivious to the delicacy of the situation.

Artemis, who had gone a little pale at these references to Oxford and the events that had happened there about eight years previously, put down her glass.

'Yes,' she said. 'I'd like to see the yacht.'

45

The two older ones were suddenly left on their own. Caroline felt a sense of relief flood over her. She found the way Artemis dominated conversations a little overpowering; at the same time she had a residual sense, inherited from her mother, that Artemis's behaviour was not quite conventional enough, and sometimes bordered on the rude. It did not do to cross-examine people you had barely met. And finally there was always the horrible possibility that Artemis might somehow say something about their father which would cause a sensation – though why she should think this, she did not know, as Artemis hardly ever mentioned her father's Oxford years.

Charles was now talking to her about Oxford. His approach was delicate – he made clear in his manner that he was not going to mention any thing or person that might have unpleasant associations for her. That was reassuring, and soon she was actually enjoying herself. She had forgotten how pleasurable it could be to listen to a sensible good-looking man talking about a place with which you were familiar, and to find out that he knew places that you had known, and that he appreciated things that you, too, had loved. It was not just the subject matter that delighted her, for he was now telling her about rowing, something she had never cared about deeply – it was rather the manner in which the conversation was conducted. Naturally she knew that her father was a brilliant man, a man who knew all about vases and philosophy, a veritable polymath, a Socrates – but he had never spoken to her in the way in which she had always wanted him to speak to her. There had always been too much brilliance in her father's conversation. Judy and the Canon were more her cup of tea, but both of them were years her senior, and a little lugubrious for her taste. But her father, her father – he held the world in disdain, and sometimes she felt that she, too, was included in that world he despised so much.

Charles was different. Charles was normal, if that was the word. 'Normal' was a term that was constantly entering her mind these days: she wasn't normal, neither was Artemis, neither was their father. But Charles was. Hieroglyphics had been, she hoped, no more than a hobby for him; he wasn't some eccentric who was so wrapped up in the Ancient Egyptians that he would dedicate his entire life to dusty inscriptions. Of course not; and that was the sad thing; for the more normal did Charles seem to her, the more did she realise that in such normality there could be no place for her. They were too different. But Artemis perhaps was redeemable, for Artemis, she was convinced, was no more than a silly girl at heart. Artemis had suffered no terrible tragedy, and Charles might be able to do Artemis good. It would perhaps rescue her character if she were to fall in love with this nice man, and realise that her happiness depended on another. That might make her summer holiday worthwhile. And as for Charles, she still hardly knew him, and so could not feel any pity for him yet. For generally she had this tendency to feel sorry for men who ran the risk of falling in love with Artemis. But this time she hoped it would be different: Artemis would fall in love with him, and not the other way around.

They talked of hieroglyphics now, and the obelisks of Rome. He was a sensible man, far too sensible to fall in love with Artemis. He was safe. But she would fall in love with him; the more she talked to Charles, the more she thought that Artemis would find him irresistible. There was no one else on this island of the same age, and he did have a yacht as well. A yacht, rather than a sensible mind, that was the detail that would appeal to Artemis. Perhaps the drink was going to her head: all this thinking about her sister, this desire to arrange things, perhaps it was a symptom of incipient middle-age. How annoyed Artemis would be if she were to know that her own sister was so busily making plans for her. She wanted to dispose of her; and at this she pulled herself up short – for though these were secret thoughts there was something in them that made her feel a little ashamed. One was supposed to love one's nearest and dearest, not want to get rid of them. But she felt both desires at once, and it made her uneasy. Artemis had always been a difficult sister, ever since she was sixteen: always rather withdrawn, always moving from man to man, ever since their mother had died. There was no fixity about her; perhaps their mother's death had unsettled her after all. But it was so hard to tell what went on behind those cold green eyes.

Thus she sat and listened to Charles, hearing herself join in the conversation, while all the time her mind raced with details of Artemis, and she busily calculated the chances the romance had of succeeding.

'That is very interesting,' said Artemis, listlessly.

'You think so?' said Gianni, who had just been showing her how the anchor chain worked.

'No, not really,' said Artemis suddenly. 'I was telling a social lie. Things mechanical aren't really my speciality. I imagine they aren't yours either. In fact, I think you have lured me out here because you have got the idea that you appear to best advantage by the light of the moon.'

He smiled.

She looked at him critically. If any man ought to look beautiful in moonlight, then Gianni was that man. It was quite absurd of Judy not to have noticed Gianni. It only went to show how money could inflate a person's importance. Of course, Charles was pleasant enough to look at, but Gianni was far more to her taste.

'I wonder why you haven't told me that I look beautiful by moonlight,' she said suddenly. 'Don't you think you ought to?'

'Do you think that I would have lured you out here if you didn't?' he asked.

She realised that he thought the honour was all on her side.

He could feel her eyes upon him, and interpreted her thoughtful expression as one of admiration. He moved closer, until his hot breath touched her cheek. Their faces were close together now, and she studied his violet eyes.

'Let me kiss you,' he whispered, using the same formula that he had used in Barbados and all the other islands they had visited.

'Why?' she asked.

From the other end of the yacht they could hear voices, her sister's and Charles's.

'Come on,' he said, impatiently, putting his arm around her, a little awkwardly in the confined space at the front of the boat.

But Artemis did not move. Gianni felt as if he were trying to embrace a statue. He put his lips against hers, and when there was no response, he took a step backwards and studied her face, being careful not to get his feet entangled in the anchor chain.

'What is the matter?' he asked.

'Nothing at all,' she said. 'Give my best wishes to the sharks, won't you?'

'What?'

She gave him a push in the stomach, and overboard he went.

'I can't take you anywhere,' said Caroline, reproachfully, as they were driving home. 'You are awful.'

'I couldn't resist it,' said Artemis, tears of laughter running down her cheeks.

'And I'd just invited them both to come to dinner tomorrow night. I don't suppose they will now.'

'Serves you right,' said Charles, looking at Gianni. 'She's the daughter of a famous man. She doesn't take to that sort of thing.'

'What sort of thing?' asked Gianni.

He was sitting on deck, in a pool of gaslight, wrapped in towels. His soaking Armani jeans, along with the rest of his clothes, were hanging on the rail.

'You know what sort of thing,' said Charles.

'Daughters of famous men, my foot,' said Gianni. 'What about that party in Grenada, where I met that girl whose father was a friend of the – '

'Oh yes, yes,' said Charles, remembering that party with something like embarrassment, and the way Gianni had disappeared with the girl in question. 'The aristocracy are different. They have no morals at all. But these high-minded Oxford atheists simply don't like that sort of thing.'

'There isn't a woman on earth who doesn't like what you call "that sort of thing",' said Gianni with certainty. 'It is just that you English are so timid. You think that they are not interested, when they are. No wonder they are all so unhappy, when all they need is a good – '

'I've heard that argument before,' said Charles. 'They have invited us to dinner tomorrow, you know. At least Caroline did before you got pushed into the sea. I think she'll quite understand if I go on my own. You might feel a little foolish seeing Artemis again.'

He tried to keep his voice grave as he said this, but the picture of Gianni, fully clothed in the sea, and the memory of that short cry of surprise followed by a splash, kept on coming into his mind.

'But I want to see her again,' said Gianni.

'But she gave you the push,' said Charles. 'She's ghastly.'

'I don't care,' said Gianni with determination. 'I'm in love with her.'

'You can't like her, surely?'

'Of course not. She's a bitch. I don't like her in the least. But that has nothing to do with it.'

'Wouldn't you much rather fall in love with someone you actually liked?' asked Charles.

'No,' said Gianni. 'I like my friends. But one should never like one's lovers. Ever.'

'I have the awful feeling that you are going to force me to hang around this island for days on end,' said Charles thoughtfully. 'What am I supposed to do while you pursue the lovely Artemis?'

'You can fall in love with the ugly one,' said Gianni. 'That will take up an awful lot of time.'

'She's not ugly, I tell you,' said Charles. 'But I don't think so. I have other ideas. And as for Artemis ...'

'Yes?'

'Oh, nothing,' said Charles shortly.

'You're trying to warn me?' asked Gianni with a smile.

50

'I think that would be counter-productive,' said Charles.

It had, after all, only been gossip. He had heard, about eight years ago now, that Mrs Duxbury had decided to leave her husband because she had caught him in the act of attempting to seduce their daughter. But that was surely no more than a spiteful Oxford rumour, the sort of thing people who were eager to believe the worst were always quick to suppose; and in Oxford, from supposition or hazarded guess to received fact was often a very short journey. It would not do to mention it now. It was true that there was something distinctly strange about Artemis, but there were surely other explanations for that, which he could not at present imagine, but he was sure existed – safe, reasonable and unshocking explanations, the type which existed in a calm and unfrightening world. English reticence forbade him even mentioning the possibility of incest; besides which, he had the uncomfortable sensation that telling Gianni the substance of the rumour might inflame him further. A whiff of incest, like an Italian's sense of morality, was a funny thing.

'You really are so irresponsible,' said Caroline, pulling at the hand-brake aggressively when they got back to Blowing Point. 'You'll have frightened them away. The next thing we'll hear is that they've gone off to the Virgin Islands, and we'll never see them again. And God only knows what Charles will think of us.'

'Why on earth should you care what Charles may think?'

'Good opinions can't do you any harm,' replied Caroline. 'Certainly not the good opinion of a sensible man like him.'

'Charles,' said Artemis, putting more contempt than she actually felt into the name. 'Milk and water.'

Their father was on the terrace, sitting in darkness, waiting for them, idly staring out to sea and smoking a cigar.

'Nice time?' he asked.

'No,' said Caroline.

'Yes,' said Artemis.

Caroline explained what had happened, finishing with: 'And

51

I'd just invited them both to dinner here tomorrow and I doubt if they'll come now.'

Then Caroline was overtaken by the realisation that all this was a little childish, and that it was late, and that she'd feel better about it in the morning. Artemis had already gone to bed. She, too, followed her sister into the house.

Duxbury was now left alone on the verandah, peace restored after the sudden irruption of his daughters. He drew on his cigar. Women were silly creatures. The Greeks had known it, and how right they had been. Women made themselves unhappy, by allowing themselves to be enslaved to their emotions, and then, with typical irrationality, they blamed other people for their misery. Usually they blamed men. How illogical; misogyny, he reflected, carried its own reward, for the more he reflected on the foolishness of the women he had known, the more apparent became his own effortless superiority.

Poor Caroline, he thought. So like his late wife, his poor wife. He thought of her always as his 'poor' wife, not because she aroused his sympathy, but rather his contempt. What a poor specimen she had been. She had been foolish enough to fall in love with him, and to think that she could change him. She had adored him, and that was why he had despised her, for she had no judgement, no sense, no personality of her own. If she had married him for any other reason, he could have put up with her, but her adoration, her devotion that refused to die despite indifference, had made him realise that she had been in some way not quite all there. And how could he have loved her in return, when she was so different from himself? How could he have loved a mental defective? If he had known at the time what she was later to become, then perhaps he would never have married her. But he had married her – partly because she was very rich, and partly because her adoration had flattered him at first. She had wanted to marry him despite the advice of her friends and relations, and that had pleased him. He had liked the idea of upsetting all those stuffy English bores. He had also liked the idea of arousing the jealousy of his colleagues; not for him a damp little house in

Jericho and a rusty bicycle, and looking forward to college dinners as an essential source of protein, rather than a tiresome duty. Not for him the slender stipend of a college fellow. Oh no, he was going to be rich; he was going to be the Trinidadian boy with the accent that had produced expressions of wonder in the eyes of elderly dons who stole a march on them all. He had determined to make them sit up and take notice of him.

Of course, it had been a disaster; with such intentions, how could it have been anything else? But how badly he had wanted to succeed, to be seen to be successful in the eyes of all those snobbish Oxford men. Their indifference had driven him to desperate measures, even into marrying a woman he did not and could not love. And even when he had done that, still they despised him. He had not realised just how much; after decades in Oxford one ceased to be aware that one was living in a piranha pool and that envy was the air you breathed. One forgot just how much they hated you. And no matter what you did, they hated you all the same. He had got the top first in Greats in his year, and they hated him. He had won the Chancellor's Essay Prize, and they could not forgive him. He had walked into a fellowship, and they could not forget it ever. He had, as a young man, and as an older one, rejoiced in the most astonishing good looks, thanks to the perfect mixture of blood that ran in his Trinidadian veins; his first Saturday afternoon as an undergraduate in Oxford had been spent in bed with a young woman who was now an acclaimed scientist and Dame of the British Empire. He had married the richest young woman of the day. They had hated him all the more.

Why?

Was it racial prejudice? He was almost as white as they were, to an untutored eye. Was it anti-colonial prejudice, the dislike of an outsider? But he had smoothed out his vowels and become as English as they were, at least to listen to. Was it class prejudice? It was true his family had not been rich, and he hadn't been to a British public school, but he had relations grander than most, and was related to half of Trinidad. What was it then? Was it simply that he was better than all of them, and they were jealous?

But how jealous, and how hateful, they were, he was only to discover when it was too late. It still surprised him, the lengths to which they had gone. It presumably took some effort and a lot of time to prepare the ground for a criminal prosecution, so that one could deliver the ultimatum 'Either resign or face charges.'

He had never really thought that it would come to a trial. That had seemed too fantastical to be true. The charges against him had seemed ridiculous. Of course, it had been inadvisable to go to Greece year after year accompanied by a host of adoring female undergraduates; some things could be open to misconstruction; but he had spent his whole Oxford career courting misconstruction. Such things could be used against him by the ill-disposed. But what he saw as more real was the sheer hatred they all felt for him. Thus he had resigned, not because he feared the unwelcome spotlight of publicity, but because he felt terribly wounded. They had failed to acknowledge his genius. It was their loss; if they could not, there were others who could. And with this rather childish thought in mind, he had resolved to go abroad.

First Rome, then Anguilla. Trinidad was the land of his birth, but he had set his face against it. He would never go back there. It was the sort of place you left, not the sort of place you came back to after decades of absence. It wouldn't do to go back to Trinidad, to be mistaken for a tourist, to be the subject of gossip by old ladies. To go back, that was to fail. Instead, he was destined to dwell among foreigners. He was a stranger amongst the tents of Kedar, as the Bible of his youth had put it. That was what he wanted to be. Only Caroline, his oddly English daughter, kept by him. She was devoted to him, poor girl. He had rather expected her to hate him, to blame him for her mother's unhappiness. That would have been altogether more neat; but life was hardly ever so tidy. Life was a mess. No one quite behaved the way they ought to, least of all yourself. Things simply did not fall into place. An action

54

that you knew to be wrong, carried on its own little life long after you had regretted it. So it would continue. He faced this summer too without hope.

IV

'I'd like to go to Shoal Bay,' said Artemis the next morning, forgetting their near quarrel of the night before.

'Fine,' said Caroline. 'We can call at the post office first.'

The post office was where you went to pick up your letters in Anguilla, if you were lucky enough to get any, and where they sold those overlarge decorative stamps that were collected by children the world over, whose philatelic mania largely contributed to the Government's solvency. But even if you had no letters, or expected none, you still went there to meet people, and hear their news. Today they met the Canon, standing in the shade of the flamboyant tree, an aerogram in his hand.

'My sister has written,' he said with a broad smile.

'How ... lovely,' said Caroline, who remembered the Canon's sister, a large unsmiling presence she had addressed as Miss Cartwright.

'She has been accepted for ordination,' said the Canon, almost gleefully.

'Gosh,' said Artemis. 'Are you pleased? We rather thought you were against all that sort of thing.'

'Well, of course I am. That's why I came here. But I am not against it as such, just against the Synod taking unilateral action on the matter. Really I am against the Synod, I suppose. Not a General Council of the Church, you know, but these silly little gatherings they have with – oh well. The point is that Maude has been accepted for ordination by the Diocese of Mogadishu and she'll be going out there for her training in theology.'

'Is there a Diocese of Mogadishu?' asked Caroline uncertainly.

'It seems there is,' he replied. 'I confess I hadn't heard of it, but the Anglican Communion is pretty far-flung. Some parts could doubtless be flung further. But it seems that Maude has got it into her head that she wants to be a missionary priest. She writes to say that Basingstoke is no longer her scene and that it hasn't quite got enough scope for her ... though reading between the lines, I imagine she has quarrelled with the Bishop.'

'I think it is admirable of her,' said Artemis. 'She'll be cutting swathes through the jungle. What has she been doing up to now?'

'She used to grow roses,' said the Canon. 'We had over three hundred different types in our garden alone. And she was very friendly with a Miss Walkenshaw who was the headmistress of the local primary school. She doesn't say what Miss Walkenshaw has to say about it.'

'I suppose,' said Caroline, 'that she grew tired of roses and tired of Miss Walkenshaw's company. Roses are so passive, aren't they? Evangelising Africa offers more of a challenge.'

'Of course, all this means,' said the Canon, 'that she won't be wanting the house any more. It actually belongs to me entirely, though in practice Maude had taken most of it over, and I couldn't sell it with her in it. A big house, an acre of garden, three hundred varieties of rose at the last count – she's going to have to leave all that behind. And now I really must get down to Sandy Ground and take Judy her copy of the *Catholic Herald*. Where are you going?'

'To swim at Shoal Bay,' said Caroline.

'Enjoy it,' he shouted, as he got into his car.

'It's items of news like this that form the chief interest of life on this island,' said Caroline, as the sisters got into their car.

'Will he go back to Basingstoke?' wondered Artemis.

'He did come here just to get away from her, and now the coast, as they say, is clear ... But even so, I hope not. Besides, Basingstoke. What on earth is there to do there? And he's so useful here. He plays chess with our father once a week. He's the only person that our father will actually see. We need the Canon. God knows what Judy would do without him.'

'And does no one need him in Basingstoke?'

'I haven't got the energy to feel compassionate about somewhere so far away,' said Caroline. 'You don't think, surely, that he might have someone in Basingstoke, do you?' she asked, horror-struck at the idea.

'He might. The Canon is really rather sweet, you know. He's so kind and concerned for people. There are all sorts of ageing spinsters in Basingstoke, who, now the coast is, as you say, clear, might well close in for the kill.'

'I can't think of the Canon – you know – getting married.'

'Sex,' said Artemis. 'It is the universal mystery. No one can resist it. And even the most unexpected people succumb to it. There are all sorts of people whom one cannot imagine having sex, yet they do.'

Caroline heard the words and wondered if they were a hopeful sign.

They arrived at Shoal Bay, a huge expanse of deserted white sand. (Duxbury, who had been there but once, and who hated the sea, had pronounced it far better than any beach in Trinidad.) There were no buildings, indeed no proper road for the last few hundred yards – only a low line of scrub, principally made up of the poisonous manchineel.

'I'd like to swim in the nude,' said Artemis.

'Anyone might come out of those trees,' said Caroline fearfully. 'And you know what people here are like.'

'People here', Artemis knew, were in the habit of dressing up to the nines on Sundays and listening to hell-fire sermons, preached for the most part in tin-roofed chapels and sweltering heat. One saw them, lumbering along the roads, squeezed into elaborate frocks that were just a little too tight, crowned with wide-brimmed hats, a look of concentration on their faces as they dragged their sometimes less than enthusiastic menfolk off to divine worship. They would not take kindly to the sight of a young stranger, pinkly naked, frolicking on the sand of Shoal Bay. But it would have been nice, all the same, to enjoy the innocence of Eve in the garden, if only for a time.

They swam, modestly, in their bathing costumes.

'Do you really think that Charles is milk and water?' asked Caroline, when they were lying on the sand afterwards.

'Yes. Is he very rich?'

'He must be. The Broughtons who make the beer – that's him. And he has that yacht which he seems to have bought just for fun.'

'But we don't need money, do we? We don't need to marry to have comfortable lives, do we?'

'It might be quite nice to have children,' suggested Caroline.

'You don't need to marry to do that,' said Artemis. 'At least not any more.'

'It is still better to do so,' said Caroline.

'Goodness,' said Artemis. 'I think it is them.'

A yacht had indeed come into view.

'Is it them? Are they stopping?' asked Caroline.

The answer proved to be Yes on both counts. The yacht was soon at anchor about seventy yards out from the beach. Two cheery figures waved and then dived into the sea. Presently Charles and Gianni were wading ashore, wet-headed and smiling.

'This is a nice surprise,' said Caroline. 'We don't deserve all this attention.'

Charles looked a little sheepish, from which she guessed that their sudden descent had been Gianni's idea.

'The Canon told us that you would be here,' said Charles. 'We met him as he was delivering the *Catholic Herald* to Judy. Amazing how news travels, isn't it?'

'Yes,' she said.

'Your father,' said Charles. 'He is Duxbury of *Ancient Attica*, isn't he?'

'Yes,' she said again, this time looking at the distant scene.

'A very fine book,' said Charles. 'I read it.'

'So did I,' she said, remembering the long chapter devoted to an enthusiastic discussion of Greek sexual habits, that still had the power to embarrass her. 'I was thinking of going for a walk,' she said. 'Along the beach.'

They set off. She felt the need to get away from the topic of her father. If Charles came too, so much the better. There would be plenty of other occasions for Artemis to talk to him. It was a very long beach; it would be a very long walk; and the prospect of talking to Charles on his own was pleasant. She did not want him to be exposed to Artemis, who presently thought he was milk and water. Artemis – who was currently wearing a mask of something called 'Total Block' on her face – had the habit of making fun of people, even people she liked. In fact especially people she liked, just as her father did. It was as if she was frightened of liking them too much. So Caroline would take Charles away, she would rescue him for now, and leave the young Italian to keep Artemis amused.

'Did you ever meet my father at Oxford?' she said, unable to keep off this topic.

'No, not at all; I knew him by sight, though.'

'You'll get sunburnt,' she said, looking at his chest and bare shoulders, wishing as she said it that she didn't sound so auntish. 'I suppose Duxbury is one of those surnames that people tend to recognise, isn't it?'

'A bit like mine,' said Charles.

'I hadn't thought of that. Broughton. It means beer and money. Victorian prosperity. Is that such a bad thing?'

'In Grenada it got me invited to a very posh party by some people I didn't even know,' said Charles. 'But generally it means people judge you before they know you; they go on your name.'

'Judgements are hardly ever fair, even if they are favourable,' said Caroline. 'A book is judged by its cover. People say it is not, but it is. People always thought my father was arrogant in Oxford,' she said, feeling herself on the verge of confiding in him. 'They did. I was an undergraduate at the time, but I knew that they did. I was able to pick it up from the way people pronounced his name. But they were just acting on an impression they got. Deep down he isn't at all like that – at least I am sure you will like him when you meet him.'

'I will try to, I promise,' he said, with a smile.

They walked on in silence.

If I had my sister's face, but not her mind, thought Caroline, this man would fall in love with me.

'Are you staying here long?' she asked, as one did.

'Yes,' said Charles. 'I mean I think so. I don't have any particular plans about going anywhere else just yet. The original plan, in so far as there was one, was to go on to Tortola or Virgin Gorda, but I think I'm rather losing my taste for islands. Island-hopping is rather nomadic, staying here a few days, then sailing on.'

'Perhaps you should go and live in Barbados,' she said.

'Why Barbados?'

'It is the best island in the West Indies. We had an uncle there. It is beautiful. His wife grew orchids and there were monkeys in the garden. Every now and then my uncle would go out and shoot one. They were childless but happy. It is the sort of place you can be happy in. Not like Trinidad. Certainly not like St Martin. Not like here.'

'Here?'

'Not that we'll stay here forever,' she said. 'By this time next year it will be overrun by tourists. The hotels will open. My father – he doesn't like people.'

She looked at him as she said this, and saw sympathy in his clear blue eyes.

'I suppose you know the entire story, don't you?' she said, feeling herself fall over the precipice into confidential disclosure.

'Yes, I think I do,' he replied, wondering how much she thought he knew.

She looked back down the beach. Her sister and the Italian were now two distant figures reclining on the sand. They were alone.

'It's all so ridiculous,' she said. 'The real reason we left England was because my father was bored with Oxford. And yet here we are. You can't get any more boring than this, can you? What on earth will you do here, Charles?'

'A boring place is often the best place to be when you haven't an idea of what you want to do,' he said. 'You can work out what you really want to do when all your distractions are taken away from you.'

'What is Gianni like?' she asked suddenly.

'Well – he's Italian. He's supposed to sail boats. We met on the Gaza strip. He sails my boat for me. He's quite ordinary really. He dropped out of university in Italy, like so many of them do. He was doing Latin and Greek, funnily enough.'

They turned to walk back.

Gianni had spent the interval of their absence in being as polite as possible to Artemis, hoping that this would make an agreeable impression.

'We have been talking about Rome,' said Artemis, when the other two returned. 'Did you know that Gianni is a Roman?'

'So was I, for four years,' said Caroline.

'Did you like it?' asked Gianni.

Caroline was thoughtful. She was aware of the perpetual cloud of depression that always materialised over her at the mention of Rome. Had she liked it? No one had ever asked her so simple a question about Rome before. Had she liked having her heart broken? This Italian, this Gianni, imagined her to be what he was, a tourist, someone on permanent holiday. You packed your bags, you arrived somewhere, you unpacked the same bags, and then after a time you packed again and went somewhere else. But she had not done that. She had left something behind her in Rome, something that would never fit into a suitcase, a nebulous something that sometimes she called her youth, and at other times her *joie de vivre*.

'I'll never forget Rome,' she said, in reply to his question.

'What have we got to eat tonight?' asked Artemis.

'Frozen chicken,' said Caroline mechanically.

'Oh good. Then there's no problem about Charles and Gianni coming to dinner, is there?'

'Of course not,' said Caroline.

Everyone smiled. Things had been arranged, and the disaster of the previous night forgotten.

When they got home, while Artemis monopolised the bathroom, as was her wont, Caroline put the frozen chicken out to defrost, and then sat in front of the mirror in her bedroom.

It was a pity about her hair; they had cut it off in Italy, when she had been in hospital. It had been as long and as beautiful as Artemis's, but the nurses had found it objectionable: she had been unconscious at the time and she had woken to find it gone. But her hair was not the only thing that had been taken from her. She had lost so much else; and she had kept her hair short ever since, even though it did not suit her, as a sign that made sense to no one but herself.

When Duxbury had come to see her there on Tiber Island – he was fond of pointing out that it was the oldest hospital in the world and it certainly felt it – when he came and saw that they had cut off her hair, he had realised then how serious the situation was. It was as if she were close to death. In novels, they cut the hair off dying Victorian maidens. But she was not dying, only wishing she were dead. The source of her anguish had not been physical pain. It had been in her heart that she had suffered.

The horrors of that hospital were still with her. The shock of waking up, feeling your head shorn, and the implication that where you would soon be going you would have no use for a head of hair; the long involved explanation that followed in rapid Italian that she had been unable to follow; the feeling that they might cut off or out something else, of equal value, such as her kidneys or eyes, and deliver the same impersonal explanation; the knowledge that her child had died, and been taken from her, without her being able to protest; all these things had driven her to the edge of complete collapse, if not beyond it.

Silvia had come to visit her, wearing a new dress, a little pool of elegance. (Her father had rung Silvia, ordering her to visit, feeling himself unable to do anything, knowing, hoping that Silvia, a woman, would know what to do.)

'It was perhaps for the best,' Silvia had said, a little sadly, referring to her still-born child.

(Silvia had never had any children; she was very smart, and just over forty; she would never have any children now. She felt the tragedy as if it were her own, but felt compelled to lie, knowing this was what convention demanded.)

'Will he come and see me?' Caroline had asked, knowing what the answer would be.

(Silvia, too, knew the answer; he would not come and see her; they would probably never meet again; and she felt angry that it was so. Truth was swallowed up in anger, and her brother, of whom she was so fond, suddenly seemed a villain.)

'He has deserted you,' said Silvia bitterly. 'He has gone away; he won't come back.'

She was his sister; she knew him better than anyone. And at that moment Caroline had felt herself truly deserted, and that the man she had loved had had no heart.

'Where has he gone?' she had asked. 'Does he know I am here?'

But Silvia had looked away, unable to answer.

That had been four years ago. Where was he now, she wondered? Was he happy and prosperous, while she at the age of thirty had come to realise that for her hope had ended? She tried to imagine what he might be doing; but the only picture that came into her mind was the memory of the first time she had seen him.

'It is my brother,' Silvia had said, stepping into the flat, a pile of shopping in her arms.

There he had been asleep on the sofa, a copy of *Il Messagero* on his chest, his face in perfect repose. Younger than Silvia, not by any means handsome; thirty years old, but balding; breathing gently, looking a little older than his years – these were the details that came back to her. Other memories she had deleted from her mind, but the way he had looked then was something that she could never forget. She remembered how his clear green eyes had opened, and how he had looked at her. Was it then that she had fallen in love with him?

'He's been up all night,' Silvia explained.

Her brother – she could not bear to think of his name, and had done her best to forget it – had been a doctor. He did things with refugees from Yugoslavia on the outskirts of Rome, with some Catholic organisation, the name of which had meant nothing to her.

How could she have known? How could she have foreseen this unhappy ending? Her father had taken to him too. Silvia was a professional classicist; her brother an amateur. Silvia's speciality had been Virgil; he had dabbled in Aristotle and Aquinas. Duxbury's hobby then had been to attack the Catholic view of Aristotle. 'You know,' Caroline had heard her father remark, 'that man doesn't really believe anything at all.' He had said it with glee. Silvia had smiled. Silvia knew her brother. Caroline had misinterpreted that smile – but how was she to have known? Silvia had smiled because she had known that there were certain things even Duxbury didn't understand. *Povero inglese* – so educated, yet so ignorant.

And Caroline too had assumed that Catholics were merely people who held untenable views about Aristotle. She hadn't realised – she hadn't been able to realise – that religion mattered. The fact that he was a devoutly Catholic doctor who was kind to refugees seemed to be part of his natural goodness. How could it possibly have stopped him loving her and wanting to marry her?

'My poor darling,' said Silvia, that dreadful day in the hospital. 'You never knew him.'

But she had, she thought she had. He had deceived her. That was how she had interpreted Silvia's words. He had seemed to love her, but all the time – there had been something incommunicable about him. There had been something she had not understood, something hidden from her. And he had left her. Why? Not understanding how anyone could prefer the company of sick and dying refugees to her own, she had assumed the worst, namely that he had never loved her at all.

She had tried to hate him for it, to purge herself of her love for him that way. But even there she had failed. Her pregnancy had nurtured the hope of his eventual return. He would grow bored with whatever he was doing. He would come back. How – she did not think. The child was her secret. To Duxbury the pregnancy, when she finally told him of it, had seemed to be the result of a lamentable contraceptive failure. He had not known what she knew. But then, even that hope had turned to despair.

Even the doctors on Tiber Island had caught something of the hopelessness of the case, and shook their heads gravely, using wonderfully vague phrases full of melancholy cadences. The shock of a sixth-month still-birth; the depression brought about by an unhappy love-affair; for these they had no cure, but could only suggest a change of air.

'Would you like to go to Naples?' asked Duxbury, a little tentatively, perhaps remembering another unhappy woman for whose death he had been blamed; perhaps wondering whether Caroline might not in fact die, so desperate did she seem.

'Further, further away,' she had said.

'Palermo?' he had asked.

'Further, further away,' she had said again. 'Beyond Italy, beyond this, to the very edge of the world.'

'Bathroom!' called Artemis, from the corridor outside, suddenly recalling her to the present.

Later, when she was examining the defrosting chicken with all the care of a surgeon, Artemis joined her in the kitchen.

'Anything I can do?' she asked.

'You could joint the chicken,' said Caroline shortly. 'I'll do the onions.'

Caroline started on the onions; Artemis prodded the chicken a little uncertainly.

'It's still frozen,' she said. 'Can I help with the onions?' she asked, because she felt she ought to.

She approached the kitchen 'work-surface' a little gingerly.

'There's only one decent knife,' said Caroline. 'And I'm using it. But you can stay and talk to me.'

'Will that chicken be enough for five?' asked Artemis. 'Don't they shrink when you cook them?'

'I'm making a curry. I'll put in bits of potato.'

'Will Gianni like curry?' said Artemis a little uncertainly. 'Generally, Italians don't.'

'Do they not?' said Caroline scathingly, chopping more ferociously. 'I am sure that he's so used to making himself agreeable that he'll eat whatever is put in front of him, even if it kills him.'

'Do be careful,' said her sister, seeing how fiercely she was wielding the knife. 'You'll cut yourself. Don't you like Gianni?'

'Eurotrash,' said Caroline, not quite knowing what the term meant, but sure it was what she felt.

'He's rather sweet,' said Artemis. 'The onions are making you cry.'

A talent for stating the obvious, coupled with a tendency to promiscuity, were valuable gifts, Caroline realised. They kept you from tears. She did not have them.

'You're such a tart, dear,' she said enviously.

'A bit of one,' admitted Artemis.

'What if you were to fall desperately in love with one of your men?'

'I'm far too sensible to do anything so foolish,' she replied. 'But Gianni is ...'

'Sweet,' said Caroline. 'Yuk.'

'He is very good-looking,' said Artemis defensively. 'Even you must admit that.'

'I will do no such thing. Italians just look good-looking, but they never really are.'

'Good looks are purely a matter of appearance, so it amounts to the same thing. I think I like superficial qualities in a man. It means that I'm very rarely disappointed.'

Caroline thought of her own experience; she had been disappointed there; Artemis would not have been.

'What's for lunch?' asked Artemis.

'Aveline is seeing to that,' replied Caroline.

Aveline was the maid, who was now sweeping the verandah

with methodic and rhythmic slowness. Caroline continued to weep over her onions, and Artemis drifted into the sitting-room. Her father was there, idly waiting for lunch.

'Caroline is making curry for this evening,' said Artemis.

'And will the Italian like it?'

'Probably not.'

'I am fond of Italians,' said Duxbury. 'They have no depth, and they are thus quite incapable of hypocrisy, once you realise that nothing they say can quite be regarded as true. They tell it as they see it; as a result they are almost completely out of touch with reality. English people can find this disconcerting.'

'Would you have liked to have stayed in Rome?' asked Artemis suddenly, wondering why her father had ever left it. She had been at university when he had done so, and had never been sufficiently interested in his motivation until now, when it suddenly seemed odd.

From the kitchen, Caroline heard the question and was still.

Duxbury smiled maddeningly, and said nothing. Artemis's curiosity passed, and soon she began to tell her father of their meeting with the Canon that morning, and the news of his sister's impending ordination to the priesthood.

But the question of Italy came up again while they were having lunch. Caroline could not get Italy out of her mind.

'We don't know anything about Gianni,' she said. 'We know who Charles is, but Gianni is a mystery. I mean, what is his surname?'

'Does it matter?' said Artemis. 'I don't need to know his surname.'

'It might be Doria, or Borghese, or something rather grand,' said Duxbury.

'One ought to know who people are,' said Caroline. 'One ought to be curious about them. A lack of curiosity is dangerous. They might have some terrible secret. Gianni might be married for all we know.'

'You are far more interested in him than I am,' said Artemis, concentrating on the plate in front of her, and using her rather blunt knife to cut a piece of cold ham.

'There are three million people in Rome, Caroline,' said Duxbury gently, knowing where his daughter's mind was leading.

Caroline looked at her plate. How ghastly ham was, this side of the Atlantic. Imported American ham; not like Roman ham at all. She wished she could stop worrying and put the past behind her. She had done her best to break the threads of memory, and succeeded for the most part; but more durable than nylon was the thread that held her still to the man who had left her to work with refugees. Every detail about him she had tried to delete; the fact of her abandonment was with her still.

V

Gianni had put on his Armani jeans and a shirt he had bought in the Via Sistina. In modest contrast, Charles was wearing a pair of knee-length shorts and a polo shirt. His legs were covered with hair that had been bleached white by the sun. The same was true of his head, a mass of curls varying from yellow to almost white.

'Shorts?' said Gianni.

'Why not?' replied Charles. 'I think we ought to stop for a drink at Judy's on the way. You never can tell with men like Duxbury – he might be rather parsimonious with alcohol.'

Charles rowed them ashore. Gianni sat in the stern, turning his face to the breeze.

'You look nice,' said Judy thoughtfully, eyeing them, when they came in.

'He's vain enough as it is,' said Charles crossly.

Gianni looked hurt.

'I suppose it is for Artemis,' said Judy. 'Prettiness always finds its own level. How long did you spend combing your hair?'

'Twenty minutes,' said Gianni.

'I am sure she'll notice,' said Judy. 'I have.'

'It makes me feel middle-aged,' said Charles. 'I wish I had some wise admonitions, but I don't.'

'Don't you worry,' said Judy, who hadn't been at the party in Grenada, where Gianni had disappeared with Lord What's-his-name's daughter. 'Just you sit back and enjoy the fun.'

'My sister and father lived in Rome,' said Artemis, conversationally. 'Where was it now?'

'Via del Governo Vecchio,' said Caroline, noticing Gianni's polite look of interest with growing suspicion. She distrusted polite young men. 'Number 43,' she added.

'My parents live in the Via Ludovisi,' said Gianni.

'And you had a great friend near the Via Merulana, didn't you?' said Artemis, showing off her knowledge of Roman addresses. 'Near St Mary Major's. What was she called?'

'Silvia,' said Duxbury.

'Silvia what?' asked Artemis. 'I was in England, at university, at the time, but I remember meeting her,' she explained to Gianni.

Caroline was silent.

'Silvia Donati,' said Duxbury with deliberation. 'She was a university professor, at the University of Viterbo. She used to lecture on Virgil, a subject of which she knew, poor woman, practically nothing.'

'But she had a nice flat,' said Artemis. 'I remember going there once. There was a roof terrace with a wonderful view, and plants, quite big ones too ...'

'I must go and look at the food,' said Caroline, suddenly getting up.

It really was too bad, she thought, as she pretended to stir the vindaloo. The merest mention of places associated with him, and she felt this overwhelming urge to run away and hide herself from view. When it came back to her in dreams, that was bearable; but to be reminded of what she had known in the midst of pre-dinner chatter was too painful. It had been so individual, so private, so much her very own. No one else had loved him, or known what she had known. In that lay the intensity of the experience, even now. No one else had felt that warm shoulder or seen the hair on the back of his head turn to a darker shade of chestnut as the dampness of sweat gathered there. That picture was hers, exclusively, incommunicably. No one else could ever know it, as it was beyond explanation. Other women had doubtless fallen in love before with handsome charming men. It was common. People discussed it, they shared a perception of what happened. They gave reasons. There were reasons to give. But in this case – how could she explain why she had loved him? He hadn't been conventionally attractive. No one else had noticed him, or loved him, as she had done, and no one else could understand it. The rest of her life, all the other things, had been taken over by her father, or by Artemis: this experience alone was entirely hers. For that reason she could not bear to hear the scenes of her former happiness even mentioned. It was the trespass of the touristic masses in hallowed ground, a heedless case of sacrilege.

'Can I help at all?' said Charles, coming into the kitchen.

'Oh no,' she said, turning to face him.

'Are you all right?' he asked, a little uncertainly.

'Oh yes. Why?'

'You look a little different, that's all.'

'I was thinking,' she said. 'Or perhaps it is the smell of the curry. The fumes can get up your nose. I think it is more or less done. I am afraid that things here are a little bit primitive.'

'So is the boat,' he said. 'Well, not primitive – cramped, rather. And Gianni is very untidy. He never puts anything away. You should see the cabin. I suppose Italian men always have a mother or an elder sister to put things away for them, don't they.'

'Yes, they do,' she said, picturing Silvia. 'Their womenfolk protect them and spoil them.'

'You didn't like Italy, did you?' he said, prodding the curry with a wooden spoon, inviting confidences.

'Italy is beautiful,' she said. 'It is the sort of place that forms pictures in your mind. You know what I mean: sun-drenched squares, people lounging on the shady side in the noon-time, smoking. My father loved it. He would much rather have stayed.'

'Oh?' said Charles vaguely, wondering why he hadn't stayed, and what Duxbury could have got up to in Rome that might have forced him to leave the country against his will. His mind quickly ran through the possibilities. Surely to be forced out of two countries in a row was something of a record. But not even Duxbury could be that bad.

'It was my fault we left Italy,' said Caroline, reading his mind.

'A fault?' he said. 'Isn't that too dramatic a term?'

'If only things could be dramatic,' said Caroline. 'But they so often aren't. They just go on, without reaching conclusions. I sometimes think it would be better if real life were like *Hamlet* – all those bodies on the stage at the end. That's one way of clearing things up, isn't it? I think this chicken is on the verge of overcooking. Frozen food does that.'

'Of course, we're English,' began Charles.

'Not my father,' said Caroline. 'He's a proper West Indian. Perhaps he likes it here; or at least he doesn't find it so odd. I mean, would you ever live here?'

'No,' said Charles, honestly.

'Where would you live then?'

'Hampstead, I suppose. But I'd have to have a house somewhere else as well.'

'I see. Well, why don't you? I mean, you can, can't you? But instead of doing that, you spend your time on a cramped yacht with someone who never puts anything away. Why?'

'It is rather odd,' he admitted. 'I do, in fact, have a house in Hampstead as it is, yet I am a nomad.'

'It is because you're rich,' she said.

'Yes, I am rich. If you are rich you can be nomadic. You don't have to worry about mortgages. I suppose some rich people do live sedentary lives, but not me.'

'It is unnatural,' said Caroline, severely. 'I am unnatural. I ought to be in one place – but instead I am nowhere. This island could be the planet Mars.'

'But where would you like to be?'

'A place that doesn't exist,' she said, thinking of Silvia's roof terrace. 'The others will be wondering where we are,' she added.

Charles followed her out on to the verandah.

'I would have voted Communist,' Duxbury was saying.

'They have changed their name now,' said Gianni. 'They are now called the Democratic Party of the Left.'

'I can't get used to name changes. I am too old,' said Duxbury grandly. 'I think I'd vote for *Rifondazione Comunista*.'

'But, *professore*, they are Stalinists,' said Gianni in mock horror.

'Precisely. A good dose of Stalinism is just what Italy needs. I like Stalinism. I feel a little thrill at the thought of five-year plans and tractor production. Heavy industry: industry ought to be heavy. The idea of light industry is simply ridiculous.'

'And who did you vote for?' asked Artemis.

'The Christian Democrats,' said Gianni.

'Goodness, how sad,' said Artemis. 'That isn't in the least bit adventurous, is it?'

'Even Silvia Donati gave them up,' said Duxbury. 'She voted for the Greens. She liked to think she was fashionable.'

'The curry's ready,' said Caroline, a little apologetically. One day she really ought to try some other recipe.

'Then let's go and sit around the table,' said Artemis, taking charge. 'Come on sit next to me, Gianni,' she ordered. 'And Charles, you go on the other side. Good. I want to persuade you to come with us to Sombrero Island. The boat goes on the first Thursday of every month. That's in a few days, isn't it? You lose track of the days of the week when you are on holiday.'

In the midst of this, the curry arrived. Gianni's plate, with a show of unkind solicitude, was piled high with vindaloo by Artemis.

'Have a popadom,' she said. 'I brought them out specially from London. They come in tins,' she explained.

He examined a popadom and smiled. He could feel a foot against his own under the table, and a hand brushing gently against his leg.

'Do be careful,' warned Duxbury. 'Sombrero Island is surrounded by sharks. They are attracted by the rubbish that the lighthouse men throw into the sea.'

'Great whites?' asked Charles.

'Hammerheads mainly. Ugly things,' said Duxbury with a shiver of disgust. 'I never go swimming. When I was young I knew someone who was supposed to have been eaten by a shark.'

Caroline tried to fathom the logic of this assertion.

'Later,' she said. 'He was eaten by the shark after you knew him.'

'Of course he was,' said Duxbury. 'They never quite knew for sure, though. One never does. But when someone disappears, that is what is generally assumed.'

'I've never given it a thought, *professore*,' said Gianni, feeling expansive and brave.

'Thoughtlessness is bliss,' said Artemis, with a rare flash of sincerity. 'There are many things I'd rather not think about.'

'Yes,' said Caroline. 'Amnesia would be ambrosia. It would make us into gods.'

'I suppose you believe in God, don't you?' said Duxbury, turning to the two young guests, fixing them with his penetrating stare.

'Well, yes, I do,' said Charles, whose family had bred several evangelical clergymen, who had gone to labour in the East End, to atone for inheriting a fortune based on alcohol.

'And Gianni's a Christian Democrat,' said Artemis, with a note of finality.

'But not a fanatic,' said Gianni, not wanting to ruin his chances.

'I think that God may have existed once in the past,' said Duxbury, putting down his fork laden with curry. 'But he has now faded away into nothingness. He made the world, and then realising how badly he had made it, he decided to take voluntary redundancy. How could God be any good at being God, if he made the hammerhead shark?'

'But if people left the poor old hammerhead in peace, it wouldn't do anyone any harm,' said Charles. 'It's only when people interfere that things go wrong.'

'And when things, as you put it, go wrong, does God step in and put them right?' asked Duxbury.

'I wish he would,' said Caroline. 'It would save us all so much trouble.'

'You're so clerical,' said Artemis, accusingly. 'And don't look at me like that.'

'But no one can save us from ourselves,' said Duxbury. 'Only that is not depressing, it's liberating. We are free.'

'Oh, what tripe,' said Caroline. 'We'd all like to be someone else, or we'd all like to be better versions of ourselves.'

'I'm perfectly happy being my own ghastly self,' said Artemis.

'And so am I,' said Duxbury. 'I rejoice in low opinions, especially my own. I don't have to worry about what anyone may think of me, because, before they think it, I have already done so.'

'Do you mean,' said Charles, 'that there's nothing that you would not do?'

He spoke generally, impersonally.

'Nothing that comes to mind,' said Duxbury, after a pause for consideration. 'Morality is purely a matter of taste.'

The curry had disappeared. Gianni was drinking a great deal of water. There seemed to be no pudding, of which he was glad. A heavy English pudding just then would have killed him. It had been hard enough forcing down the over-generous helping that Artemis had given him.

'I am afraid I had rather forgotten pudding,' Caroline explained. 'But there is some ice-cream in the freezer. Or did we have to throw that lot away the last time the generator broke down?'

Ice-cream was politely but universally refused. Caroline wondered whether this meant the dinner had not been a success. She made another effort, trying to tempt them with coffee, and was rewarded with greater success. She got up to go to the kitchen. Soon she was fiddling with mugs – there were no cups and saucers here, for the house was equipped as if for a camping holiday. She waited for the kettle to boil and thought about God. If he did exist, he certainly had not arranged things very well. She supposed he might exist. Perhaps the one man she had ever loved had left her for God after all, and not his career. Or more accurately, he had left God for her, briefly, and then gone back to him. Perhaps if she were to think of it in that way, defeat would be slightly easier to bear. It was better to think of your successful rival as omnipotent, immutable and all wise, rather than some Other Woman. But Silvia, who had always seemed so clever, had blamed her brother's heartlessness, not God. How harsh families could be. Yet Silvia had always spoiled her brother; she had done everything for him, always; had she really thought him so ruthless? Was cruelty the sort of thing sisters admired in Italy?

The kettle boiled. Perhaps the truth was this: you loved people, you knew them; and yet you continued to love them, even when you knew how unlovable they could be. She poured the hot water on to the coffee granules. Why was it all so illogical? Why couldn't she love someone worthy and good? Why not just pack her bags, and leave this island and her father? But she would be alone then, and solitude was the last thing she wanted. Solitude without amnesia would be hell.

She put the coffee mugs on to a tray and carried them out to the verandah. There was a little commotion at the table as she arrived. Duxbury was getting up to go.

'Don't get up,' he said to the others. 'I am rather tired, but you continue enjoying yourselves.'

But one guest, ever eager to be agreeable, had got up. Gianni was now holding out his hand, which Duxbury had taken, and rapidly expounding his great pleasure in meeting the *professore*. And indeed his violet eyes seemed to be sparkling with pleasure, and the whole posture of his body spoke of flattery. Duxbury was clearly pleased. It was, after all, very gratifying to be treated in this way. The elaborate politeness of this young man and his flowery phrases produced a delicious sense of contrast with his intentions, which, Duxbury surmised, were totally dishonourable, and if he knew Italians, possibly illegal too, at least in English law. But Italians were like that: their words and their actions were completely at variance, and yet they were utterly sincere. In addition there was the amusing thought of the way Gianni was paying court to the father, in order to win the daughter: so much for the rights of women! The flirtation was transposed, from daughter to father, and the father was delighted.

'*Fai il tuo volere*,' said Duxbury by way of reply. '*Saro contentissimo*.'

Gianni smiled radiantly, and then, with great reluctance, let go of Duxbury's hand. Caroline, feeling a little sick, wondered if he would stoop and kiss it.

'*Grazie, professore*,' said Gianni.

Duxbury left. Caroline could not but feel annoyed. Her father had given *carte blanche* to Gianni, as if Artemis herself was a mere chattel to be disposed of. What on earth was he thinking of? And to tolerate Gianni's flirtation – that was the only word she could think of – was almost too much.

Artemis, who knew no Italian, but merely thought that Gianni was over-polite and a little ridiculous, not understanding the transaction that had taken place, said:

'It would be quite nice to walk out to the point. There might be a breeze.'

'Yes,' said Gianni, looking expectantly at Charles.

'I am quite happy here, at least for now,' said Charles.

After they had gone, Charles turned to Caroline.

'Your father seemed to take a shine to Gianni,' he remarked. 'Or, at least, that is what Gianni thinks.'

'Yes,' she said. 'My father is a bit of a tease.'

He realised, as she said this, that it was true. Duxbury delighted in being thought much worse than he, in fact, was. He revelled in imputed crimes that were not his own.

'Gianni wouldn't realise that,' he said.

'No,' she said. 'I suppose he wouldn't. You must think us a bit odd,' she added.

'Why?'

'We're hardly a normal family. My father is a tease, so is Artemis, I think, and I am their hanger-on. We're a bit of a freak show.'

'You are certainly odd,' said Charles, helping himself to a cigarette from Gianni's pack, and lighting it. 'What I mean is I don't quite see what category you fall into. There's nothing wrong with you; there's simply something wrong with the world.'

His words faded into silence. Sitting there with him in the tropical darkness, she felt the sudden need to speak.

'Once, I was in love,' she said. 'I thought that was it. I saw myself married to him and having his children; I had this feeling that somehow I had arrived, that I had found what I was looking for. We had our secret world. We belonged one to another. Then it all went spectacularly wrong. I got pregnant; he left me, because he couldn't go through with it. And then the child was still-born. That was the worst thing of all. It all sounds rather bald when I tell it to you, but it wasn't. We left Italy. I insisted. If the child hadn't died, I think I wouldn't have minded so much: there would have been something to show that it hadn't all been a terrible illusion. I don't know why I am burdening you with all this. Artemis doesn't know. She wasn't there at the time. And even if I told her, I rather doubt that she would be able to grasp the point of it all. I'm afraid she rather upset me, talking about Rome just now; she knows nothing about it. To her men are just another form of leisure activity, like roulette or knitting. I really don't think she's capable of falling in love. I did hope that you would take her on and teach her to be different.'

'Gianni has got to her first,' said Charles. 'He told me that he is in love with her.'

'And is he?'

'It is possible. People do fall in love at first sight, I suppose. The only thing is that Gianni seems to do it rather a lot. I think he sees her as something of a challenge.'

'He's been listening to Judy Blomberg,' said Caroline. 'Judy has great influence on this island. But why didn't you fall in love with Artemis at first sight? Judy would have preferred that, and so would I.'

'Would you?'

'Yes.'

'I have tried falling in love at first sight, and it doesn't work,' he said. 'Or rather it works too well. You can do it again and again, the way that Gianni does, but the point is that you should do it just once and for all. It's like taking a degree: if you decide to take a second degree, as I did, people always assume there was something wrong with your first one, and they are generally right.'

'Artemis wouldn't agree,' said Caroline. 'Her view is the more the merrier. The trouble with that is that you never really fall in love with anyone that way. You are always moving on. It should be eternal, but it hardly ever lasts more than a week. Nothing seems to last. I sometimes wish that I had been born religious, then at least I would have had some idea of permanence.'

'Hasn't Canon Cartwright converted you yet?'

'He wouldn't dare try,' said Caroline a little sadly. 'He's too timid. He's not at all evangelical, you know. His sister is. She's going to be a priest out in Africa. George, the Canon, says that she's going to convert people, that she's full of zeal. There used to be an evangelical church in Oxford, didn't there? They used to convert people too.'

'Yes, they did,' said Charles. 'Warm handshakes, broad smiles and guitars.'

'But the Canon's sister isn't at all like that,' said Caroline. 'She's never smiled in her life, and I doubt she can play the guitar.'

'Not warm?'

'No.'

'I think you have to be, to be a real evangelical,' said Charles. 'You're also expected to play the guitar. Perhaps the less musical can get away with banging a tambourine, or shaking one of those lavatory rolls filled with rice. It's called making a joyful noise to the Lord, as in the hundred and fiftieth psalm.'

'There was nothing joyful about Miss Cartwright,' said Caroline, beginning to feel sorry for the Diocese of Mogadishu.

'Then she must be Zwinglian,' said Charles with determination. 'Or like John Knox: harsh mountain terrain and intransigent theology. Swiss or Scottish.'

'That's why the Canon is here; to get away from her. They used to share a house in Basingstoke. Having breakfast with John Knox or Zwingli every morning can't have been much fun. If there had been any spinsters in the congregation sighing over the Canon she would have seen them off pretty quickly. But now she's going to Mogadishu to evangelise natives and to terrify cannibals into vegetarianism.'

'The Canon will use the opportunity to get married, I suppose,' said Charles.

'Could he?' asked Caroline. 'Marry? I can't imagine him … you know what I mean.'

Charles did. Nowadays sex was an activity confined to the young and beautiful – or at least it was meant to be.

'I wonder what Gianni is doing?' he said, thinking aloud.

'Are there sharks?' Gianni was asking.

'Of course not,' said Artemis contemptuously. 'You sound like my father. There aren't any sharks in the Caribbean. At least there aren't here, so close to shore. Sharks are miles out to sea.'

'And how do you know?'

'I just do,' she said. 'Do you honestly think that they'd build hotels on beaches and tempt rich silly tourists to come all the way out here if there was the slightest chance of them being eaten by sharks? Don't be ridiculous. They'd sue them for every penny they'd got.'

'How could they? They'd be dead,' said Gianni, who was after all Italian, and thus much interested in litigation.

'Oh, do shut up,' said Artemis. 'And come in.'

She was standing in the sea as she said this; the water came up to her knees; her clothes lay in a pile on the beach, and Gianni stood next to them, a little uncertainly.

It was an extraordinary idea of Artemis's, to go swimming after so heavy a meal.

'Take your clothes off,' she ordered, as if she were a warden in a nudist camp.

Gianni sat down on the sand and began to undo his shoe-laces. Artemis, unwilling to wait any longer, plunged into the waves, leaving Gianni to fumble with his shoes. Soon he could feel the cold wet sand against his bare feet. This should have been a delightful sensation, but wasn't. He was feeling cold. He had eaten far too much curry and he felt sick as a result. What was more, in his eagerness to go for a walk with Artemis, he had left his cigarettes behind on the verandah. He was beginning, disastrously, to long for a cigarette, so much so that he could not really see any point in going for a nude moonlit swim with Artemis if his stomach felt too full, and if he could not have a cigarette afterwards. Besides, the water looked cold. If that were not enough, he had not quite liked the way she had ordered him to undress. It was very peremptory of her, and not in the least romantic. He was not used to being told to strip.

Artemis appeared, wet, hair flowing, naked, fresh from her swim.

'You're a coward,' she said, standing in front of him, like some goddess that knew no shame.

A hundred yards away he could see a solitary light. That was the house. He felt a sudden desire to go back there, to be in the safety of human company and away from this odd, though beautiful girl. He was unable to concentrate on her beauty: perhaps it was the curry; but he felt no excitement, only the feeling that he might suddenly be sick – or worse.

'Goodness, you are cold,' said Artemis, advancing and touching his cheek.

'I'm feeling a little bit ill,' he said lamely, conscious of failure.

'My mother's family made their money in sugar,' Caroline was saying. 'There wasn't actually any connection with the West Indies on her part; my parents met at some sort of conference. My maternal grandfather introduced them.'

'What sort of conference?' asked Charles.

'Something socialist or philanthropical, I think. My grandfather was like that. It almost killed him when my parents decided to get married. I mean, my father wasn't rich, and my mother was loaded, and no one knew who my father was. And then they suspected that he was a little too dark.'

'It boils down to money in the end,' said Charles.

'And race,' she said. 'When they took the wedding pictures, my grandmother apparently insisted that the photographer over-expose the film so that my father looked less dark; but all that happened was that my mother disappeared – her face melted away into her dress. She was very blonde and rather insipid-look-ing, I think, when young.'

Caroline considered the strange history of her parents in si-lence. So did Charles. Their concentration was only interrupted by the sudden return of Artemis.

'Where's Gianni?' she asked, a little out of breath, plonking her shoes, which she had been carrying, on the table. 'I seem to have lost him.'

'You didn't walk here barefoot?' asked Caroline. 'The place is full of land-crabs.'

'They are only in the scrub,' said Artemis defensively, remem-bering the horrible hermit crabs that came out at night. 'I kept to the path.'

'I'd better find a torch,' said Caroline.

'Not a successful evening,' said Charles, when they were back on the yacht. 'A bit like the evening in Grenada, in fact, when I was last to leave because I couldn't find where you'd got to.'

'It's not my fault,' said Gianni. 'At least not this time.'

Charles grunted.

'You can't possibly imagine that I somehow wanted that to happen, do you? I'd much rather that one of those crabs had in fact bitten me on the toe.'

'You shouldn't have eaten that curry,' said Charles severely. 'You only did it to impress her.'

'Oh God,' said Gianni, struck once again by the image he had of Artemis, wet and naked, getting out of the sea. How beautiful she had looked; how she had turned his stomach to ice; and how foolish he had looked, illuminated by the powerful beam of Caroline's torch, leaning against a tree, hand on stomach, doubled up in curry-induced agony. How on earth would Artemis ever take him seriously again? And yet he was now haunted by that vision of her, naked on the moonlit beach.

'There seemed to have been some commotion last night, after I went to bed,' observed Duxbury at breakfast the next morning.

'There was,' said Caroline, without elaborating, glad that Artemis was still in bed.

'That nice young Italian,' said Duxbury. 'I did like him. In fact I liked him very much. Such a polite young man. I suppose he will go with you to Sombrero?'

'I suppose so,' conceded Caroline.

'It's almost enough to tempt me to come too,' said Duxbury, watching for her reaction, sure that this would annoy her.

But Caroline refused to be drawn.

VI

The sun was high over Road Bay. Judy looked out of the doorway of the bar, staring at the insignificant islands that lay out to sea. It was still too early for the first drink of the day, being only a few minutes before ten. The Canon was with her. He was in a light mood, an unusual mood. He was talking of marriage, and its desirability. Judy was thinking of marriage herself as she half listened to him, and remembering what a disaster her own had been. What was he doing now, she wondered. What indeed had he ever done? Marcus Blomberg was not the sort of man you associated with activity. He had been so lazy. When he had ever done anything, he had always done it with such deliberation that she had felt that he was doing it to annoy her. He had driven her into a state of contradiction. One moment she had wanted to tell him to stop whatever he was doing; the next to rebuke him for never doing anything.

'What do you think, Judy?' she heard the Canon say to her.

There was a pause. Some sort of answer was expected of her. This was rather difficult, as she had not actually been listening. What did she think anyway? Most of the time she simply thought it was time for a drink. At other times, and this was one of them, she was wondering why she had come to the West Indies, when she had never particularly liked the sun. But the Canon was waiting for an answer.

'I don't really know,' she said, being utterly truthful and hedging her bets at the same time.

'I mean,' said the Canon, 'she can't really enjoy it here, can she? I'm sure she'd go back to England, if she had something to go back for, that is.'

'That is logical,' said Judy, hoping it was indeed so, wondering to whom the Canon was referring.

'And I know she wants children,' continued the Canon. 'And so do I.'

'How do you know that?' asked Judy suddenly. 'Men always seem to think they know that sort of thing,' she added, remembering how the unfortunate Mr Blomberg had always been so knowing, the type of man who had been able to explain everything, and leave no room for mysteries.

'She told me,' said the Canon, defensively. 'I was telling her about the Sunday school, and she said that she'd always thought that she would have made a good teacher. We were discussing children. I know that was what she meant: I told her we had thirty in the class and she looked wistful.'

'I look wistful all the time,' said Judy. 'Not just on the odd occasion.'

'I think she wants to go back to England, get married and have children,' said Canon Cartwright, refusing to be deflected, stating his position.

'Caroline is in love with her father,' said Judy. 'That's her reason for being here.'

'Oh nonsense, Judy.' Nevertheless the Canon sounded somewhat shocked. 'You don't think, do you, that Caroline, or Artemis ...'

There was a profound silence.

'Perhaps it is nonsense,' said Judy at last. 'Perhaps I'm in love with Duxbury.'

'But you don't even know him.'

'I've seen him. Outside the supermarket, standing under the flamboyant tree. He is so good-looking.'

'He's well over fifty-five,' said the Canon.

'So am I. So was Laurence Olivier once, and all the famous film stars. Amelia Churchill is over fifty-five, I'll bet.'

'Who?'

'The film star. The one who does tropical adventures.'

'Duxbury,' said the Canon, again feeling the conversation

88

drifting off course, and determined to take it under control, 'isn't a nice man.'

'No one ever loved anyone because they were nice,' said Judy. 'In fact, usually it is quite the reverse. And why do you say he's not nice, to use your own word? You play chess with him every week. You're the only person on the island he associates with.'

'He frightens me,' said the Canon. 'He's destructive. He's one of these men who has seen through everything, and holds nothing sacred. But – anyway, I am going to ask her.'

'Ask who what?'

'I am going to ask her to marry me.'

'Ah,' said Judy.

'What do you mean by "ah"?' he asked, after a slight pause.

'I'm just a little surprised, that's all,' said Judy. 'But I think it is a very good idea.' (She, in fact, thought the exact opposite, but felt she would rather have died than said so.) 'But don't do it just yet. I mean, test the ground, prepare her.'

'I have been preparing her,' said the Canon. 'But it isn't some sort of exam, you know. I want to marry Caroline Duxbury. She was so pleased when I told her that Maude was going to Mogadishu. Her face lit up.'

'Let's have a drink,' said Judy, thinking that the occasion could excuse the hour.

'There are some men,' she said, when they had both settled down with beers, 'that you can never get away from.'

'And do you think Duxbury is one of those?'

'Yes. I do. His wife wouldn't leave him. Caroline has always lived with him. Artemis comes back to see him, time and again. But he's just the sort of man that ought to be left. He's addictive, like cigarettes. You know that they are deadly, but you can't live without them. You co-operate with your own doom. Duxbury is an *homme fatal*.'

'Of course, I won't say a thing about it to him,' said the Canon.

'Good,' said Judy. 'It is your job to rescue her.'

I am morbid, thought Judy, as she stood on the jetty later that morning, looking down at the bright blue sea through the wooden slats. I think impossible thoughts about a man I have never even spoken to; my mind is filled with dark suspicions that cannot possibly be true.

'Are you coming to Sombrero Island?' asked Charles, who had appeared next to her.

'Has your Italian friend abandoned you?' she asked.

'Gianni? I've abandoned him. He's on the yacht, feeling ill. He ate too much curry last night, and he's not used to it.'

'Is it love-sickness?' she asked, noticing that there was no sympathy in Charles's voice.

'You mean Artemis. Yes, I suppose it is.'

'And she is going to Sombrero, isn't she?'

'Yes, she is. Gianni has to go too, even if it kills him. What about you?'

Judy stared out to sea.

'I belong on land,' she said. 'I am sure the Canon will go, though.'

'A clergyman is always useful,' said Charles.

'You went to Duxbury's last night,' she said. 'What do you imagine he does here all the time?'

'He's a secretive man, I think,' said Charles.

'I can't think what he has got to be secretive about,' said Judy peevishly, though she could, only too clearly. 'Perhaps he is one of those men who is secretive so that he'll appear interesting in the eyes of his neighbours. The very thought of him drives me mad. I know it is unreasonable of me, but he does. I wish people would act in a simple and straightforward way. It is so unreasonable of them not to. We are all a bit funny here, aren't we? We need someone to sort us out, to tell us what is what. Living on an island like this is bad for one's imagination.'

'Have you asked the Canon? To give you moral guidance?' said Charles.

'Oh, the Canon,' said Judy crossly. 'He's as bad as the rest of us. He's now got it into his head that he ought to marry Caroline.

I've never heard such nonsense – but he seems to think that it is a good idea. Middle-aged men ought to know better, especially when they are clergymen. He plays chess with her father, for God's sake. And please don't tell me that Caroline is just meant to be a vicar's wife, because if you do, I'll scream. Anglicanism,' she continued, 'is such a ridiculous religion. It's so full of compromises. The Canon is so typically Anglican he drives me mad, much as I love him. Thank God I'm a Catholic. At least you know where you are then, even if you are damned.'

'Damned?' said Charles. 'Surely none of us are damned?' He looked around Road Bay: the sea, the sand, the wooden houses, the salt pan beyond. 'No one here could possibly be damned,' he said.

'Perhaps we ought to be,' said Judy. 'I think I ought to be. I ran away from Mr Blomberg, when I said I would stick by him till death did us part. That was wrong of me.'

'But you wanted to leave him, didn't you?'

'I think you have said it there,' said Judy. 'Of course I wanted to. I wanted to get away from respectable Mr Blomberg and become an international vagrant. We're all doing what we want to do. You wanted to buy a yacht and cruise the Caribbean. Gianni wanted to come with you and chase girls. Duxbury wanted to snub Oxford. Artemis simply wants to do as she pleases, and seems to succeed. We are all doing what we want to do. That's why we're all in hell, because what we want is so very undesirable. It's like worshipping the Golden Calf. It seemed like a good idea at the time, but in the end … In the end you realise that it's just a golden calf after all, and it's jolly boring.'

'I wish I did want something good,' said Charles. 'But you know, Duxbury doesn't want to be here. I think he's here because Caroline wanted it, not the other way around. And if she were to marry the Canon, then Duxbury would have no reason to stay here, would he?'

'You don't honestly think for a moment she would, do you? Marry the Canon?'

'The Canon is no oil-painting, I suppose,' began Charles.

91

'The Canon is a dear,' said Judy, interrupting him. 'The Canon is ideal: nice and sincere, and he wouldn't drink or gamble or break the speed limit or do any of the other awful things that men do. He wouldn't chase other women. But she'd die – of boredom.'

'What would interest her, then, do you think?' asked Charles.

'Love,' she said. 'And now I'm tired of standing in the sun. It is time for a drink.'

She turned, for one last Parthian shot.

'If the Canon had any sense, he'd marry Artemis,' she said. 'And if Artemis had any sense, she'd accept him.'

'Why?' he asked.

'Because he's normal,' said Judy. 'It would do her good.'

Evening was falling over Blowing Point. Soon the lights of St Martin would be visible over the channel, which, guarded by sharks, separated the two islands.

Duxbury was sitting on the verandah sipping a glass of water. He had given up alcohol. In Oxford once he had drunk port on Guest Nights and whisky in Senior Common Rooms; in Rome there had been wine; but now there was only water. Food, too, had shrunk. Gone were the opulent dinners of years past – now he lived on meals that Caroline cooked from expensive frozen ingredients imported from far away, and sold for inflated prices in the Galaxy Supermarket. But he no longer cared what he ate or drank. The body and its functions, once so important, had shrivelled into insignificance.

What was important now? (From the house he heard the gurgle of water – one of the girls was having a shower.) He had never meant to have children. That had been his wife's idea. He had not, when young, seen the importance of having children. They were an encumbrance; he remembered all the trouble they had given him. Artemis had been sixteen when her mother had died, and when he had gone to Rome. She had been lodged in a boarding school for her last year, and had not, thank God, been thrown out for pregnancy or drug addiction. In fact, she had been remarkably little trouble despite what he had feared to the contrary. What trouble there was had come from Caroline, much to his surprise. She had never reproached him for her mother's death, at least not openly, but it had always been the great unmentioned subject between them. Artemis had been utterly unaffected by it, from which he had concluded that Artemis had been as glad of the tragedy as he had been.

But even if both his daughters had never been born, what then? What would he have done? How would the resulting freedom have been filled? And would it have been any different from the echoing liberty he had, in fact, always enjoyed?

That life was a void to be filled was something that he had always felt, but he managed to fill it, even now. He kept himself amused. Over the years his amusements had changed, but not his ability to entertain himself. *Ancient Attica* had kept his interest when he had been young: he had prided himself on the perversity of his choice even then. Other men had been playing hockey, or going to the cinema, or doing whatever ordinary people did, while he had pored over the fragments of the pre-Socratic philosophers. Fragments – there was something satisfying in the knowledge even now that the very first geniuses that humanity had ever produced had left behind no more than enigmatic scraps. They had kept their mystery, those old sages of Ionia, just as the Archaic sculptures did, smiling, puzzling, defying the reductive logic of the crowd. There was something so vulgar in explanations. Socrates – now there was a man. The man who searched for the meaning of things had had to be put to death by drinking hemlock. What was surprising was not the fact that he was executed but that people had had the patience to put up with the old bore for so long. Plato. Yuk. Aristotle. 'A great mistake at the beginning becomes a greater one at the end.' That summed up Aristotle. The whole of Aristotle was a huge mistake, magnified, all based on the initial mistaken idea that everything that existed was somehow intelligible. Oh dear. How Greece had gone off the rails once this mania for explanations had taken root. As

93

far as Duxbury could see, nothing was intelligible. All was mystery, darkness and fear. And God, if he existed, was a monster.

The biggest lie of all was the myth of love. Silly Caroline. Even Artemis didn't believe there was such a thing as love. In Artemis he could see glimpses of his younger self. Love was a monstrous invention, designed to tame Man's natural nobility and reduce it to domestic middle-class North Oxford bliss. 'All you need is love,' they had sung, even at the other end of the social scale. The fools. His wife had looked at him accusingly, wondering why, when the rest of the world did it, he could not or would not love her. Caroline, too, had allowed love, that most dehumanising of emotions, to ruin her. It was a disease which he had spent his entire life trying to avoid.

Imprisoned by the domesticity of marriage, he had taken up adultery as a form of rebellion, as a way of raising his banner against the cult of love. Shortly after Artemis's birth, he had embarked upon a series of amorous adventures. He had avoided affairs with dons' wives, seeing them, quite rightly, as merely another form of domestic routine. Instead he had concentrated on the seduction of undergraduates from women's colleges. He soon found that he had a way with young women, and he became practised in seducing and throwing away each girl within the space of a term. His name became famous in Junior Common Rooms, and notorious in Senior ones. The Dean of St Anne's (always the least staid of women's colleges) went so far as to brand him a villain, which, when her edict became public, caused him immense amusement, and an increase in reputation amongst his prospective victims which the Dean herself could hardly have intended.

His status as a Don Giovanni figure was not simply a matter of personal vanity. As a young man, Duxbury had possessed that sort of almost unearthly beauty that is sometimes given to those of mixed race. Well into his forties, he was still considered one of the most handsome men in Oxford; but he cared about this as little as he cared about most public opinions. He saw his physical charms as a weapon, his chosen instrument in causing pain to those he despised, chiefly his wife, but after her, all women.

Like most truly successful atheists, he had been brought up as a strict Catholic. He had abandoned all pretence of religious belief at the age of sixteen, but he still remembered the passage in the Scriptures where the rebel Absalom had, as the ultimate sign of his disdain for King David, lain with the royal concubines. That was what he aimed to do: he was polluting his enemies' womenfolk.

His wife had at first done what everyone had expected of her, namely taken it like a martyr and received the sympathy of her friends with dignified restraint. It was this, her refusal to be drawn, her refusal to hate him, that provoked his final assault on the sanctity of love, home and family. He had realised when she was still quite young that Artemis was like himself, and he made her his ally. When Artemis was sixteen he had turned his attentions to her, not for reasons of passion, but more out of a spirit of perverse curiosity, a desire to see how much his wife would put up with. He did not commit with his daughter what the Catholics in their precise Aristotelian way called a mortal sin, or even a 'completed act'. It had never come to that; rather it had been an elaborate tease, an assumed flirtation, a conspiracy between the two of them against her mother. It had worked: between them they had driven her over the edge. Talk of incest was only then just coming into fashion: he never knew whether his wife presumed the worst, or whether the mere fact that he could assume such a pose had made it so terrible in her eyes.

And then – what then? The whole joke had turned sour. The Dean of St Anne's, a ghastly woman whom he had long suspected of seething with unrequited passions for himself, had been the one to persuade an undergraduate to approach the police with tales of sexual harassment, and the sheer pettiness of their morality had driven him away. After that he had been glad to leave Oxford: the knowledge that Oxford was still so conventional a city had made it suffocating. Rome had been freedom indeed after Oxford. It was the most pagan city in the world. It was the solid refutation of all that Catholicism and Christianity stood for. St Peter's itself, huge and hideous, towering over the Apostle's tomb, in its gaudiness mocked the Fisherman's bones. Galilean simplicity was crushed under the weight of human pomp and glorious bad taste. Those wonderful Renaissance Popes, the Barberini, the Pamphili, those splendid Roman names, had done more for paganism than any philosopher. And in the Via del Governo Vecchio, where he had chosen to live, in the warren of squalid streets that was as yet untouched by modernising hand, paganism reigned. In those days he had made his wicked way to the Vatican Library, armed with his special ticket of admission, over the bridge between Bernini's angels, comfortable in the knowledge that however dilatory his own researches might be, they were made redundant by the life of the Eternal City itself.

Behind him the gurgle of water had ceased. His elder daughter had emerged from the house to hang a bath towel in the hot rays of the late afternoon sun. Her hair was wet and dark; her face moon-shaped and severe; and for a moment her plainness annoyed him. She had only become so plain since the day they had cut her hair in hospital. But hair grew again; it was almost as if she wished to make herself ugly, to proclaim to the world her wounded status. It was a reproach, either to herself or to him – which, he could not determine. But it was not his fault at all. He had done everything she had wanted to do when things had gone so disastrously wrong. When she had begged him to take her away from Rome, he had done so. She knew that he had not wanted to leave. He had not taken to the sacrifice at all gladly, it being the first sacrifice he had ever made, but he had made it all the same. He had never done anything similar for his wife – but with his daughter his sense of daring failed him, and he had done for Caroline what he had neglected to do for her mother. The reproaches of the past hung between them even now. Caroline reminded him of his poor wife; even her looks were sometimes reminiscent of hers.

'We're going to Sombrero tomorrow,' said Caroline. 'The boat leaves at six.'

'I see,' he said, gravely receiving this information. 'I once asked the Canon,' he added, 'why the hammerhead shark existed. Do you know what he said?'

'No. What?'

'Divine Providence. What it is to have faith, eh? It changes the world.'

'I suppose it does,' she said. 'It explains things.'

'It explains everything,' said Duxbury.

'It gives you a language,' said Caroline. 'If you had faith, you wouldn't sit here mulling over your shark-obsession. You would be free of it.'

'I'd have a God-obsession instead.'

Caroline suppressed the desire to point out that he had that already. She sat down on one of the rickety chairs. She looked out to sea and contented herself with saying:

'The Canon is a nice man.'

He wondered in silence whether she had a clergyman-obsession. She was only thirty, but she was getting spinsterish, turning into an excellent woman, destined to marry a vicar, if only her destiny had been different.

It was now completely dark.

'What is for supper?' he asked, not that he cared.

'I've been rather busy making up the picnic for tomorrow,' she said. 'Would something like scrambled eggs do? We can have the smoked salmon that Artemis brought out with her. It needs eating.'

Silence fell again. The darkness was thick around them; each sat there wrapped in impenetrable thoughts.

Duxbury's mind, like the sharks he so feared, was never still. Stillness would mean death. It ranged freely over the dark and empty spaces, flying through the air, seeking a branch to settle on.

'No one knows,' he said, 'how long sharks live for. I wonder what happens to them when they die?'

'What do you mean – "what happens"?'

'To their bodies. Perhaps other sharks eat them when they grow

97

old and slow. That is what monsters of the deep generally do. They eat each other. Not a nice thing to do.'

'Can't you think of anything more cheerful?' she asked, a little accusingly.

'It's your trip to Sombrero Island. It has started off a train of associations. Who else is going?'

'The Canon. Charles Broughton. Gianni the Italian.'

'Gianni,' said Duxbury, for a moment considering that particular young man. 'Is he in love with Artemis?'

'I imagine he is,' said Caroline. 'Most people seem to be at one time or another.'

'Now that's a cheerful subject,' said Duxbury. 'Artemis is beautiful. Men love her. I've even noticed that the Canon appreciates her.'

'Men are rather fools when it comes to beauty,' said Caroline. 'They don't realise that it is only skin-deep.'

'Surfaces. I've always been happy with surfaces. I suppose you prefer soul, my dear. A most regrettable preference, if you don't mind me saying. Your mother thought that I had great soul. The truth is that I have no soul at all. I have a mind and a body and nothing else. She disliked the first and mistook the other for something ethereal. But there was never anything there – ever. Beauty is only skin-deep, as you so rightly observe, simply because it can't be anything else. You must realise the complete truth, my dear, or else you will continue to be unhappy. I've noticed you, you see. Signor Donati, now. Did he have a great soul? Was there something he had that you could not reach, that eluded you? Was there some Holy Grail, that you glimpsed for a moment, but which you will never see again? No, there wasn't. That is the only possible answer. Men are just men. We have no souls. Artemis realises that. Sex is simply sex, and can never be anything further.'

It was the first time that his name had ever been mentioned between them since their arrival in the West Indies. It came as something of a shock to her to hear him spoken about by her father; she had grown used to thinking of 'Signor Donati' as her own, exclusively so. But what had seemed to be so entirely hers was not so after all; it was public property, to be analysed, to be weighed up, to be discussed. The sanctuary had been violated. Suddenly the picture she had of him in her mind began to crumble; she saw him, for a moment, as a more ordinary figure, just as she had first seen him, asleep at Silvia's.

'Do you mean love is impossible?' she asked.

'Yes, I do mean that,' said Duxbury. His mind reviewed his own amorous past. 'Sex can only ever be sex. It can never be anything else. The body is only the body. It can only do bodily things. A body can never cease to be a body. Love, by contrast, is to do with the mind. Mind and body are like oil and water – the two cannot be blended; a physical action can't have a spiritual meaning. And the body is only fully itself when it is freed from restraints imposed by the mind. That's when sex becomes pleasurable.'

'I think that is one of the most depressing things I have ever heard,' said Caroline.

'Freedom is frightening,' said her father. 'That is why men invented religion. It comes from the Latin *ligare*, to tie. Religion is the safety-belt for the frightened. They also invented the idea of shame at the same time. Shame is the feeling that unless sex is made respectable by love then it is sinful.'

'And if I hadn't loved him, would I be happy now?' she asked.

'Yes.'

'And have you never loved anyone?'

'No one. Not a single one of them.'

'But it was love that made it all worth it,' said Caroline.

Artemis came out on to the verandah.

'What are you talking about?' she asked. 'And why are you sitting here in the dark?'

'Sombrero Island,' said her father, feeling that the conversation had gone far enough.

VII

Gianni was the first to get up the next morning.

'There's a swell,' he told Charles, prodding him with his foot.

'What?' asked Charles.

'There's a swell. And before you ask, it is half-past five.'

'I wish to God you'd keep this cabin tidy,' said Charles, sitting up in bed, looking for a pair of shorts. 'Are these yours or mine?' he asked, examining the contents of the pockets.

'Mine,' said Gianni. 'Anyway, get up.'

There was indeed a swell. As he dressed, Charles bumped his head twice against the ceiling of the cabin. On deck there were two mugs of coffee merrily slopping around.

'It's not much of a swell,' he said, hopefully.

'Yes, but the ladder,' said Gianni.

Both of them thought of the ladder. Sombrero was a mere rock, bound by cliffs, the only access being provided by a steel ladder fixed into one of the cliffs. In rough weather, far out in the Anegada Passage, jumping on to the ladder from a frail, heaving boat was something of a challenge. If one were to fall – but no one had ever fallen in, so it was not worth thinking about; no one had fallen in, simply because no one had tried the jump in anything more than the mildest swell.

'I could make it,' said Gianni, maddeningly.

'I don't see why I shouldn't,' said Charles, feeling his pride stir.

'The captain of the *Warspite* is very careful about letting inexperienced people try in rough weather,' said Gianni. 'He's a part-time policeman, and he hates accidents. He wouldn't let the girls try. Not if there was a swell. And as for the Canon …'

It was, thought Charles, hard to see how the Canon would

make the agile leap from rowing boat to slippery steel ladder even in the best of weather. As for an accident – he could see that happening. He could see it all.

'We'll just have to see what the captain of the *Warspite* says,' he concluded. 'Policemen always know best,' he added, piously.

The captain was waiting for them on the jetty. He was a tall man, somewhat gaunt in appearance; he was accompanied by two lighthouse men, both in uniform.

'You sure you want to come?' asked the captain. 'Last time it was like this, all our passengers had to stay on board, and that included Mrs Demmer. She didn't like it. Perhaps you would like to wait to next month?'

'We're good sailors,' said Gianni, not liking the implicit comparison with Mrs Demmer, who sounded just the sort of woman who would get in the way on any ship. 'And,' he added, hoping to impress, 'I used to be a mountaineer.'

'Of course, if you think …' began Charles, in more conciliating tones.

'Just as you please,' said the captain, who was accustomed to dealing with those who sailed for a living, rather than those who sailed just for pleasure. It would be no skin off his nose if two more silly foreigners spent six hours vomiting their way across to Sombrero, only to find they could not land when they got there. He turned to the two lighthouse men, with whom he had been discussing barracuda. Tourists did not hold his attention for long.

Presently a car arrived, disgorging Artemis, Caroline and Canon Cartwright, the last carrying a picnic hamper.

'We've got plenty of food,' said Artemis, seeing Charles's expression. 'Enough for you too, I should think, don't you, George?'

'Yes,' said the Canon, who had clearly been pressed into service by Artemis.

'The trouble is, there is a swell,' said Charles.

'Only a little one,' she said, looking out to sea, in the way every beautiful woman did when faced with a minor inconvenience that she did not intend to allow to impede her will.

'What he means is,' put in Gianni, desperate to assert himself, 'that it might be impossible to land when we get out there. I mean I would be able to, but it would be impossible for you to do so.'

'Oh, nonsense,' said Artemis. 'I am wearing proper shoes.'

Caroline now came up.

'What's the matter?' she asked.

'Mr Masculinity here thinks that it may be dangerous for the weaker vessels,' said Artemis.

'It might be uncomfortable,' said Charles, diplomatically. 'You see, it may not be possible to go ashore if the swell is more than a foot or two. I mean the captain would not allow any of us to do so.'

'I am not afraid of being uncomfortable,' said Artemis.

'It would be pretty awful if we couldn't get off the *Warspite* once we got there,' said the Canon. 'There doesn't seem much point going all that way, if, at the end, there's nothing there, if you see what I mean.'

'We could always have the picnic somewhere else,' said Caroline sensibly. 'That way we could swim as well. You can't even swim at Sombrero.'

'I am going aboard,' said Artemis, cutting through the good sense, ignoring Caroline's embryonic arrangements. 'The *Warspite* sails at six, and it's almost that now. Come on, George, help me carry the picnic.'

The Canon, forgetting his misgivings, obediently bent down to lift the heavy basket. And the rest of them prepared to follow where the food led.

'It's all your fault,' said Charles crossly to Gianni. 'If she falls in and gets eaten by sharks, you'll bloody well have to explain it to her father. He might not be so pleased with you then.'

'My fault?'

'You only have to tell a girl like that that she ought not to do something because she's a woman, and what will she do? The very opposite.'

'Yes,' said Gianni. 'She has spirit. I like.'

'What you call spirit is simply the desire to be stubborn and resist good sense,' said Charles. 'And you should be wearing long trousers,' he added, still in admonitory mode. 'The sun will be terrible.'

'You're an old woman,' said Gianni, teasingly.

'Old women are often wise,' replied Charles.

The other three had settled themselves a little uncomfortably at the front of the schooner, whilst this altercation was going on. The captain was getting ready to cast off from the jetty, and the men were shouting to each other in unintelligible accents. Caroline was dispensing tea to the Canon from a thermos flask. Artemis was arranging her hat and anointing her face with opaque sun cream, from the tube marked Total Block.

'I hope you have all brought books,' she said. 'I have.'

Once her face was done, she took out a very thick paperback and a glossy magazine from a straw basket, and with a look of self-sufficiency put on her sun-glasses. She was wearing a long white dress, and looked at Gianni's bare legs a little pityingly before turning to her book.

Gianni hadn't brought a book. He had not in fact read a book since he had dropped out of university some years previously. He had brought a small rucksack with him though, out of which he pulled his only possible form of amusement, a packet of American cigarettes.

They set sail.

The Canon sipped his tea, thinking how provident Caroline was. Behind them Anguilla slipped away. Within twenty minutes it was merely a brown line on the horizon. After half an hour it could not be seen at all.

'I've brought a book of poems,' said the Canon, finally breaking the early morning silence.

'Do read one to us,' said Caroline, putting down her book, *The Charterhouse of Parma*, a cast-off of Artemis's.

Artemis, underneath hat, glasses and Total Block, was inscrutable. She reluctantly laid aside her blockbuster. (She had reached that stage of her holiday where all pretence at serious reading had been abandoned.)

'Yes, do read a poem,' said Charles, nudging Gianni, who woke up.

'As we're out of sight of land, I think I will,' said the Canon. 'It's one you all know; they are always the best sort.'

The Canon had a splendid voice, deep, resonant and dignified, formed for Cranmerian cadences. The familiar phrases rolled over his audience, and they settled down to listen. Even Artemis, who had never been read to since the nursery, found that she could not help listening. Only Gianni, who was unfamiliar with English poetry, felt he was witnessing some mystery into which he had not been initiated. He could not quite settle, but lit another cigarette, looked admiringly at his long brown legs, and tried to make out the shape of Artemis's bust beneath her flimsy kaftan.

It was a very long poem, a poem about the sea, as far as Gianni could tell, a story about an old sailor. At the end of it there was silence.

'What is an albatross?' Gianni asked Charles when it was over; the word 'albatross' had struck him as strange.

'It's a sea-bird,' said Charles in low tones.

The *Warspite* was now ploughing through the waves, and they could feel the happy reverberations through the wooden deck on which they lay. The rhythm comforted them.

'You see,' said Caroline, feeling she should explain the poem to the poor foreigner, lest he be left out, 'The albatross is a symbol of Christ. He shot Christ with his crossbow and that was why he had to be punished for it.'

'It is about purgatory,' said the Canon. 'A doctrine that rigid Protestants do not accept.'

'But aren't you a Protestant?' asked Gianni, picking up the disapproval he had heard in the Canon's tone. He felt a little adrift: Christ had somehow been a sea-bird; and now the Canon was abjuring his religion.

'No, I am Anglican,' said the Canon. 'That means I am theologically Catholic, liturgically Cranmerian, and when it comes to Church discipline, I am an Erastian.'

'Ah,' said Gianni, without comprehension.

'But what is purgatory?' said Artemis all of a sudden. 'No one has ever explained it to me.'

'Purgatory,' said the Canon, 'is one of the most hopeful doctrines in Christianity. Of course, Calvin couldn't see that. You see, if you believe in purgatory, you believe that everything in the end can be made good, and that nothing is past redemption.'

'That is comforting,' said Caroline. 'Or would be if it were true.'

'Do you mean,' said Artemis, 'That if someone commits a crime, they can pay for it in purgatory and still be saved? Yes? But what about the victim of that crime? How will purgatory benefit them?'

'That's a different question,' said the Canon.

'People can't be redeemed,' said Artemis. 'You can't undo the past.'

'You're your father's daughter,' said the Canon.

Artemis was silent. There was something of a pause. Then Charles spoke.

'The Mariner didn't kill Christ, did he? It happened years ago, in Palestine. It's part of history now. I mean, how can one say that the poor old Mariner was responsible for the death of Christ?'

'It's all history,' agreed the Canon. 'We are history too. Anyone who kills love kills Christ.' He quoted:

> 'He prayeth well, who loveth well
> Both man and bird and beast.'

Artemis, insofar as anyone could, underneath sun-glasses and Total Block, looked wounded, as if all this talk of loving one's neighbour was some monstrous conspiracy designed to ruin her life.

'I am going to walk around the boat,' said Gianni, who could now feel the sun burning his legs. 'Perhaps the men have caught some fish by now.'

He got up and stretched himself. Charles got up too to accompany him. Off they went.

'You can't be in love with her under that hat,' said Charles. 'She looks hideous.'

'I am in love with her,' said Gianni.

'What about that girl you met in Grenada?'

'Oh, that …' said Gianni. 'That was weeks ago.'

'But you seemed pretty keen on her at the time,' said Charles.

Gianni ignored this. Charles's rationality was simply too pitiable. No wonder he had no success with women; he was simply too scrupulous.

The men at the back of the boat had a bite on one of their lines, and were hauling something in. Charles and Gianni watched in silence. It was a barracuda, a small one, a little less than two feet in length. On to the deck it fell in wide-eyed surprise, its mouth open, its teeth razor sharp and needle thin. One of the men hit it on the head, removed the hook, and then, taking a knife, sliced a fillet of flesh from its silvery side, which he then used to bait the hook once again.

'Is it dead?' asked Gianni, watching the dark droplets of blood ooze from its wounded side.

Charles did not answer.

They walked on, and made the circuit of the boat, coming back to the other three. There sat the Canon with Caroline and Artemis, like some happy bison that had found permanent sanctuary.

'Won't you come and watch the fishing?' said Gianni to Artemis.

'Is it exciting?' she asked.

'Not really,' he replied. 'But come and see.'

So she got up and joined the two young men in their wanderings, leaving her sister and the Canon deep in theological discussion. The truth was, such discussion made her uncomfortable; she had rather hoped the Canon would act the part of her

107

personal slave for the day, but could now see that Caroline was eager for his attention. It seemed only fair to let her have her share. She would spend her time with the two young men, who were, each in his own way, beautiful and at the same time rather dull.

'So you never thought of becoming a Catholic?' Caroline was saying.

'Yes, and no. Judy says I ought to become a Catholic, but she thinks everyone ought to. I don't think I would be fitted for a life of perpetual celibacy.'

'Oh,' she said, sensing sex on the horizon. She didn't want to talk about sex. There had been far too much sex in the Duxbury family as it was. And here was the Canon, a clergyman of advanced years and weight, the only person she knew who seemed sexless, about to confess to her that he too, like all the rest of them, was not immune to the siren song of the senses.

'I mean,' continued the Canon, not realising the trepidation he was causing as he hesitated on the conversational brink, 'I think that the clergy should be married. It's not too late for me yet. I am forty-two. And now that Maude has gone, or is about to go, to Mogadishu, the principal obstacle to my happiness is about to be removed. People who go to Mogadishu never seem to return. At least I have never met someone who has. I don't dislike my sister, though I do find her rather dominant. You've met her, so perhaps you know what I mean.'

'Yes, I think so.'

'And when she joined the Movement for the Ordination of Women, goodness, there was no stopping her. She found allies then; she went to meetings and she came back armed to the teeth with ideas that she would use to torment me. It wasn't domestic bliss, I can tell you. That's why I came here.'

'And now she has gone, or is going, will you go back?'

'Basingstoke,' he said, contemplating the Caribbean sea and sun. 'I'd have to look for a job. Perhaps London. Some nice vicarage; some parish that was fairly high, but not too high. The

Bishop of London is a nice chap. I used to know him slightly years ago ...'

A thought struck Caroline. If the Canon had wanted to get away from his sister, why hadn't he gone to London in the first place? But she couldn't think of the Canon now, or of the logic of his life. Her mind had involuntarily turned to another man who had lived with his sister, in Rome. How different the Canon was, with his talk of Basingstoke and London, and of how he had last seen the present Bishop of London at Pusey House some ten years ago, when they had both attended a meeting about the life and work of C.S. Lewis.

At the other end of the schooner, they were discussing food.

'Judy cooks from time to time,' Artemis was saying. 'Fish mainly. We ate red snapper there once. And another time we had something that came in steaks; no one seemed to know what it was. She bought it off some fisherman.'

'We could sail over to St Martin for dinner one night,' said Charles. 'There must be some decent restaurants on the French side.'

'The Dutch side is all hamburgers, as far as I can remember from last year,' said Artemis. 'Caroline and I went over on the ferry. She thought it might amuse me, but it didn't.'

'I was thinking of Marigot or Grand Case,' said Charles.

'There's nothing there,' said Artemis. 'My father looks at them with his binoculars every now and then. He's never been. He hates boats.'

'Why?' asked Gianni. 'Wouldn't he come with us to St Martin, do you think?'

'He wouldn't. He says he is frightened of drowning or being eaten by sharks. One can never tell whether he is joking or not. I mean, there are no sharks here, are there?'

'No one gets eaten,' said Charles, 'but that's only because black people never swim, and the few whites who do never go far from the shore. But it is possible. People do get attacked by sharks.'

Artemis looked at him. 'I thought you were so brave,' she said, contemptuously. 'But you are cautious.'

'And I suppose you are not frightened of sharks at all, are you?' said Charles, ironically.

'Well, of course not,' said Artemis.

Indeed, she wasn't. She had heard her father talk about sharks so much that they had lost their horror for her. It was a superstition that she had grown out of.

'What is the time?' asked Gianni.

'Look at the sun,' said Charles.

'Look at my watch,' said Artemis. 'It is not yet ten.'

It was not yet ten. Duxbury stared out to sea, imagining his daughters on the schooner, half-way across the Anegada Passage. He was at Road Bay, having ridden there on his motor-cycle; he had just been to visit the Chief Minister, his landlord, to pay the rent. Time hung heavy on his hands. There were at least two hours to kill before lunch; so he stood under the shade of a tree, studying the sea.

He heard steps behind him, and turned to see a white woman of about his own age, smiling at him.

'Won't you come in for a drink?' she asked.

'Come in where?' he asked, a little rudely.

'The bar,' she said. 'The sun isn't over the yard-arm, or whatever it is supposed to be, but it is so hot. Besides, Caroline and Artemis have an account. They'll be paying. You don't need more reasons than that, do you?'

'You are Mrs Blomberg,' he said.

He appraised her critically. She was wearing a loose shapeless frock, and her hair, greying and rather disordered, was caught up in a bun. Her eyes, though, were large, dark and sparkling. He wondered if she were a little mad. There was always something a little odd about women in general, he thought. But this one, living alone on a beach, serving beer to strangers, was odder than most.

'Call me Judy,' she said, as no doubt Judith had said to Holofernes.

'Judy,' he said, savouring the sound of it.

110

He followed her into the bar.

'I saw them go off early this morning,' she said as she poured him his drink, a beer, without asking him if that was what he wanted.

He took the beer with a grunt, not disposed to conversation. (Indeed, he had never bothered to make himself agreeable to strangers; he had never seen any reason why he should.) Down they sat. She lit a cigarette. He looked at her again. He was used to his daughters, but he hardly regarded them as women any more; they were simply his daughters. But women ... when he remembered women, a train of associations came into his mind. He thought of their infinite capacity for suffering. Their bodies were so soft, so ill equipped to deal with the harshness of life. A man might break his leg, he thought, but when a woman did so, the quick power of recovery was beyond her. A woman's pain could never be forgotten, could never be treated as if it had not happened.

Their eyes betrayed their true nature: his wife had looked at him with those pain-filled eyes again and again, as if to try and force him to love her. How could he have done so? He could never have loved anyone so in need of his love, anyone so unlike himself. Weakness killed love. His wife had had a weakness for him. Her death and the manner of her dying had been her revenge. The whole of Oxford, which had ignored her while alive, had taken her part when she was dead, thanks to the efforts of the girlfriends with whom she had shared those fatal final drinks. He had committed the unforgivable sin, and they had driven him out, finding what pretext they could. He had not respected the sacredness of women; that had been his crime.

He was a law-breaker, and such transgressions always carried their own punishment. He had not been able to do to Caroline what he had done to her mother. He had been unable to commit the same crime twice. That was why he was here. He had felt himself forced to take her away from Rome, when she had begged him to do so. Anger at his own weakness, at the sense of compulsion and guilt, had made him bring her to the most inhospitable island he could find.

'Do you like it here?' asked Judy, thinking the silence had gone on long enough.

'No,' he said. Feeling that this was too blunt, he made an effort and added: 'I can't swim, you see. Never learned. When I was a boy in Trinidad, we didn't. At least some did, but we lived inland. Sometimes we went to the sea, when we went on holiday to Tobago.' He remembered those nightmarish holidays. 'I don't like the West Indies much. It's only the Europeans who think that the Caribbean is paradise; all real West Indians leave as soon as they can and go to London.'

This, he knew, was a slight exaggeration, but he felt it was true. There was something ridiculous about the mess he had allowed himself to land up in, stuck here in Anguilla, living in a concrete bungalow, and now drinking beer at ten o'clock in the morning with a complete stranger; it was as if he had never left the West Indies, but spent his entire life like this – as if everything he had ever done had never taken place. But it had – he was still a law-breaker – and nothing could undo that.

Who was Judy, he wondered? Had she chosen this sort of life? Did she sip beer all the time? He was old enough to think of beer as a man's drink, not fit for a lady. How could she be happy? She had to be mad.

'Of course, Trinidad is very different from this,' she was saying.

'Have you been there?'

'Years ago, on a cruise. We stopped at Port of Spain, and we were driven inland for miles to see the Pitch Lake. I suppose you have seen the Pitch Lake, haven't you? It's the most famous thing in Trinidad, isn't it?'

'It might be,' he replied. 'But I have never seen the Pitch Lake.'

'You haven't missed a thing. It's like a huge car-park. One corner, I seem to remember, was a little liquidy. Mr Blomberg was amused.'

'Why do you call him Mr Blomberg?'

'I don't like to remind myself of his Christian name,' she said.

Duxbury understood; he himself never thought of his poor wife by her name. A name was sign of intimacy.

'I suppose Sombrero Island will be another Pitch Lake. Something tourists go and see, but those who know wouldn't dream of visiting.' Then he added: 'Caroline is crazy.'

'To go to Sombrero?'

'Yes.'

'The Canon has gone too.'

'Was that the reason for Caroline going?'

'They might enjoy each other's company,' said Judy.

This seemed a reasonable proposition; he supposed they might; it was a possibility that had never occurred to him before now.

'Caroline's a romantic,' he said shortly. 'She nurses a broken heart. It runs in the family.'

He felt he ought not to say more. It would not do to discuss his wife with Judy Blomberg. He was silent.

She looked at him, dying to ask more about broken hearts. Whose heart, in particular, had been broken besides Caroline's? Had Duxbury come here with a broken heart too? Suddenly it seemed as if the island was littered with these strange organs – hers, Duxbury's, Caroline's, perhaps even Charles Broughton's as well. Why else would someone come to so remote a place unless they had some deep interior wound to hide? How handsome Duxbury was, how different from his blond daughters. The dark curl of his hair, the penetrating brown of his eyes, the wonderful tone of his skin that seemed to have escaped ageing, all these things made him look arrogant. Beauty *was* arrogant; but underneath the beauty, what vulnerability might be hidden? The sight of him, sitting there in her bar, was enough to make her hope that he was suffering from a broken heart and that he had been speaking of himself.

His thoughts had moved along different lines. Broken hearts were of little interest to him. He had watched Caroline break hers without being moved by the spectacle. Her pregnancy had annoyed him considerably, being, to his mind, the result of culpable

113

ignorance. The still-birth had frightened him with the prospect of her death, or, once that passed, the thought that she might kill herself in her unhappiness. Duxbury knew that killing oneself for love was something of which he was not capable. But Caroline might be. He felt a slight sense of distaste now, thinking of it, sitting in the bar with Judy. Some bond was being formed between them by the very fact that he was sitting there with her in what seemed to be companionable silence. They were drinking together. Once you had a drink with someone, a certain intimacy was usually unavoidable. But he did not want to be intimate with Judy Blomberg. He noticed that a sliver of cigarette ash had fallen on to her generous bosom, and was lying there unregarded. Bosom. What a word. What a thing. No wonder the Greeks had never really bothered with the female form, but had left that sort of thing to the degenerate Romans. He thought of pregnancy, childbirth, miscarriage and menstruation, all the pain and agony that they involved. The life of a woman was one long illness, with no redeeming nobility in it. How different was the life of a man. And how very like the Catholics to exalt the female figure above that of the male. Didn't they even stop and think about it? The very concept of virginity, when you realised what it meant – yes, that – was enough to make your flesh creep.

'I must be going,' he said, knocking back his beer.

'Won't you have another?'

'No,' he said. 'Thank you,' he added. 'I very rarely drink these days at all.'

Serve him bloody well right if Caroline did go off with the Canon, thought Judy. He deserved to be left. Caroline was too good for him. But no matter how arrogant Duxbury was, how little disposed to communication – he had hardly said a word all the time he had been there – the fact remained, that with such a father, Caroline was hardly likely to choose such a husband.

'Good-bye,' she said, standing up. 'Do come again,' she added, in what she hoped was a nonchalant tone.

'That young Roman,' said Duxbury suddenly. 'What do you know about him?'

'He's just someone who attaches himself to rich people, as far as I can see,' she replied.

'Oh,' he said, and turning, left.

'I think I can see it,' said the Canon.

'Not a mirage?' asked Caroline. 'Can you get mirages at sea?'

'You get something,' he said. 'Terrible delusions. People go mad and jump overboard. But I don't think they are called mirages.'

The captain confirmed that the brown spot in the distance was in fact Sombrero Island.

'Well, of course it is,' said Artemis, when they told her. 'That's why it is called Sombrero – it looks like a sombrero sticking up out of the sea.'

But the captain was glum as he peered through his binoculars. He could see a thin line of foam at the base of the rock. At such a distance, that was a bad sign. It might be very difficult to unload supplies, hauling them up to the top of the cliff with the block and tackle, if the swell were that bad. It would be even harder with inexperienced people getting in the way.

Caroline, who had the sort of mind the intelligence of which had grown adept at foreseeing disaster, interpreted the captain's glum looks and sighed. If there was a swell, and there was, for the *Warspite* was buffeting the waves even now, it would be all very well for the younger ones, by which she meant Gianni, Artemis and Charles, but it would be hopeless for the Canon. She simply could not imagine the Canon jumping from a heaving boat on to a slippery ladder, with white surf foaming around his legs. Nor would the captain allow it, she was sure. A drowned clergyman wouldn't do any of them any good. And if the Canon were to be confined to the *Warspite*, it really would be too unkind to leave him on his own. After all, the Canon had come all this way, she was beginning to realise, to keep her company. She had to return the compliment somehow.

For a moment she almost wished that the swell would be enough to keep them all on board. Two hours' tête-à-tête with the

115

Canon on a hot deck was not her idea of fun. Yet Artemis would expect it. Artemis always did. Artemis was quite content to get the Canon to carry the picnic basket, but would expect Caroline to stay aboard with him if circumstances demanded it. Ever since their mother's death, when she had been sixteen, Artemis had unconsciously placed her sister in the older generation. Caroline had become the sort of person who would fuss over boarding school lists, give advice, see to the dull details that no one was interested in, and chat to ageing or unwanted friends of the family. Caroline was in short the daughter of the house, the one who did the respectable things that Duxbury and Artemis themselves could not be bothered to do. It was into this role that she had been cast. And now, she realised, she was expected to spend two hours alone with the Canon. It was enough to make her feel resentful. Of course, she liked the Canon. That wasn't the point. What she resented was the presumption that she did not like or appreciate the company of men her own age, and that Gianni and Charles were fit companions for Artemis, but not for her.

'I'm thirty,' she said, suddenly out loud.

'So am I,' said Charles. 'It is the perfect age.'

'Why?'

'Because once you're thirty you are past the traumas of youth, you've settled down, and yet you're still young. At least that's the theory. Whether it is in fact true, I am not so sure.'

'It may be true for a man,' she said. 'But I am already old.'

She thought of her father, who, both in Oxford and in Rome, had never shown his age. In Rome, he had pretended to be working on a book, *Ancient Latium*, a companion to *Ancient Attica*, but he had spent most of his time doing other things. But how stupid this was, to think of age as something connected with the ability to have sexual intercourse. Charles was thirty; she was thirty; but a world of unhappy experience separated them, just as it separated her and Artemis. It was not that she was ugly, it was that she was unhappy – that was what made her so sad.

'Do you think we will be able to land?' Charles was asking.

'I am not sure all of us will,' she said, trying not to sound gloomy; but she couldn't help it; she had got into the habit of expecting the worst, and in her experience the worst was what usually happened.

'Of course Gianni will try,' said Charles, 'even if it kills him. He's very keen to impress your sister. If it does kill him, it will mean he'll die as he's lived.'

'Couldn't you get him not to?' she asked, feeling that she ought to do something to avoid so pointless a death.

'It would be nice if he would listen to reason,' said Charles. 'But there is no chance of it. In fact it would be counter-productive. But who does listen to reason? Can you blame him? And if it is really dangerous, I am sure the captain won't allow him off the *Warspite*.'

'You're right,' she said. 'I'd never try and dissuade Artemis. She's so headstrong. It would just make her more determined. I think there's something terribly wrong with human nature, don't you, when you realise that people simply don't listen to reason. I wish I was more reasonable.'

'And if you were, what would you change?' he asked.

You couldn't change the past, she knew; and the past was all that mattered. But this was another glum thought and she tried to throw it off.

'I am resolved to be very reasonable from now on,' she said.

The Canon heard her say it and took note.

Artemis, who hadn't been listening, shouted: 'We're getting really close, Look!'

They looked. The rock was now visible in all its plainness. They could see the lighthouse, the cliffs, the steel ladder. They were almost there. There was a flurry of activity on the *Warspite* as the schooner made its final run into the lee of Sombrero Island. It was a little past eleven o'clock in the morning.

Jamie Duxbury was in the post office, where he had collected his daughters' letters. There had been none for him. There hardly ever were. Gone were the days when the post had brought disquieting missives from strangers, all of whom seemed to expect something of him. Now he stood under the shade of the flamboyant tree, where he had left his motor-cycle, wondering who on earth wrote to Caroline. The letter had an English stamp, so it wasn't Silvia. But as far as he knew, Silvia had never written to Caroline. Five years ago, or perhaps six, he had had an affair with Silvia; and while he and Silvia had been spending time at her house on the Lago di Bolsena, or doing whatever they had done to pass the time, Caroline had turned her attention to Silvia's brother. What a disaster that had been. Caroline had inherited her mother's ability to fall in love with men who were not in the least suited to her. She had none of Artemis's hatred for them. He knew, standing there outside the post office, that Artemis did hate men; he was a man himself, and felt her antipathy. One day Artemis would end up marrying the least manly man she could find – perhaps some tame old sheep like the Canon. That would be a good joke, to have the Canon for a son-in-law.

He turned his attention back to the letter he was holding, away from these disquieting moments of insight: whoever had written to Caroline, it wasn't Silvia. It wasn't some remote voice from the past, but probably an accountant or someone equally dull. It was probably not even worth the trouble of opening the letter and reading it.

Someone behind him was coughing in an apologetic English manner. He turned. It did seem to be a day for meeting people. A man with a beard, wearing a crisp open-necked shirt, was holding out his hand to him, expecting it to be taken.

'I don't think we have met,' said the Beard. 'But I am John Demmer.'

Duxbury put out his hand and took it back again as soon as he politely could. Mr Demmer was Her Majesty's Commissioner. He knew who he was, but what could he possibly want?

'Perhaps you would like to come up for drinks tomorrow?' said Demmer. 'At about seven.'

'Ah,' said Duxbury, who had received an invitation to drinks before and never answered it, now searching for some excuse. 'My daughters are staying with me,' he said.

'We'd be delighted to see them too,' said Demmer.

A horn sounded from a car on the other side of the road.

'My wife,' said Demmer.

Duxbury looked and saw a pretty young woman at the wheel of a station wagon.

'Until tomorrow,' concluded Demmer, and hurried uxoriously away.

Duxbury was left under the flamboyant tree. He had been caught. Why on earth should Demmer have the presumption to think that this invitation was in any way pleasurable? The whole idea of drinks with the Demmers was too suburban. He hadn't come to the most desolate island in the West Indies to indulge in small talk with strangers. First Mrs Blomberg, now Demmer. It was getting too much. Why wouldn't they leave him alone? They made him feel like a thing in a freak show. Perhaps he would get on his motor-bike and see if there were any flights to Puerto Rico, or somewhere like that, in the next few days. He'd treat himself. The girls could look after themselves; they might even enjoy meeting the Demmers, improbable as that seemed. With that in mind, he got on his bike and rode off in the direction of the airfield.

VIII

The swell had dropped somewhat, and the captain of the *Warspite* had no objection to letting Artemis kill herself if that was what she really wanted to do. The schooner lay at anchor in the comforting shade of the cliff, shade that was rapidly disappearing as the sun reached its zenith, and from the deck Caroline, the Canon and Charles watched the launch take the lighthouse men and Artemis and Gianni to the perilous steel ladder.

Gianni, if truth were to be told, would much rather not have gone. The shady water worried him. Shade attracted fish; small fish attracted the larger ones that ate them; and with them came the sharks. A slip of the rubber-soled foot and you would be someone's lunch, and some monster of the deep would become your living tomb. But pride was pride, and had overcome fear; Artemis expected him to come with her, and he would rather have died than let her know that he was not as courageous as she was.

The small boat drew level with the ladder. The swell seemed to be about two feet, or three at the most. At regular intervals the boat rose and fell to the altitude of four rungs.

'You get that rung there,' said the captain, pointing. 'You get a lower one, and the undertow will get you, right? So when the boat is up, you jump, OK? John'll show you.'

John showed them. On the crest of the wave the sailor jumped, held fast to the ladder and was away. The gap that he had jumped, between boat and ladder, was about four feet.

'OK,' said Artemis cheerily, wishing nevertheless that she had been wearing trousers, and not her kaftan.

The swell rose, and she was suddenly gone. She held on to the

121

ladder and then climbed up it swiftly until she was out of sight. On the *Warspite* Caroline breathed a sigh of relief.

Then it was Gianni's turn. It reminded him of some of the terrible things he had had to do when he had been a conscript in the army. Up went the boat; he hesitated; down came the boat.

'Get on with it,' said the captain, unsympathetically.

Up came the boat again. Gianni jumped, thinking that if he missed this opportunity, he would certainly be thrown on to the ladder by the impatient captain. That would be too undignified. Better to die, crushed between cliff and boat, or eaten by a shark, than to look a fool. Besides, Artemis was looking at him, he was sure, from the top of the cliff. And Charles and the others would be looking from the *Warspite*. He could not afford to fail. So he jumped – his hands grasped the rung, and his feet struggled for a foothold; then, recovering from the petrifying fear, he rather shakily began to climb upwards.

'Well, there you are,' said Artemis, when he got to the top. 'Come on, I want to explore.'

They were in a different world now. Above their heads screamed the gulls. The sun was still bright, but high on the exposed rock in the middle of the sea, the sharp wind blew away the heat. A concrete path lay before them, which led to the only building on the island, the lighthouse, a concrete cube with a cylindrical tower perched on top of it. Everywhere else there were craters, the legacy of years of guano extraction. Grey rocks and craters: it was like the surface of the moon. There was not a plant in sight. They had come, Gianni realised, all the way for this.

'There doesn't seem to be much to see,' he said.

'What did you expect?' she said.

He followed her down the path. The captain and the light-house men had joined them now, and they formed a little procession towards the concrete cube.

'How long do you spend here?' Artemis asked one of the men.

'Three months,' was the answer.

'There, you see,' she said to Gianni, as if to rebuke him for being childish.

The lighthouse had little to recommend it. The two tourists were advised to admire the view from the tower. The lamp, they were told, was fully automatic. The men were only there in case it should go out, which since its installation in the early 1970s it had never done. So Artemis and Gianni climbed the metal staircase to view this masterpiece of reliability. There it stood, all on its own, deprived of human company, in a glass-walled room, surrounded by an air of neglect. The view was one of uninterrupted sea.

'I can't see the *Warspite*,' said Artemis.

'It is under the cliff,' said Gianni.

She had the sudden feeling then that no one could see them, and that they were in a place that no one had visited for some time. She wondered now whether he would make some sort of an advance. It was all rather absurd. They had come all this way to see something so very unremarkable – and the others had come simply because she had wanted to come, for no other reason. She had led them all off on this wild-goose chase – and now what?

She turned away from staring at the sea, and looked at Gianni. She leaned against the glass. He was looking at her now. She knew then that he found her attractive. She smiled.

He continued to look at her for a moment and then he turned away. The floor of the room they were in was strewn with dead flies; the sound of the wind and the sea was excluded by the encircling glass. This was a goldfish bowl, he thought. Goldfish were such tedious creatures: they always did what was expected of them. There never yet was a goldfish that hadn't swum round and round in its glass bowl, opening and closing its mouth, eating and excreting, until overtaken by the fate that was common to Man and Fish alike. Nor would there ever be. Goldfish conformed. So in their way did sharks. When a shark ate you, it wasn't an act of unkindness, it was simply in its nature. A shark could be neither evil nor good – it was simply a shark: grim, determined and unfree. A shark never chose to do what sharks did – grow a second row of teeth, eat smaller fish, or swim eternally. Oh no. And neither did he ever choose. It was nature

123

that had led him here. He had swum and swum, all the way from the Via Ludovisi to this fly-blown lighthouse top, by jet, by yacht, by clapped-out schooner, because that was his nature. He had never once stopped and thought; two decades of unthinking choices had led him here; twenty years of freedom that hadn't been freedom at all.

'Let's go,' he said suddenly, wishing to escape, feeling the overwhelming urge to get away. 'Let's go and see what the others are doing.'

The others were still on the *Warspite*. The Canon and Charles were discussing the swell, wondering whether it would keep them on board all day, wondering whether they should risk attempting to land, having seen the apparent ease with which Artemis and Gianni had done so. Caroline was picking up clothes – Artemis's clothes. She was neatly folding a brightly coloured cloth, something called a sarong, which her sister had let carelessly drop, and was putting it away in one of the bags. Clothes, she remembered Silvia saying, were the person. What you wore was what you were. Silvia had said that to her one day in her elegant flat off the Via Merulana, as if delivering a great truth. Silvia's clothes had been superb. Whilst the memory of Silvia herself grew dim, she could still picture her stunning Jos Vercruysse leather coat, her Salvino Biolo dark glasses and her Gianfranco Ghirlanda evening dresses. Aeneas's shield in the *Aeneid* had been a fashion statement, according to Silvia. (Her father, when he had heard this, had sniffed in a marked manner, and announced that he couldn't tolerate new theories about old poets at his time of life.) But Silvia had believed it. The clothes were the person; fashion was faith, and she had even bought a hugely expensive bathing costume by the Californian Futurist Brian Morris to prove her point. But if clothes were the person – who then had Silvia been? What was she?

Caroline herself had never dared go near any of the Roman clothes shops on the Via Condotti or the Via Sistina. Silvia's Salvino Biolo dark glasses had cost over a million lire – and even if you only had a vague idea of exchange rates and could not cope with all those noughts, even then you still knew that a million lire was a daunting sum to pay for a pair of sun-glasses. That was why she had always let Artemis buy clothes for her in England and bring them out to Rome. She had put herself – hadn't she always? – in her sister's hands, and as a result had ended up as the owner of countless frocks that flowed, usually designed by Laura Ashley, just at a time when Laura Ashley was going out of fashion. That was how Artemis had seen her – as a rather faded don's wife, gracing dull garden parties in Canterbury Road. While this was a thousand light years away from the wickedly expensive and often minimalist creations of the Californian Futurists, it was perhaps not the disaster that it might have been. She had, as Silvia put it, become an exponent of *il look inglese*. She had even been admired.

But Ciriaco, Silvia's brother, hadn't been a fashion victim. The nature of his work had demanded a more practical approach. Only his name had hinted at baroque extravagance. Ciriaco – difficult to pronounce, faintly reminiscent of cheerfulness, in English 'Cyriac', in Latin 'Ciriacus', the name, he had explained, of a saint done to death by Diocletian or perhaps another wicked emperor, now forever revered, no doubt, in some Campanian village by devout old women dressed in black.

Ciriaco. The sheer ridiculous poetry of his name made her want to cry, even now. No wonder she had tried to forget his name; now, in this very moment, it had come back unbidden to disturb her peace. He had been her saint, she his pilgrim. 'But you know,' he had said to her several times, explaining the practicalities of the situation. She had not listened or understood. He had tried to tell her that her expectations were irrational. But love was irrational, and she had been in love. Common sense had made no sense to her. His refugees, and the fact that he planned, even then, to go away, and that she could play no further part in his life – these things he had explained to her. But she hadn't understood. She had blocked her mind to his reasonings. Had she really loved him? She had not wanted him to be free, but to be hers. Was possession compatible with love?

She quickly finished putting away Artemis's sarong, feeling she was being ridiculous. If only she could tidy away life, and put away the bits that she and others had dropped.

'What do you think?' she heard Charles asking, realising he was talking to her. 'The Canon thinks the swell is wearing off, or whatever swells do.'

She found herself drawn into intelligent everyday conversation, something she was so bad at – her father never discussed anything, he pontificated; and presently she was agreeing that they ought to go ashore after all.

They went ashore, taking the picnic with them, and it was considerably easier than they had thought possible.

Artemis was quite glad to see them.

'There's nothing on this island,' she said, clearly not finding things as amusing as she had hoped.

Gianni hung around in the background a little sheepishly as she said this, trying to make himself useful with the hamper.

There was only one place for the picnic, the narrow strip of shade created by the lighthouse. Here they sat on the concrete path that bordered the building, their various baskets and bits in their midst. There seemed to be an enormous quantity of chicken sandwiches, all made with the bread sold at the Galaxy Supermarket, white, spongy, easy to cut but strange to eat. As she dispensed the chicken sandwiches, Caroline was driven to reflect that the bread was not her fault. The Galaxy was not the Harrods food hall, even if it was almost as expensive. And no one else had offered to make the picnic.

'Ice? Chutney?' she said in slightly aggrieved tones, doing two things at once, which never helped.

'What is chutney?' asked Gianni, suddenly intrigued, coming out of what Caroline suspected could have been a sulk.

She explained it to him, opening the jar, inviting him to poke its contents with a spoon. The little cloud of bad temper that she had felt, no bigger than a man's hand, vanished from the horizon. Gone was her sudden discontent with the quality of Galaxy bread. Instead she was doing what she liked best: talking intelligently of a subject about which she knew something, in this case mangoes. A conversation developed, the sort that only those with quick minds can have. They spoke of the way Poirot had demonstrated the correct way to cut a mango in one of the Agatha Christie books; how mangoes grew in swamps; how Mussolini had drained the Pontine Marshes; the countryside around Rome; and how the Lake of Bracciano was to be preferred to that of Albano. On that, as on other subjects, they were agreed. This was a pleasant surprise. She remembered how pleasant agreeing with people could be – for too long had she dwelt among those who had loved discord. Artemis and her father always disagreed with her. Theirs was a spirit of contestation. 'It will rain today,' she might say; 'You're so depressing, dear,' Artemis would reply, quite ignoring the uncertainty of the weather. But facts meant nothing to them – facts were merely obstacles to be jumped over. They were rebellious subjects, enemies to peace – and they were not going to allow facts to stop them. If her father were to meet God face to face, he would still persist in atheism, still talk about 'what Aristotle really meant', oblivious of the reality before him.

Gianni bit into a chicken sandwich laced with chutney feeling contented. Why did he so little realise what was good for him? Artemis, thank God, was now some distance away, devoting herself to Charles in a marked manner. He had offended her. This was not at all what she had expected. She was beautiful, and had expected him to behave accordingly, but he hadn't. It was odd. For once the long chain of expectations had been broken. But Gianni could not regret it – at least not now. He would later regret the missed opportunity in the tower, but for the moment he was enjoying talking to Caroline, someone who actually listened, rather than doing what Artemis expected of him, no matter how beautiful Artemis might be.

'What was the name of your friend in the Via Merulana?' he asked suddenly.

'Silvia. Silvia Donati.'

'Who is Silvia? What is she?' asked the Canon, feeling at a loose end, now that Artemis was monopolising Charles and ignoring him.

'Silvia was a fashion victim,' said Caroline, her mind returning to previous thoughts. 'She was also my father's mistress. She taught Virgil at the university.'

'Really?' asked the Canon.

Gianni, imagining a mistress's function to be purely educational, nodded.

'It is an old-fashioned word, isn't it?' said Caroline, registering the Canon's surprise. 'But what other words are there? "Girlfriend" sounds awful. One really must not be too modern about such things. To be modern is to risk being ridiculous. And,' she said, in case that was what was worrying the Canon, 'neither of them was married, and they were both over twenty-one.'

Gianni began to get the picture. How strange the English were with this almost clinical dissection of the human heart. It was as if they were discussing the price of vegetables. He wondered about Silvia Donati, who she could be, what she could be like. He wished he could ask. Who was this woman who had been the mistress of the Professore Duxbury? That the Professore Duxbury should have a mistress did not in the least surprise him: the *professore* was rich, very handsome and charming – Gianni could see that. Lucky Silvia Donati. Donati was something of a famous name. He thought for a moment and felt the desire to ask a question about this Donati. But the Canon was talking, and the name slipped from his mind. The Canon had said something he had missed, and Caroline was replying.

'He will never marry again,' she was saying. 'And if he did, it would be a disaster. He didn't actually like Silvia that much, you know. She was just a little bit too clever for him. I don't mean she was a genius, only he doesn't like clever women. He thinks that Aristotle had the right idea – they are a lesser form of life, or whatever it was that he said. My father says that you can only love your equals, and a woman can never be the equal of a man. Therefore, one can never love a woman. He wouldn't admit any woman could be as clever as he was. When Silvia showed signs of it, it annoyed him.'

'It's a very Greek theory,' observed Gianni. 'The bit about like liking like is Plotinus.'

'Neoplatonism,' said the Canon, very disapprovingly. 'The classics are so unhealthy.'

This descent into Ancient Greece left them in a little pool of embarrassment. The Canon thought it was a jolly good thing that Greek was dying out in English schools. As for Caroline, she felt constrained to silence by the fact that she had criticised her father in public, in front of Gianni too, a virtual stranger. She had stepped over a limit and transgressed. They hadn't all come to this God-forsaken rock to hear from the lips of his daughter just how awful Jamie Duxbury was. Picnics, wherever they were held, were designed for polite conversation, and nothing more disturbing than the indigestion caused by overeating in the open air. It was a shock to find a conversational chasm yawning at your feet when all the time you ought to be discussing the weather. Thank God Artemis was out of earshot; she would have been furious. And neither had Charles heard, of which she was glad, for his pity would have killed her.

Only Gianni was not embarrassed, but happily immune from the discomfort that Caroline and the Canon felt. He used the silence to think, to try and set his mind in order. Of course, the *professore* was one of those strange Englishmen perhaps ... but he heard voices behind him, voices that belonged to Charles and Artemis. Her voice in particular commanded his entire attention. She was flirting; he could not hear what she was saying, as the wind carried her words away, but the tone of her voice told him all he needed to know. This then was the woman who had all but offered herself to him not an hour ago in the tower above their heads. He felt a sudden pang of jealousy. Thoughts of Duxbury evaporated to be overtaken by the awful thought that somehow this Artemis, this girl, might come between himself and Charles.

He got up at once and made towards the place, a little apart, where Charles was sitting with her. There was no telling just by looking at the back of his head what Charles was thinking. Perhaps he was smiling at her, entering into that secret world of complicity and love. He would no longer need anyone to sail his yacht if he had Artemis. He would no longer be amused, as he had been in Grenada, when Gianni had disappeared with the girl at the party. Artemis threatened the entire world that they enjoyed together. She would ruin everything.

Gianni stood behind Charles and put his hands under his chin, and then drew his head back, and held it tight.

'*Alzati*,' he commanded. '*Andiamo per una passegiata.*'

'What are you saying?' asked Artemis.

'I said we are going for a walk and that he had better get up,' said Gianni, using his grip to force Charles to his feet.

'Then I'll come too,' said Artemis, getting up as well, now every inch a school prefect.

'We're only going to examine the phosphate diggings,' said Gianni distantly.

'I adore worked-out mines,' she said coldly.

Charles smiled. He had always suspected that it would end like this: at least, not quite like this, but that it would end in some argument. Both of them seemed out of temper, quite why he was not sure, but he enjoyed the spectacle it provided. They moved off, a discordant trio, in search of exhausted diggings.

Caroline, still in her cloud of silence, realised that she had been left alone with the Canon. The others had disappeared, round the other side of the lighthouse. Here they were, the Canon and she, alone on the wide, wide sea. She could not quite remember ever being alone with him before. Judy had always been there, pouring beers; or her father; or Artemis. Anguilla was like that; it had only six thousand inhabitants, but despite their modest numbers, people seemed to congregate in little groups, never pairs, as if knowing that if two people were left alone together, something untoward might result.

But what could happen if someone were left alone with the Canon? Even the barest of acquaintance with the popular press was enough to make one realise that clergy could be dangerous – but the Canon was so respectable, so very Anglican, one couldn't imagine him doing anything remotely scandalous. The clergy were not men, but those strange twilight figures, a sort of Anglican compromise between the sexes, a third sex, a class of their own. Just like a vicarage tea party: for what was tea? Not lunch, not dinner, but a useless little interlude hovering between the two.

'Caroline,' he said, breaking the long silence.

'Yes, George?' she asked, feeling she ought to use his name, and not the half-jocular ecclesiastical title he rejoiced in. After all, where was he a Canon of? She had asked him once, but didn't remember his answer. Surely there was no cathedral in Basingstoke.

'Have you never thought of leaving your father?' he asked her.

A simple question: but what was the answer?

'My mother wanted to leave him,' she said. 'She never quite did. She had made up her mind to do so, but she was killed before she could tell him. I wonder if it's Fate that no one can leave my father.'

'You can't believe that.'

'I can't. But perhaps I'd like to. I could go and live in London tomorrow. I've got the money. I could have a job and a flat and a life, just as Artemis has. There's nothing to stop me. The fact that I'm here rather than there, though, shows that there is no particular reason for me to go.'

'Then you want to be here?'

'The alternative is so empty. Look at Artemis. She's young and beautiful and I'm neither. But she's empty; ever since she's been sixteen, she's been so cold. I could never do that.'

'You wouldn't have to,' said the Canon.

'One day my father may realise that what Aristotle did or did

131

not say does not really matter; none of that matters; he may just notice me,' she said. 'He may just see.'

'See? See what?'

'That in the end love is better than unkindness and that if we stop wanting the wrong things we will be happy.'

'But you want all the wrong things,' he said forcefully. 'You want to devote your life to Duxbury, you want to spend your time worrying about Artemis. There are other things you could want, like – '

A husband and children, he was on the point of saying. But she interrupted him before he could.

'How can you know what I want?' she said. 'You are trying to look into my soul. Not that I believe in souls,' she said, her Somerville pride asserting itself. 'And I don't care what Aristotle says.'

'Damn Aristotle,' said the Canon. 'I want you to come to England with me and be happy.'

'Oh, Canon,' she said, after a pause. 'If only you knew ...'

'Knew what?'

But he could not know and she could not explain. She could only love Ciriaco.

'I can't marry you,' she said. 'Or anyone else. It is impossible.'

'The world is full of impossible things,' he said a little desperately.

'I suppose it is; but not for me.'

Why not, he wanted to ask; but the time for confidences was past; the others were coming back, looking hot and for the most part bothered. He could not urge the case for his house in Basingstoke now; and perhaps he would never have another opportunity.

'It must be time to go back now, surely,' said Artemis, plonking herself down in the shade.

'Sombrero has failed to amuse you,' observed Gianni.

She did not reply.

'If we go to the other side, we can see if the sea is in the shade,' said Charles. 'Shade attracts fish, you know.'

No one had a better suggestion, so the disconsolate little party made its way back along the concrete path. Along the cliff edge, the men from the *Warspite* were fishing, their long lines dangling in the shady waters beneath them.

'We've caught nothing,' said the captain. 'There's something down there frightening them away.'

'Something?' asked Charles.

'Sharks,' said the captain.

They peered at the water, expecting to see a dorsal fin break the surface at any moment. But there was nothing to see. The sharks, if they were there, were deep down, out of sight.

'It's shark-infested,' said the captain grimly, used to causing dismay with such statements.

But today, for some reason, the oohs and ahs of excited horror were not forthcoming. An atmosphere of almost Soviet joyless-ness hung over the day-trippers. Each was discontented and longed to be gone. Even Charles, who had the least to be un-happy about, could feel the sunburn on his neck, and was beginning to long for the shade that only a more substantial island could provide.

Duxbury was at home, sitting on his verandah, drinking a cup of tea. This was the nearest he ever came to domesticity. He had got used to the taste of UHT milk, which came in plastic bottles with blue tops. You got used to everything in the end. He no longer missed Rome, or Oxford, just as he had long ceased to miss the Trinidad of his youth. They were countries that no longer existed; but the past had the habit of never entirely going away. To look at Caroline was to see her mother, his wife. Artemis was a more cheerful prospect. Artemis, even though she was a woman, was his younger self. But in other ways, too, the past intruded. He had gone to the airfield this morning, to find out about flights to Puerto Rico or wherever else the planes might be going – the airfield was a little like a hitch-hikers' station. But he had not asked. He had got back on his motor-bike and ridden away as quickly as possible. For he had witnessed, bags in hand, someone arriving, being met by the Demmers, someone he knew. It was the Master of an Oxford college, the college that had been his own, a man called Peacock. The sight of Peacock with Demmer had immediately made him think of the Commissioner's invitation for drinks. And he had fled, shaken, back home to a solitary lunch.

Reflection over his pig's tail soup had led him to the conclusion that Peacock had not come to Anguilla with any particular intention in his regard. It was ridiculous, albeit easy, to imagine that Peacock's arrival was part of some plot, that the past had come to track him down. And doubtless Demmer, in inviting him to drinks, merely had in mind the rather fatuous thought that two Oxford men would enjoy meeting each other so far from home. Stupid Demmer: Oxford men, Duxbury knew, never liked meeting each other anywhere. Why on earth should two Oxford men want to meet in the West Indies, when the chances were they hated each other like hell back amidst the dreaming spires?

Of course, it would be stupid not to go to the drinks. Was the prospect of meeting Peacock so very frightening? He had hardly known the man at Oxford. Peacock had been a scientist, rather beneath his notice – God alone knew who had had the bright idea of making him Master. It was quite possible that their slight acquaintance, renewed at such a distance in time and space, would discomfit Peacock more than it would discomfit Duxbury himself.

Now that he sipped his tea, he wondered why on earth Peacock was here. It would be too much of a coincidence if he were a relation of the Demmers. Perhaps he was here to do 'research', to waste university money, enjoying himself. Dons were experts at that sort of thing. He supposed Peacock must have had some speciality in the days he had actually taught undergraduates something. He had the feeling now that Peacock had been a biologist. What an unglamorous occupation. How very hard it must have been for Peacock to rise to the top with such a handicap. Natural scientists were such a dreadful bunch of people – they were badly dressed, run down, and usually looked mad.

134

Peacock, however, was none of these things, being the sort of man who had doubtless made his career by flattering the right people, an occupation that would be impossible if one had had bad breath and dandruff. But all the same it was comforting to think of the odious Peacock as a scientist; no doubt he had some very restrictive speciality (what?) designed to distract one's mind from the thought of anoraks, dismembered rabbits in laboratories, and riding rusty bicycles through the Oxford rain after a hard afternoon studying the reproductive habits of small furry animals.

Through the burning heat of a Caribbean afternoon came the *Warspite*, bearing its cargo of thoroughly bored Europeans. Gianni had curled up in a corner and gone to sleep, once he had seen that Artemis had retired behind dark glasses and a book for the duration of the voyage. The Canon and Charles, sitting in the few inches of shade that had now appeared on board, talked a little desultorily about Egyptology. Caroline, alone, stood at the prow, watching the schooner cut through the water. From where she stood, she could, by craning her neck, see the Canon and Charles in conversation. It was clear that the Canon was giving her space, giving her a chance to think about his extraordinary proposal of marriage. She had not imagined that what was happening now had been in any way possible. She was in a state of shock. Ageing clergymen (he was forty-three or four, wasn't he?) did the most extraordinary things after all. And now she had to think about it. No one in her family had ever thought about anything, as far as she could remember. They just did things. She had not been brought up to reflect – but it was what she had learned to do: she was now always thoughtful, cautious, a little depressed. Common sense, that little interior voice that counselled thought, had taken her over.

She kept on thinking until they arrived at Road Bay. She loaded her thoughts into the car with the picnic things and her sister, and they drove off after brief good-byes, made easier by the fact that Judy was there to meet them, bearing an envelope for Charles from Mr Demmer. But even that little bustle didn't stop the Canon from reminding her that he would see her soon – a quite unnecessary remark, really, when for the last four years or so they had seen each other almost every day. At least he didn't ask for a lift, as she half feared he might.

This desire to get away from the Canon did not augur well. How could you consider marrying a man who, no sooner than he had proposed, you wanted to get away from? It made no sense. But the proposal itself – if it was so very ridiculous, and she had rejected it out of hand, why did it still trouble her? Why couldn't she put it out of her mind?

The Canon resurfaced as they sat on the verandah after dinner.

'Not a good day?' asked Duxbury, sensing something had gone wrong, judging by their silence, and wanting to know what exactly.

Artemis said nothing. It had not been a good day, but she had suggested the trip in the first place, and she was not going to admit that it had been anything less than a success. Besides, there had been more to the failure than she cared to contemplate: she thought of Gianni in the tower and wondered what had gone wrong.

'The Canon,' said Caroline, with hesitation, unable to speak of anything else, 'has asked me to marry him.'

'Oh dear,' said her father, a little gleefully, imagining his fat friend sinking to one knee.

'And what did you say?' asked Artemis appalled.

'I didn't say anything at all,' lied Caroline. 'I was too shocked to speak.'

'He's mad,' said Artemis, feeling deeply annoyed. As far as she had been able to tell from the day's activities, the Canon far preferred her to her sister. Hadn't he carried the picnic basket when she had told him to? How dare he be so disloyal?

'Of course, you told him ...' she began.

'Told him what?' asked Caroline.

'That he was mad. I mean the Canon – he's so unromantic.

He's a clergyman. He's the last person to propose marriage to anyone. I just can't imagine him ...'

'Can't imagine him what?' asked Caroline levelly.

'I suppose he is a virgin, isn't he?' said Artemis. 'How absolutely ghastly.'

'But he may be your brother-in-law soon,' said Duxbury. 'Don't forget that, much as you disapprove of sexual continence, my dear.'

Caroline was silent. She felt she ought to defend her admirer; the fact that the Canon was so scorned by her sister reflected rather badly on herself. But what could she say? Could she mention his steady character? (She presumed he had one.) Or his valuable house in Basingstoke? Neither of these, she felt, would cut much ice with Artemis.

'Are you in love with him?' asked Duxbury in a spirit of philosophical enquiry. Was she, he wondered, doing what her mother had done, namely, forming an unfortunate attachment?

At the thought of love and being in love, Caroline was struck dumb by remembrance.

Duxbury knew. He knew she was thinking about Ciriaco Donati. Artemis, who did not know, thought the silence was a bad sign, and felt a wave of impatience. Still Caroline did not speak.

'You can't possibly think of marrying him,' said Artemis, thinking that this was what was going through her head.

'Why not? Have I got anyone else to marry?'

'You've been in love before,' said her father in detached tones, thinking of Ciriaco, who, if the truth were known, he had liked, insofar as he had ever liked anyone. 'But the first time it was tragedy; this time it is farce.'

It was the truth of this comparison that made it so cruel to her ears.

'Marry him if you must,' continued Duxbury. 'Live in England, be a vicar's wife, run church bazaars, be civilised. But is that what you really want to do?'

'How could she?' asked Artemis. 'It is ridiculous.'

Even Duxbury was rather taken aback by the vehemence of Artemis's condemnation of the Canon as a future husband.

Caroline, still not speaking, still leaving them wondering, got up and left the verandah. The thought that Artemis might somehow pick up her father's reference to Ciriaco and turn her attention to him was too much to bear.

'She won't, will she?' asked Artemis, after she had left, still thinking of the Canon, and quite uninterested in her sister's other experiences, which were beyond her horizon.

'Anyone would think you wanted him yourself,' said Duxbury. 'There's no accounting for taste, I suppose. Caroline has never been conventional.'

Conventional taste, in Duxbury's view, meant the Greek Ideal, those cold marbles in the Vatican Museum. Ciriaco Donati, though a nice enough chap, had been the wrong side of thirty, too balding and too tubby to be mistaken for a Greek god. His pleasant smile had been his only recommendation.

'She wants to have children,' said Duxbury, with his usual distaste for such matters.

'How do you know?'

'I know,' he said firmly, thinking of the state she had been in in the Tiber Island hospital. 'She wants a child. Some women do; your mother did.'

'I will never have a child,' said Artemis. 'If I did there would always be the chance that it might turn out to be like its father. I couldn't have that. You'd be stuck with the replica of some ghastly man for the next eighteen years, and you'd be reminded of how stupid you'd been every day.'

'That's true,' said Duxbury. 'That's how I feel looking at you and Caroline. I'd made a ghastly mistake.'

'You inherited her money,' replied Artemis, realising as she said it that she had done so too.

'Those who marry money earn every penny,' said Duxbury sententiously. 'I suppose I had one daughter who was like myself, at least in character.'

She smiled at that, ruefully. She knew she was like her father.

He was the one who had formed her character, and made her what she was now. She never felt the temptation to dislike herself, but disliked him instead. He had created her faults; for one moment, she wondered if it could ever have been different.

'Peacock is here,' said Duxbury, reminded now of Oxford and things past.

'Who or what is Peacock?'

'An Oxford man. And we have been invited to drinks tomorrow with the Demmers. Peacock is staying with them.'

'Oh.'

'I imagine everyone will be there,' said Duxbury. 'A party.'

'Everyone isn't very many, at least not on this island,' said Artemis.

She wondered if Charles and Gianni would be there. She hoped not. That had not proved to be a very rich seam. But because everyone meant so few people, it was more than likely that the Demmers would have invited them. And so would the Canon be there; where there were drinks, there was the Canon. Would she be able to resist teasing him about Caroline? Or would she not speak to him at all, but concentrate on Charles and Gianni? What a choice! She sighed at the absurdity of island life.

IX

Peacock was the sort of man who specialised in making himself agreeable, and had spent the first few hours of his stay on the island doing his best to charm his young hostess. He had had lots of practice: dons always did. His first love had been marine biology, but with the approach of early middle-age devotion to scholarship had given way to a penchant for the comfortable life a don's salary could hardly provide. Unlike Duxbury, he hadn't married money; he had, in fact, married a rather faded woman, who, whenever he could, he made sure he left behind at home in Canterbury Road. Having made this one youthful mistake, he had spent his mature years correcting it. Hours spent in the laboratory and on tedious field trips to unglamorous locations were supplemented by hours massaging important egos and espousing fashionable causes. By the time he was fifty he had sat on important committees; he had made a name for himself as an environmentalist; he had had luncheon with members of the Royal Family. When the Government had been Labour, he had been socialist; when it had been Conservative, he had found himself to be a Tory at heart; and for being so universally agreeable, he had been rewarded by being made Master of his college: for, when names came up for consideration, no one had been able to say anything bad about Bryan Peacock, except that they didn't like him much, an opinion which might have been universally held, but was certainly universally concealed.

As for money, that essential commodity, Peacock had been streets ahead of his nearest rivals. He had used his knowledge of marine biology and his contacts with a few well-placed friends to advise film-makers. After several years of unrewarding toil, he had reaped his reward. His apotheosis had come when his name had appeared in the credits of one major success, a Hollywood movie, the villain of which had been a great white shark, played by a cunningly constructed fibreglass dummy, carefully checked for realism by Bryan Peacock, MA, DPhil, (Oxon).

It was on the set of the shark film that he had met Amelia Churchill, the famous actress; from that moment, he had never looked back; he had arrived.

With such achievements, and bearing in mind the fact that he was in Anguilla to rendezvous with Miss Churchill, he could quite afford to feel what he thought of as polite curiosity when Mrs Demmer said:

'Jamie Duxbury is coming to drinks tonight. I persuaded my husband to invite him.'

'Duxbury?' he asked. 'Is he here then? I had rather lost track of him.'

Peacock smiled, as if to signify that Duxbury was some dear old friend, rather than a former rival from the shark-infested waters of Oxford.

Mrs Demmer, having mentioned the name of Duxbury, seemed to become slightly excited by it. It was as if she had broached some forbidden topic.

'Yes, he lives here,' she said. 'We see him from time to time.'

That much was true. She did see Duxbury from time to time, usually in the post office, and mostly at a considerable distance.

'Oh. He's a millionaire, you know,' said Peacock knowledgeably. 'He can afford to live here. His wife's family made sugar lumps, or something like that. A nice man,' continued Peacock with glittering insincerity, 'but something of an eccentric.'

'Oh?' said Mrs Demmer, fishing for details, scenting dirt in the offing.

'From what I remember,' said Peacock, 'his leaving Oxford, though unfortunate, was nevertheless opportune.'

Peacock spoke with a cultivated drawl, which some years previously had replaced his native Nottingham accent.

'He's a very good-looking man,' said Mrs Demmer in the most

offhand manner she could manage. 'His younger daughter is pretty, the elder one rather plain.'

Mrs Demmer, being pretty herself, thought the status of Duxbury's daughters important. The prospect of discussing the father seemed to be receding.

'And how is Miss Churchill?' she asked, feeling Duxbury could wait. 'Everyone is so excited about her yacht calling in here,' she added, in best Foreign Office fashion.

Peacock, who had noticed no signs of fevered excitement during his air-conditioned drive from the airfield to the house, nevertheless recognised the compliment and smiled his best courtier's smile.

'I spoke to her last when she gave me a ring from Los Angeles,' he said, knowing a transatlantic call, so casually mentioned, could not fail to impress. 'I am not quite sure if Amelia will have time to come ashore.'

Mrs Demmer looked suitably crestfallen.

'But,' he added, with the generosity of one giving hope where none was possible, 'I think she's bound to invite you on board when I tell her who you are.'

Mrs Demmer smiled the smile of the socially gratified. Like Amelia Churchill, she was something of an actress herself. She wondered how on earth she would explain away the prospect of drinks on Miss Churchill's yacht to her husband. He hated drinks parties, which was awkward for a diplomat, and sometimes thought longingly of the alternative careers that might have been his in the quieter reaches of insurance or accountancy.

Even Judy had got to hear about the drinks party at the Demmers'. She had not been invited, but she knew about it all the same, gleaning facts from various sources.

'They've got a man called Peacock staying,' she said, as she bent over the open fridge, feeling the bottles for coldness. 'He's something important. And this actress creature is turning up too. Name of Churchill. I got that out of one of the maids that lives

143

locally. Apparently she was eaten by a shark – Miss Churchill, that is. It was her most famous role.'

'How old is the actress?' asked Gianni with a flicker of interest.

'She must be sixty,' said Charles. 'She used to be on telly years ago.'

'I gather that she's become frightfully grand since then,' said Judy. 'I can't imagine her coming here. She's got a huge yacht. This Peacock seems to be her hanger-on. He's about fifty, her younger man. I suppose the Duxburys have been invited to the drinks this evening,' she added, wistfully.

The two men were silent.

'I was rather surprised that the Canon went home yesterday without calling in for a drink,' said Judy suddenly. 'So did the girls. I hope nothing went wrong on Sombrero Island.'

Gianni and Charles stared into their drinks. Judy reflected that things were becoming complicated. Had the Canon proposed? What had been the result? Why were Gianni and Charles so sheepish all of a sudden? At points like this one really needed some efficient military man to intervene and make everything clear, using diagrams on a blackboard, as they did in NATO military exercises.

'I see that you have quarrelled,' she said, trying to establish what exactly was going on.

Charles kept his eyes fixed on his glass; Gianni looked up, shrugged and smiled.

'I knew this would happen,' said Judy, picturing a duel on a moonlit beach. 'Both of you have fallen in love with Artemis.'

'Oh really, Judy,' said Charles in remonstrance.

'I am certainly not in love with Artemis,' said Gianni. 'I think she's ... corrupted.'

'Oh, Catholic claptrap,' said Charles with the asperity of one who had spent his school holidays at the seaside, accompanied by evangelical nannies, where he had been forced to enjoy the harsh cold waters of the English Channel.

'People can be evil,' said Judy, rallying to the defence of her co-religionist.

'She's a perfectly ordinary girl,' said Charles. 'Anyone would think she's a witch from the way you talk about her. She's had an odd upbringing, that is all. It must have been difficult seeing the way her father treated her mother. But I am certainly not fleeing the island to get away from her. That is what he wants to do.'

'We've been here long enough,' said Gianni.

'We're staying for drinks with the Demmers,' said Charles, going over old ground.

'Oh dear, you have quarrelled,' said Judy. 'It would be so flattering for her if she were to find out. No one has ever quarrelled over me. I have had such an ordinary life.'

'You say that hoping we will contradict you,' said Charles.

'Nonsense,' said Judy. 'I am past flirting. I am too old. I am saying it because it happens to be true. Women do have ordinary lives. It is only men who go off on yachts and think they have great souls. Don't deny it. I can tell. You think that you are important, that your feelings matter, that somehow you are the centre of the turning world. Men are such egotists. But women aren't like that – we know that it is so ordinary, no matter how tragic it may seem to you. It's commonplace for us. Look at Caroline. And yet her father, a man who has never had to suffer anything in his life, thinks he is the reincarnation of Lord Byron. And as for Artemis, Gianni is right, there is something terribly wrong with her.'

'What?' asked Charles.

'She is corrupted. She's masculine. It's the worst thing I could ever say of a woman.'

'She's not masculine to look at,' said Gianni.

'But her soul is,' said Judy. 'I need another drink.'

Gianni felt pleased; he could feel that Charles had been defeated. Charles contemplated the remains of his beer with some discomfort. The knowledge that he possessed a masculine ego was not a pleasant thought; how much better it would be if instead of sailing the world, imagining one had a great soul, one could make sense of someone else's sufferings, understand their feelings, and redeem them from ordinariness. Why had Caroline suffered? That was what he wanted to know. Could he make that commonplace experience in her something sacred, worthwhile, unique?

'The Canon will marry her, you know,' said Judy, pouring out three more beers. 'Caroline will marry the Canon.'

'That would be a waste,' said Charles.

'It would be better than spending the rest of her life with Duxbury,' said Judy. 'Duxbury is awful,' she added feelingly.

Duxbury was awful. She knew it. She was after all in love with him.

'I don't like Anglican clergymen,' said Gianni. 'I mean the idea of them. They are not like priests at all. The Canon is a nice man – but being nice isn't something I associate with priests.'

'Yes,' said Judy, who knew what he meant. Priests were meant to go off and get martyred in foreign parts, not to lead lives of quiet domestic bliss. She tried to imagine St Ignatius Loyola settling down to breakfast with his wife and kiddies, but failed to do so.

'What we need are heroes,' said Judy.

'You can't be a hero any more,' said Charles. 'Not today. There's nowhere left to go if you feel the urge to be heroic. People like the Canon are the best we can hope for.'

'You can go to Bosnia and tend the wounded,' said Judy. 'But people don't, on the whole. They're always making appeals for volunteers in the *Catholic Herald*.'

'Who are?'

'Doctors. Not for money. For people.'

'Well, I'd send a cheque,' said Charles. 'But I'd only get in the way if I went myself. I mean, what on earth could I do in a refugee camp?'

'I know the feeling,' said Judy. 'We are defeated. Morally defeated.'

Gianni felt a twinge of conscience, possibly because he had not had much sleep the night before. He and Charles had stayed up late quarrelling about Artemis – if their desultory conversation could be called anything so definite. You needed principles to

146

quarrel: without them, one just offended people, leaving oneself with the vague idea that there was some stand that one ought to take, if only one knew what it was.

Bosnia, he thought. Here they were, failing to agree over Artemis, instead of worrying about what was far more important. Artemis didn't matter: he knew that, but it only deepened his discontent at his own failure to get her out of his mind. The trip to Sombrero had convinced him that he ought not to stay on the same island with her if he could help it. She frightened him, yet fascinated him. But Charles was stubborn, unwilling to move; half regretting it, and half anticipating it, he knew he would have to face the pleasures of Artemis and not run away.

Where was there to go? He wasn't a hero. He wished he could be. But he was condemned to follow his passions. Once, he had controlled them; now they controlled him. How wonderful it would be to join the Italian Red Cross in Bosnia, instead of chasing girls whom he didn't even like. It would be a liberation. But Artemis, who he was sure had no soul of her own, was despoiling him of his.

Caroline came in on silent feet, and stood in the middle of the bar.

'How quiet you all are,' she observed.

'We were thinking about Bosnia,' explained Judy gravely.

'Oh, how interesting,' said Caroline, who never read newspapers. 'The girl nearby has just done my hair. For the Demmers' drinks party. Artemis suggested it. I thought I'd show you, Judy.'

'You look wonderful,' said Judy sincerely. 'Now you must tell me exactly what she did to it.'

For Judy was dying to hear about the Canon's proposal, which had surely taken place by now, and thought that a discussion of hairdressing would be bound to drive the two men away.

It did. They got up to go: Gianni with a rueful smile, for he understood female conspiracies, and Charles with an air of disappointment. He felt, irrationally, he was sure, that he was being excluded from something – quite what, he did not know. The

147

private world of Caroline's experiences seemed suddenly mysterious and interesting.

'We'll see you at the Demmers',' he said, as they left.

The Demmers' house, as befitted the residence of a colonial Commissioner, was the nearest thing that the island of Anguilla could boast of to a luxurious abode. The kitchen had the sort of fridge that made ice automatically; the bedrooms were air-conditioned; there was even a swimming-pool. In these circumstances, and in such comfort, making oneself smart was not difficult. Both Peacock and Mrs Demmer were able to take up their positions in the drawing-room confident that they would outshine their guests. Duxbury's bungalow at Blowing Point had, they supposed, one of those bathrooms in which you doused yourself with buckets of cold water. And as for the Canon's house, it was doubtful whether that had any bathroom at all.

'How people manage, I can't think,' said Mrs Demmer, with an elegant little shiver; the type that their superiors keep for the times when they are simply forced to think of the lower orders.

Such hygienic considerations, and Peacock's well-crafted reply, were interrupted by the arrival of the guests. As is often the case with small drinks parties, the guests arrived *en masse*. All six of them were suddenly there at once – Duxbury and his daughters, the Canon, looking a little ill at ease, and the two young men from the yacht. This sudden influx was not at all what Mrs Demmer had hoped for: she had imagined welcoming them singly, putting each one at their ease, in the manner of a professional hostess. She had had it all planned in advance. Naturally, her husband had been earmarked to take care of the Canon; she herself felt little interest in the Canon; but as for the lugubrious Mr Demmer, entertaining clergymen was his department. Nor did she have any plans to talk to the two girls. They, too, failed to interest her. Of course, Artemis was very pretty, and deserved to be acknowledged as such, but Peacock could do that. No: it had been her carefully laid plan to speak to those two beautiful young men, and to Duxbury. She had been looking forward to it all day. Ten years of marriage to Demmer, and being polite to nonentities whom you hoped you would never have the misfortune to meet again, had inculcated in her a spirit of ruthlessness when it came to cocktail parties.

Duxbury was attractive. She could see him now at the other side of the room, listening to the Canon, his sardonic gaze taking in the rest of the company. She ought to go and rescue him. There was something in the curve of his mouth and the expression of his eyes that excited her. He was so very dark. She was his hostess, it was perfectly legitimate for her to go up to him and prise him away from the Canon. This was merely a social duty she was performing. But somewhere in the depths of her soul, she longed to be antisocial. She longed to rend her Laura Ashley summer frock, expose her limp pale breasts to the eyes of all present, and dance before them, heedless of their shocked silence.

As she made her way towards Duxbury, she wished she could seize him, regardless of what anyone might think: he was twenty years her senior, he was supposed to have something of a past, she hardly knew him. How true: but in that lay his attraction. She wished she could shock the world, but knew she never would. She was doomed to be her usual self – boring Mr Demmer's pretty little wife. She would talk to this fascinating stranger of impersonal, neutral subjects, and do her duty as hostess.

Peacock had followed her across the room to where Duxbury stood. Duxbury was wearing a rather ancient off-white linen suit, which made him look like some cocoa planter from the hills behind Port of Spain. The linen complemented the darkness of his skin, and the curl of his hair. Beside him the two beautiful young men were as nothing.

'You know Dr Peacock?' she found herself asking, as she offered Duxbury a limp hand, feeling her bowels turn to ice as his dark brown eyes fixed on her.

'Yes, I do,' said Duxbury, somewhat warily, turning from her to

Peacock. 'And how is Oxford?' he asked, as if enquiring about some unloved and half-forgotten place.

'Unchanged,' said Peacock.

Oxford thus disposed of, the next question could be broached with the same polite lack of enthusiasm.

'What brings you to Anguilla?'

'I am helping some film-makers,' said Peacock.

'Oh, how?'

'My subject, you know – or rather my speciality,' said Peacock, a little mysteriously.

'And what is your speciality?' asked Mrs Demmer, though she knew; but she felt she ought to fuel the conversation between these two great men.

'Marine biology, and in particular – '

'No Oxford man really likes talking about his chosen field,' said Duxbury suddenly, interrupting. 'Still less does he like discussing anyone else's. There's something rather shaming in the realisation that you might have devoted perhaps forty years to studying something for no better reason than the fact that no one else has bothered to study it. Can you imagine looking at rows of cadavers in a laboratory or piles of broken stones, and thinking that was your life's work? That's why whenever dons meet at High Table, which they can't avoid doing, they usually speak about something utterly infantile, like football.'

Mrs Demmer assumed a pained expression. Duxbury began to think that it would have been better not to have come to this ridiculous party after all. He must have been made to have come, especially as he had known that Peacock would be there. Peacock reminded him of the ghastly tedium of Oxford life. And as for Mrs Demmer, with her glassy smile and her prissy frock, he could sense that she was fainting with lust. She repelled him; he hadn't come all the way to the West Indies for this. He had to get away; looking around the room, he saw the Italian boy talking to Demmer. He would rescue him.

'He murdered his wife, you know,' said Peacock, as soon as Duxbury had gone.

'Did he?' asked Mrs Demmer, enthralled. 'How?'

'She was run over when crossing the High Street. He drove her to it.'

'You mean he was driving the car and ran her over?'

'No. He didn't kill her literally. He made her life a misery. And after her death he couldn't stay on in Oxford. He was forced to leave.'

This little anecdote merely increased Duxbury's standing in her eyes. He was an anarchist, and she a prisoner of respectability.

'Come and talk to Dr Peacock, dear,' she said to Caroline, who now came into range, trying to avoid the Canon. 'Do you remember him from your Oxford days? He's the world's leading expert on sharks, you know.'

'How lovely,' said Caroline.

She was wearing one of Artemis's frocks; that, and the fact that the girl at Sandy Ground had worked something of a miracle with her hair, produced a glint in Peacock's eye.

'I knew your mother,' said Peacock. 'She was a friend of my wife's.'

Mrs Demmer wondered if this was the right thing to say. Her eyes wandered round the room. The pretty Artemis was stuck with the Canon, and looking as if she resented it. Duxbury was talking to the Italian. Charles, the good-looking – but how colourless compared to Duxbury! – brewing heir seemed rather bored, no doubt because he was being entertained by Demmer. But she felt no compulsion to rescue him from her husband. She sipped her drink and felt the Bacchic frenzy rise in her again. How pointless people like Charles were, compared to Duxbury. She became suddenly aware that Caroline was talking to her, attempting to draw her into the conversation; by her tone, it seemed to be one of those conversations which no one is particularly interested in, but which is nevertheless undertaken out of a grim sense of duty.

'Do you like Anguilla?' Caroline was asking.

'Yes, it's delightful,' replied Mrs Demmer, her mind clouded

151

with visions of dusty roads, exorbitant prices and a desiccated husband. 'We love it here,' she heard herself saying, invoking the matrimonial 'we', that telling pronoun that spoke to strangers of shared connubial joys.

'If I were married ...' said Caroline suddenly, realising that the Canon, who wanted to marry her, was not far away; but if she were married, what then? How could she finish this awkward sentence? If she were married, what, if anything, would change? Would the world suddenly become a happy place?

'Aren't you married already?' asked Peacock, in the ingratiating tones that he had learned in Senior Common Rooms, using the voice he kept for the wives and daughters of dons.

'No, I am not,' she said a little defensively, feeling that he thought that she ought to be.

But such a thought was far from Peacock's mind. Marriage in his view ruined a woman. One had only to look at the dreary females who inhabited North Oxford, women like his own wife, to see that. He smiled at Caroline conspiratorially. It struck her now that this ghastly man, this marine biologist, this shark expert, who was old enough to be her father, was attempting to flirt with her. A second realisation followed. Peacock, unless he was the sort who flirted with every female he met, must find her attractive. She felt her fingers tighten around the stem of her glass and wondered if she dared, as she now very much wanted to, to throw her drink in his absurd face. That would wreck the drinks party. There would be a moment's pause in the conversation, a little whimper of horror from Mrs Demmer, and the certainty of never being invited again; and the knowledge that the next time she saw her hostess in the supermarket or at the post office, she would be cut dead. What a delightful prospect – to be free forever of the chains of polite social intercourse; to have the liberty of the outcast, and to know that from then on one need only be polite to people one actually liked. That was what her father had done.

But something stayed her hand. The upbringing she had received from her mother triumphed. She wouldn't assault Peacock after all; she would suffer in silence; perhaps she would content herself with a cutting comment instead.

'Don't you find Oxford stultifying?' she asked. 'It must be like living in a very small pond full of piranha fish.'

'Some people do find that they don't fit in,' he replied, with a slight edge to his voice.

Caroline sensed an allusion to her father's exit from the city of the nightmarish spires. She looked around for rescue and found the Canon next to her. Simultaneously, Mrs Demmer began to steer Peacock away. But whether this was an improvement, Caroline could not tell. She had been doing her very best to avoid meeting the Canon, since their fateful trip to Sombrero. He had been remarkably patient: after all, he had proposed marriage, and doubtless wanted to try again. And here he was, large, over-weight, slightly hot and bothered, wanting to marry her, not content with further evasion. (Over his shoulder, she noticed that the odious Peacock had now latched on to Artemis.)

'You look beautiful tonight,' he said.

'Tonight, yes,' she said. 'Usually, no.'

But what he had said was true, once you overlooked the hyperbole. She hadn't suddenly become beautiful, but she was presentable: a decent frock, and the fact that someone had taken her hair in hand (she had got into the habit of cutting it herself, with nail scissors), a certain amount of make-up, these had done the trick. Her usual self was more a product of neglect than of nature. And here was the Canon admiring her. Much as she had not actually wanted to attract his attention, she ought to thank him. That was the expected thing. Wherever she turned she met convention. There was no need for thought any more; one need only do what was expected of you. Life was a labyrinth, but the signposts were clear.

'I'm no good for you,' she said, tearing her mind away from the pictures of mazes that it was already forming. 'I am too uncon-ventional.'

'What on earth do you mean?'

'I mean I would hate it.'

'Hate what?'

'I'd hate being a vicar's wife. It would be absurd. I'd have to be polite to people, living in Basingstoke, meeting other vicars' wives, wondering what impression I was making. The whole of my life would be one long exam. I don't even believe in God; at least I don't know if I do; I certainly don't believe in the Church of England. It is all too tame for me.'

'You've been listening to Judy,' he said. 'I mean about the Church. But I'm not asking you to marry the entire C of E, just me.'

He looked around him, realising that this wasn't the place to make his apologia, but that he had no choice. He might get no other opportunity. He plunged in again: 'I could quite easily get a college chaplaincy in Oxford. Wouldn't you prefer living in Oxford to all this?'

'This', she knew, had few attractions. (She could now see Peacock positively leering at poor Artemis.) The West Indies might mean paradise to the people who believed travel agents' propaganda, but they meant nothing to her. This wasn't paradise; happiness was within: whether you lived in Basingstoke or Anguilla, Rome or Oxford, there was no difference. You could be unhappy anywhere.

'You must think I am mad,' she said, 'but even though I ought to marry you, I won't.'

Once she had been in love with someone else. She had seen the far-off vision, and until such a time as she should see it again – and she might never do so – she would stay as she was. She would be faithful to what she knew to be true.

The Canon sensed the finality of her words.

Artemis now approached.

'I am not enjoying this,' she said. 'That ghastly old lecher.'

Caroline sympathised. It really was rather ungallant, she felt, of Charles and Gianni not to have rescued Artemis from the awful Peacock. What else had they found to do? Charles had spent most of his time with Demmer; and God alone knew what Gianni had found to talk to her father about.

'I suppose we could go home,' she said, looking at her watch cautiously.

Home seemed like an excellent idea. She did not want Peacock foisted on her again; refusing the first and perhaps last proposal of marriage you were ever likely to get was enough for one evening. Besides, it was well past nine thirty.

Right on cue, Duxbury hove into view, looking unusually convivial.

'We're thinking of abandoning this dreadful party and going down to Judy's for some proper drinks,' he said.

'I won't,' said the Canon.

'Sermon to write?' asked Duxbury.

'Yes,' lied the Canon.

'I am not coming. I want to go home,' said Artemis, hurt by the way Gianni in particular hadn't spoken to her all evening, but had devoted himself to her father instead. It was too galling.

'I'll come with you,' said Caroline dutifully. 'Perhaps if George could drive us ...'

The party was clearly breaking up. The maid opened the front door for them as they made their good-byes and spilled out into the little pool of light outside. There the six guests divided. Duxbury and the two young men got into one car and drove off at speed into the thick darkness. The Canon helped the two young ladies into his station wagon, and drove off carefully down the unmetalled drive.

'What did you think of Duxbury?' asked Mrs Demmer, watching the Canon's tail-lights being swallowed by the darkness.

'Very much the same,' said Peacock, considering scandals past, in tones of envy.

X

Within two hours, the verdict that Duxbury was just the same as ever would have been one, had he been there, that Peacock would have found hard to sustain. As far as both Charles and Judy could see, Duxbury was changed. They put the transformation down to the consumption of four or five bottles of imported beer. Gone was his previous abstemiousness. Whereas the first time he had appeared in Judy's bar, he had driven her mad by hardly saying anything, now, with drink inside him, he was far more sociable. But Judy was not sure if she found the change an improvement. Charles was inclined to agree; Duxbury had been rather dull for the last two hours. Having established that Gianni had been educated at the best of Rome's Classical Lyceums, the Visconti, and then gone on to La Sapienza to study what Gianni called 'Ancient Letters', Duxbury had been led into a series of anecdotes about the Italian education system, and his old friend Silvia Donati ('she knew nothing, absolutely nothing about the *Georgics*' – a judgement Caroline, had she been there, would have felt was most undeserved) followed by a disquisition on *Ancient Attica*, both the place and the book of the same name, as well as its still unwritten successor volume, *Ancient Latium*. Samnites, Etruscans, Latins, Greek colonists and the possible site of Alba Longa were dealt with in quick succession. Finally the conversation lapsed into Italian, and Duxbury told Gianni of a funny thing that had once happened to him outside the Villa Giulia Museum. At this point, Judy, who didn't speak Italian, turned to Charles with a question.

'Where are the girls?' she asked.

'They went home,' he replied. 'The Canon gave them a lift.'

'Oh. Why?'

'I think Artemis was in a fit of pique,' said Charles cautiously. 'That man Peacock was rather attentive towards her.'

'Surely that's just what she enjoys?'

'I don't think so. You see she was rather hoping that Gianni would talk to her, but he wouldn't.'

'Oh,' said Judy, looking at Gianni. 'I see. You'd better explain. I thought he'd simply love to spend time being attentive to her.'

'In a perfect world, yes,' said Charles. He noticed that Gianni was quite wrapped up in what Duxbury was saying, and would not hear him. 'You see, Gianni is in love with Artemis. He has told me so. Artemis is in love with him – at least he's sure of that. But they both dislike each other so thoroughly that neither will admit it. Artemis tried to make Gianni jealous by flirting with me. He got so angry that I daren't even talk to her now. Gianni strongly disapproves of the idea of a woman coming between two men like that. So the upshot is that we are both ignoring her, and that is why she has gone home in a fit of pique.'

'That's awfully complicated,' said Judy. 'And rather funny.'

'Not for me,' he said. 'I would quite like to stay on this island, but he says he won't hear of it.'

'Because of her?'

'Quite. He says he wants to get away from her. Of course, it's not true. The real reason is that he feels she has defeated him.'

'Why do you put up with him?' asked Judy. 'Can't you just …'

She left the question eloquently unfinished.

'That has crossed my mind,' said Charles. 'But I need someone to sail the boat. It's not much fun on your own on a yacht. I'd feel like the Ancient Mariner, alone on the wide, wide sea. I could get a replacement, but … And besides, how could I let him go off on his own? How on earth would he ever get back to Italy? He's got no money and no brains.'

'None at all?'

'He's utterly irresponsible,' said Charles severely. 'You couldn't just leave him. His parents might never hear of him again.'

Judy imagined rich well-dressed parents, sitting in Roman elegance, worrying about their only child. He had to be an only child. His mother probably adored him. Italian mothers always did. And he was such a charming young man.

'Is he a good sailor?' she asked.

'Not a bit of it,' said Charles. 'I let him do the cooking.'

'You could leave him here with me,' said Judy. 'I could do food in the bar. An Italian trattoria on the beach. More drinks?'

More beers were dispensed. Gianni and Duxbury were now deep into discussion of the World Cup, and had discovered a mutual passion for Lazio. Judy distinguished the word 'Gascoigne' in the fast-flowing dialogue.

'What about the Canon and Caroline?' she asked. 'Not like them to go home early. It's not even midnight.'

'I don't know why they went,' said Charles a little resentfully. 'I suppose they were tired. They looked it.'

Judy, wondering at the uncharacteristic behaviour of the Canon and Caroline, assumed the worst. The marriage she had tried to arrange would not now take place.

It was not quite midnight. At Blowing Point, Artemis was sitting on the verandah with a bottle of rum and the Canon. Caroline had gone to bed as soon as they had got home. Artemis, feeling grateful for the lift, had invited the Canon in for a drink. He, feeling the need of company, had accepted. That had been two hours ago.

Before them lay the black sea, relieved by a line of white surf that marked the reefs, and in the distance the lights of Marigot and Grand Case on St Martin. In this setting confidences had been inevitable.

'I feel miserable,' she said. 'I've got everything I want or should want, but I'm miserable all the same.'

'Are you in love with him?' asked the Canon.

'Of course not. I'm suffering from a demeaning passion. I suppose he must have hidden depths – he couldn't be that superficial and still be human – but I'm not interested in his hidden depths. I want superficial things and that annoys me. I ought to be more like Caroline, I suppose.'

'Yes, Caroline,' he said, a little wearily.

'You're not really in love with her, are you?'

'No. I suppose not,' he admitted. 'I'd like to be in love with someone, though. But wanting to love and actually loving are not the same thing. Whether I stay on here, or go back to England, isn't a very interesting question for anyone but myself.'

'That's freedom,' said Artemis. 'I can do what I like too, without anyone being able to object. I like that. That's why I hate Gianni so much. I want to possess him. Possessions weigh you down.'

'But if you like being free, my dear, why are you so infatuated with him?' asked the Canon, genuinely puzzled.

'I can be contradictory if I want to. That's part of being free too. Like the Greeks: they expressed their freedom by owning slaves. I'd have Gianni as my slave any day – but I never want to be his. I want to do to him what he wants to do to me.'

'It's a power struggle. I'd have been quite happy to have been Caroline's slave,' he said.

'She'd have been yours, George.'

They sat in the dark silence for a few moments, both feeling a sense of loss.

'I wonder what my father is getting up to,' said Artemis. 'We'd better have another bottle, hadn't we? I think he'd like us to wait up for him, don't you?'

'Those Etruscan tombs,' said Duxbury. 'Have you seen them? I mean the ones at Tarquinia. They are generally reckoned to be the most interesting ones.'

'No,' said Judy.

'No,' said Charles.

'Yes,' said Gianni.

'Oh, but you must, you know,' said Duxbury.

'Right now I think I must shut up shop,' said Judy, feeling an attack of bad temper coming on. 'It's almost one in the morning and I don't want my licence taken away.'

'Do the police come round?' asked Duxbury.

'No, but there's always a first time,' said Judy.

'Look, sell us a case of beer,' said Duxbury. 'Charles will pay. He's a millionaire. He owns a brewery in England.'

'I most certainly will not,' said Charles, who, like Judy, was bored to death with Etruscan tomb talk.

'Oh,' said Duxbury, slightly, but only slightly, put out. 'Then put it on my daughter's account.'

'Very well,' said Judy, 'and then I am going to lock up and go to bed.'

Within ten minutes, she had done just this. Charles, Gianni and Duxbury stood outside the bar, Gianni carrying a case containing twenty bottles of beer.

'Inhospitable woman that,' said Duxbury. 'I don't mind telling you that I stole her bottle opener when she wasn't looking. Reminds me rather of a very disapproving woman I once knew who was Lady Margaret Professor of something or another. Very snooty she was. I once had her in a punt on the Cherwell, or was it the Isis? Some river in Oxford, anyway. She never forgave me.'

'I'm not bloody surprised,' said Charles.

'Oh, Carlo,' remonstrated Gianni.

'I think it's time we got on our boat,' said Charles, who was beginning to feel very sober.

'No,' said Duxbury. 'Let's sit on the jetty, away from the houses. We don't want the police turning up, do we? Besides, I don't like boats one little bit.'

'Yes, let's sit on the jetty,' said Gianni. 'And the *professore* will tell us stories about Oxford.'

So they sat on the jetty, under the light of a brilliant moon, the water under them. It was now so late that the night seemed to be getting hotter. They opened three more beers, using the stolen opener. Charles resolved to be agreeable.

'Tell us about the *professoressa* in the punt,' said Gianni when they had settled down.

'No,' said Charles, rather sharply. 'Don't.'

'No,' said Duxbury, 'I won't. I'll tell you about the Etruscan

161

tombs instead. My book is going to be about Ancient Latium, the period before the Roman Republic. No one else has bothered with that up to now. There's an awful lot of work to be done. When I did *Ancient Attica* I went to Greece every summer with an army of undergraduates, and got them to do the work for me. I was merciless. Go here, go to that museum, photograph that pot; and they all did it for nothing too, just so they could have something to write on their CVs. But Italy is different. English people can't handle Italian museum staff. You turn up at some famous museum and find it's all closed up, no one is expecting you, they say they never got your letter. You lose your temper – that isn't the way to work in Italy, is it?'

'Not at all,' agreed Gianni. 'You have to flatter and cajole, but in the end you get what you want through persistence. It is the same with everything. It merely takes time.'

'Are you going to write this book in Italy?' asked Charles. 'Or here?'

Duxbury was perturbed by this question from the serious young man, for the question presupposed that the book was in fact going to get written; whereas for years the book had been something talked of, a phantasma, an idle concept for an unoccupied hour. But the thought that someone like Charles was taking him at his word was off-putting. Charles actually assumed that he, Duxbury, was going to settle down and write the definitive tome on Ancient Latium – an enormous project, the labour of a lifetime. Charles was in short taking him seriously, and Duxbury felt constrained to reply in all seriousness.

'One could write it here, but all the research has to be done in Italy. I'd have to fly back and forth. It might even be an idea to go and live in Italy again. You see, most of the places one has to go to are outside Rome; Rome is the only convenient base; Rome or Viterbo; and unless you are on the spot, it is almost impossible to make an appointment with anyone. Letters never get answered – you know how it is.'

'Then come and live in Italy again, *professore*,' said Gianni enthusiastically.

162

Duxbury suddenly felt the heaviness of alcohol upon him.

'Caroline would never go back to Italy,' he said.

'Why not?' asked Gianni.

Charles looked at Gianni disapprovingly; there were questions one did not ask; but the young Italian was not to know that.

'Caroline was unhappy in Italy,' said Duxbury. 'She fell in love with a man called Ciriaco Donati, the brother of this Silvia we used to know. He would have fallen in love with her, but he went away instead, overseas. He was a Catholic and a doctor, and he left her pregnant without knowing it – all very accidental – and the child was still-born and she said she would never live in Italy again. Ridiculous, because Ciriaco isn't even there as far as we know. In fact, he's in Bosnia, working in some refugee camp.'

This brief reference to tragedy was followed by silence. They helped themselves to some more beers. Charles lay on his back and contemplated the bright light of the tropical moon. No wonder Caroline was unhappy. She had fallen in love with a hero. Gianni and Duxbury began to talk to each other in Italian.

'Of course,' Gianni was saying, 'I can take down inscriptions in Latin and Greek. My Greek isn't what it used to be, but I can read Latin at sight. I did three years at La Sapienza before dropping out.'

Duxbury considered. There was something rather interesting in the idea of having this young man as his acolyte. The whole idea was very Somerset Maughamish, just like the now very crumpled suit he was wearing. He could flit between the West Indies and Italy, taking Gianni with him. Goodness knows, he could afford it. And it would annoy the hell out of Caroline and Artemis, Artemis in particular. He had noticed her attitude to this young man. All his life he had loved annoying people. This seemed to be the ultimate provocation. If Artemis was in love with Gianni, how annoyed she would be to have him hanging around all day, if he wasn't returning her interest. (That's why she had gone home early from the Demmers', he now realised.) And as for Caroline, she would die. His elder daughter was so obsessed with the idea of what other people thought – and what would other people think if he suddenly took on Gianni, this elegant Italian, as his personal assistant? Somerset Maugham indeed.

Gianni, having outlined his qualifications, opened his packet of cigarettes, to find it empty. He swore under his breath. Duxbury, seeing this, and seeing that Charles was still looking up at the stars, took out of his pocket what seemed to be a large snuffbox. Within a short time both of them were smoking hand-rolled cigarettes.

The world seemed a very pleasant place to Gianni just then. A delicious sense of well-being crept over him, a gorgeous lassitude. He had always lived a life devoted to pleasure and ease, and now a new vista was opening up before him. The *professore* would give him a job; the *professore*, he knew, was very rich, and also, as this evening proved, far more interesting than Charles. Carlo, *poverino*, was so English: he didn't like doing anything that he might enjoy. But *il professore mulatto* (Gianni could tell that Duxbury was of mixed race) was different. He was an anarchist. What fun they would have together.

Charles was thinking different thoughts, thoughts of sadness and death. Ciriaco, this stranger, had gone to Bosnia – but what had he ever done? The levity of the other two, their conversation in Italian, failed to lift his spirits. He did not feel drunk; he only felt the depressing after-effect of alcohol. His family fortune was founded on beer – at which he sat up, feeling he couldn't blame himself for all the ills of the world – he sat up and the sudden movement made him a little dizzy. He saw Gianni and Duxbury sitting cross-legged, smoking, like serious Red Indian chieftains engaged in delicate tribal business. He looked at his watch. He saw that it was very late indeed. His head felt strange.

'Why don't we go for a swim?' he suggested, longing for the purity of water.

'I don't like the sea,' said Duxbury, with a mild shiver, thinking of the sharks that never slept.

'You go, Carlo,' said Gianni. 'I'd drown.'

'Oh,' said Charles.

There seemed to be something very relaxed about Gianni and Duxbury, Charles thought. Perhaps they were drunk; they had to be drunk. The case of beer was almost empty.

'Well, I'll go for a swim,' said Charles, realising he was rather drunk and desperately tired himself. 'How deep is the water here?'

'Deep enough,' said Duxbury with authority. 'Dive straight in.'

Charles stared into the black depths. The sea was still, like velvet, reflecting the pale light of the moon. To dive in would be to dive into the waters of Lethe, the stream of forgetfulness. He took off his shirt, preparing for this second baptism.

'I need to piss,' said Gianni with sudden realisation.

Gianni got up, and made his way towards the landward side of the jetty. Duxbury took out his box and began to roll some more cigarettes. Life was delightful. There was a small splash: he raised his eyes from his task to see that Charles had disappeared, leaving a little pile of clothes on the jetty.

Judy heard the splash too; the night was so still that, though the jetty was a good hundred yards off, the sound carried. She looked at her watch: it was well past three. She had been unable to sleep, but had lain there for hours, it seemed, aware of the voices in the background. Would they never go home, she wondered?

The splash drove her to get up and go to the window. It might assuage her bad temper to find that Duxbury had fallen in the sea and drowned; Caroline had told her once that her father couldn't swim. But from her window she could see Duxbury sitting on the jetty in his white planter's suit; and underneath her window she saw another figure, Gianni, engaged in the act of urination. This was the last straw. It had not been a good evening. If Caroline and the Canon had decided to marry; if she hadn't been so annoyed with Duxbury for making her fall in love with him; if, if, if; if so many things, then perhaps she wouldn't have decided to phone the police. But she did. With anger in her heart, added to the bad

temper provoked by insomnia, she resolutely made for the telephone.

XI

Caroline woke early the next day, refreshed after what had been, she realised in the quiet moments of reflection she enjoyed lying in bed, a disappointing evening.

Still in her nightdress, she padded into the kitchen. The first indication that something was wrong was the sight of two empty rum bottles on the verandah table. A second indication was the gentle noise of snoring coming from the sitting-room. Further investigation led her to discover the Canon, fat and unshaven, asleep on the sofa. She looked at him, and presently, feeling he was being watched, he awoke.

'We were waiting up for your father,' said the Canon, feeling some explanation was necessary, lest she jump to the conclusion that he was pursuing her.

'And ...?'

'He didn't turn up, at least, he may have turned up since ...'

The Canon's voice trailed away in embarrassment.

Then the telephone rang.

It was Duxbury.

'I know it's early,' she heard him say. 'I tried to get hold of the Canon, but he wasn't at home. I thought it would be better.'

'He's here. Asleep on the sofa,' said Caroline. 'Where are you?' she asked, feeling like the aggrieved mother of an errant teenager.

'Me? Yes, well, I am with Gianni and Charles.'

'On the boat?'

'No. Not exactly. We're in The Valley.'

'Ah,' said Caroline, very patiently, waiting for the whole truth. (The Valley was the island's capital, a little collection of Government buildings.)

'We're at the police station,' said Duxbury. 'Perhaps if the Canon's car is there, you could come and pick us up.'

'Have you had a car accident?' she asked, imagining drunken driving and battered lampposts.

'Not an accident as such,' said Duxbury.

'Perhaps I'd better come,' she said. 'The Canon isn't fit to drive. He seems to have spent the night drinking on the verandah with Artemis,' she said in tones of disapproval.

'Thanks,' said Duxbury, handing the telephone back to the policeman on duty, who was their old friend the captain of the *Warspite*.

It was destined to be a morning of recrimination and hangover.

'I can't believe it of you,' said Caroline. 'Three grown men. And Charles being charged with indecent exposure. It is not at all like him, surely.'

Duxbury, having just admitted to being drunk and disorderly in a public place, in lieu of being charged with possession of illegal substances, was not disposed to argue.

'*Povero* Carlo,' said Gianni contritely.

'*Povero* Carlo my foot,' said Caroline. 'He wasn't *povero*, he seemed furious.'

This was, in fact, the case. Charles, after spending a night in the cells, had been driven off in a taxi, without speaking, white with anger.

'Yes, yes, most unfortunate,' said Duxbury suavely. 'I mean, coming up out of the water when the captain was with us. He should have stayed in the sea. Or he should have worn his underpants. They take a very dim view of skinnydipping in these parts. It's something to do with their religious prejudices, I suppose. And they don't like white people doing it.'

'But what were you doing?' asked Caroline, aggressively changing gear.

'We were just having a quiet drink,' said her father.

'Yes,' said Gianni loyally, mightily thankful that smoking ganga was considered an offence that could be overlooked, unlike appearing naked before a policeman. It really was too bad of

168

Carlo to be so annoyed about it; true, once it got out, as these things did, that he had been charged with indecency in the West Indies, he would look foolish, but his anger had been something of an over-reaction. And he had seemed to blame Gianni, taking the view that the severity of his treatment was a result of their crime, not his. It really was kind of the *professore* to take him in at this juncture. There was no question of going back to the yacht, not with Carlo in this mood.

'Carlo' was certainly more angry than he had ever been. The circumstances of his arrest and imprisonment had been such that, when actually taking place, had defied credibility. He had gone for his swim, a long relaxing swim in the dark tranquil Caribbean, leaving Duxbury and Gianni to their frankly childish conversation about Etruscan tombs. He had been aware, in a vague sort of way, that they were smoking; he had, he now realised, assumed at the time that it was ganga, but not wanting to appear a killjoy, tried to overlook the offence. Naturally he did not approve, but being years Duxbury's junior, hadn't liked to point out the fault. In fact, he thought that going for a solitary swim was rather a good way of showing his silent disapprobation.

He had swum, filled with deep relaxing thoughts. He had emerged from the sea and walked along the beach to the jetty to retrieve his clothes. It was only then that he had realised that someone else had joined the party. Perhaps it had been a mistake to approach the captain of the *Warspite* and hold out a hand in greeting when the captain was dressed in his police uniform, and he, Charles, was dressed in nothing at all. His public-school frankness had led him astray. Only later, in the privacy of the police lock-up, did it strike him that the captain had been gravely embarrassed to find Duxbury and Gianni together, smoking dope; and that if anyone was to be charged with a crime, he was a suitable sacrificial lamb.

What was so annoying was the knowledge that both Gianni and Duxbury had taken his own misfortune so calmly. They had not been able to see how an indecency charge levelled at him was simply not the same as a drunk and disorderly charge pinned on them. People frankly expected someone like Duxbury to be drunk and disorderly once in a while; Gianni had no reputation to lose; but he, Charles Broughton, was someone who had never been anything but respectable. And then they had had the cheek to urge him not to make a fuss, lest the captain insist Duxbury empty his pockets. He was meant to take the rap: when he considered how Gianni had lived off him for months, this was rather a presumption.

The very thought of Gianni filled him with cold fury. No sooner was he on his own yacht than he went down to the cabin and began to pack away Gianni's possessions into whatever bags he could find. He thought of the way Gianni had behaved in Grenada; the way Gianni had involved him in his designs on the ghastly Artemis; the way Gianni had shamelessly flirted, if that was the word, and he rather suspected it was, with Duxbury. Damn Artemis, damn Duxbury, damn Gianni, he thought. They deserved each other. Presumably that was where Gianni now was; let him stay there; he would regret it. Then, gathering all the stuff, he resolved to take it to Judy's whence Gianni could pick it up at his convenience.

'But he isn't going to live here, is he?' asked Caroline, when she was alone with her father, once they were back at Blowing Point.

'I don't see why not,' said Duxbury, in that infuriatingly vague way of his.

'Do you mean to say,' said Caroline, 'that you have arranged to have him come and live here as your research assistant, without even asking me? Or Artemis?'

'But I know you like him, dear,' said Duxbury with pained naïvety. 'I know you do. You invited him here to dinner. It will amuse you to have a new face around the house. We always had lots of people round in Rome, didn't we?'

That was true; who they had been, and where her father had found them, she had never really wanted to know.

'But you can't just pick people up,' she said. 'And you don't need a research assistant. You're not even writing a book, are you? Or are you? Isn't this all a bit sudden?'

'Not at all,' said Duxbury. 'I should be writing *Ancient Latium*, but I've neglected it for years. Now I've got an assistant, I'll have to get on with it. It will make me work.'

'But isn't Charles expecting him back?'

'No, not at all,' said Duxbury, remembering how Charles had left them that morning.

'But what about Artemis?' said Caroline, trying another tack.

'How on earth could it upset her? She's only here for a few more weeks, anyway.' Duxbury smiled blandly.

'But don't you see how difficult it will be for her to have him here in the house?'

'I don't see that at all,' he replied.

'She's infatuated with him,' said Caroline. 'I think he turned her down; she can't bear being strung along by him – '

'My dear Caroline, Artemis's sexual behaviour is her affair, not mine. Do you think I can spend my entire life worrying about you two girls? I had to leave Rome because of you and Ciriaco. Am I to do without a research assistant, simply because Artemis fancies him?'

'I didn't know we were such a burden to you,' she answered.

'That is the sort of thing your mother used to say. And now, if Gianni is ready, I intend to go with him on the motor-bike to fetch the car and his stuff from Broughton's yacht. Frankly, I don't think Broughton has behaved at all well; and the fact that Gianni is an excellent scholar will be much to my advantage. Good-bye.'

Presently Caroline heard the sound of the motor-cycle. The same sound must have woken Artemis, who, within a few moments, appeared in the kitchen.

'Slept well?' asked her sister. 'I saw the empty bottles,' she added by way of explanation. 'It must have been quite a night.'

'It was,' said Artemis.

Caroline compassionately set about making a cup of tea, which she presently set in front of her sister along with two aspirins.

171

'The Canon's good company,' said Artemis, gratefully sipping her tea. 'I quite like him after all.'

'Good. I always knew you would.'

'We waited for Duxbury to come back. Did he?'

'Yes,' said Caroline. 'He did. He had something of an adventurous night. I had to go and pick him up at the police station.'

'Oh.'

'And another thing, Gianni has quarrelled with Charles, so he's coming to stay here. In fact, he has already been here. They've just gone now to collect his things.'

'You'd better explain,' said Artemis, putting down her tea.

Caroline explained.

'I'll go back to London,' said Artemis quietly. 'Today.'

'Darling, you can't,' said Caroline.

'I don't see why not,' said Artemis. 'If he's going to behave like this ...'

'But Gianni – '

'I don't mean Gianni, I mean him,' she said bitterly.

'Of course, he's never been conventional,' said Caroline. 'But you don't think, do you ...'

'What?'

'I mean, Gianni is just going to be a research assistant, isn't he? He's not ...'

'Nothing would surprise me,' said Artemis. 'He's doing it to humiliate me. He knows that this is the worst thing he can do to me.'

Artemis began to weep into her tea.

Caroline stood by helplessly, wondering what on earth Charles would think of this sudden theft by Duxbury. Indeed, if this was Artemis's reaction, what would anyone think?

As a consequence, when the new household assembled for lunch, there was some tension in the air. Only Gianni was completely at ease, almost triumphant. Here he was, arrived in their midst. Artemis had done her best to ignore him so far, but she was now forced, if not to acknowledge him, then at least to see him constantly. There was no avoiding him. How this would annoy her! (How it had annoyed her already: her face had been as inexpressive as a granite cliff at table.) The idea of annoying her, of driving her out of her self-control, filled him with delight. She had ruined his self-composure, and he would do the same to her. He would defeat her: she would have to come to him eventually, on her hands and knees, metaphorically, perhaps literally. She would be forced to admit that she couldn't live without him, and this unconditional surrender would be the high water mark of his amatory success to date. The fact that he neither loved her, nor even liked her any more, was quite immaterial. This was a war: the fruits of victory that he would enjoy after the battle was over were of secondary importance. He no longer thought about what he was fighting for – but simply of the fact that he had to make her feel what he himself felt, the hopeless slavery to passion.

It was war. Artemis could see it. And she could also see defeat staring her in the face. He had outflanked her brilliantly, and arrived in the midst of the enemy's tents when her back had been turned. This was the time when sensible commanders sent out peace feelers, and negotiated for an honourable surrender. But in this particular war there could be no honourable terms. It was a fight to the death. She would rather be damned than be added to his list of conquests. But the worst thing of all was his smiling assured presence, and the suspicion that, much as she hated the thought of surrender, submitting to him might have its consolations.

After lunch, the table on the verandah was cleared, various boxes of notes were unearthed, boxes that Duxbury had brought with him from Italy, but hardly looked at since. A start was being made to *Ancient Latium*. There was talk of a synopsis. But was her father really interested in the Sabines and the Samnites? Or was he more interested in adding Gianni to his entourage? He had been most decisive, going to Road Bay to pick up Gianni's things, cementing the breach with Charles.

Of course, Artemis knew that her father was unconventional, to use her sister's coy phrase. Sex embarrassed Caroline; but

173

Artemis thought of sex, usually, in a spirit of scientific detach-
ment. Her parents had been unhappy together; her father had
been an accomplished adulterer in Oxford: these were facts she
had grown up with. They left her unmoved; the tragic aura which
for Caroline surrounded their mother simply did not exist for her.
She did not have Caroline's gift for empathy, or indeed her
capacity for embarrassment. Other people's lives were walled
gardens into which she did not see. Occasionally one came across
a wall, one assumed there was something behind it, but she had
never felt curious enough to wonder just what was on the other
side. She had felt herself born to be self-contained. For twenty-
four years she had lived in the world, shut in, unbreached. No
one had penetrated her inner nature, and she had never specu-
lated about anyone else's.

But now, what was happening? Was her father interfering in
her inner life? Had she an inner life? Had he? What was he up
to? Did her father know what she felt about Gianni, and was that
why he was introducing him into the house? Was this an example
of his famous talent to annoy?

Leaving their father and his new assistant, she and Caroline
went and sat on the deserted beach. There was no one there:
there never was. They were two female Robinson Crusoes, alone,
untouched by the touristic hordes that would surely one day
arrive.

'You don't still want to go back to England, do you?' asked
Caroline.

'Not really,' she admitted, knowing that flight would mean an
admission of defeat. Besides, she could not tear herself away.

'Do you think Gianni is beautiful?' she asked, bringing to the
surface what was most on her mind.

'Yes, and no. Yes, he is. And no, because he's far too keen on
being admired. He is too vain. That sort of quest for admiration
can lead one into trouble.'

'All Italians are like that,' said Artemis.

'Not at all,' said Caroline, defending Ciriaco's memory. 'Some
are taken by surprise when they are admired. I don't think you

can love someone unless that is, in fact, the case. If you love someone who expects you to love him, he won't see any merit in your love. To him it will be the usual tribute. But if it takes him by surprise, if he thinks you are giving him something that no one else can, then there is something there. Our father was the best-looking man in Oxford. He expected our mother to fall in love with him. He's a narcissist, in love with himself. Perhaps he and Gianni deserve each other.'

'And you accuse me of psychobabble,' she said.

'Charles is good-looking,' said Caroline meditatively. 'He's slightly diffident. I wonder how he's taking Gianni's desertion?'

'With relief, if he's got any sense.'

'I think he'll be hurt. Gianni doesn't have much loyalty.'

'Gianni is a shit,' said Artemis, realising that this was one of his most alluring characteristics.

XII

Evening approached, and Caroline continued to worry about Charles. Eventually she suggested to Artemis that they drive to Road Bay and see him. But he wasn't in Judy's bar. Judy assumed he was on the yacht. Judy seemed to be much moved by the idea that Charles was sitting on his yacht, too embarrassed to leave it, in the wake of being arrested for indecent exposure. It was this that prompted Caroline to step out of her beach-dress, under which she wore her bathing costume, and swim out to him.

'I've come for a drink,' she said, hauling herself aboard by the rope ladder. 'I left Artemis with Judy. We wondered where you'd got to.'

'I've been asleep all day,' he said. 'Have a towel.'

'Have you ever been to Virgin Gorda?' he asked her, once he had poured the drinks.

'No. I've been to Trinidad, to St Kitts and to Barbados, but not to Virgin Gorda.'

'I'm thinking of going there. It is the next stop on my journey.'

'Are you on a journey?'

'Yes.'

'I mean a proper journey, from a place called A to a place called B?'

'Not really,' he admitted. 'I am just sailing the Antilles, from Barbados up to Florida, I suppose. I am a vagrant of no fixed address and with no fixed plans.'

How purposeless it all seemed. Was there nothing he could do, except sail the world?

'My father was born in Trinidad,' she said inconsequentially, interrupting the silence. 'But he's never wanted to go back.'

177

'I never want to go back to places either. I merely want to go on. If I ever got to Florida, I don't know what I'd do then. The general idea was to sell the boat there and then put Gianni on a plane back to Italy. But now ... I don't suppose you would consider coming to Virgin Gorda with me, would you?'

She was silent.

'I mean, it was just an idea,' he said, lamely, wondering if he had offended her somehow.

'I am savouring your invitation,' she said. 'It's a delightful sensation.'

'Then you would come?' he asked.

'I'd love to. But would I be any use to you?'

'Don't think about usefulness, it is a mercenary consideration,' he said. 'But there is something I feel I ought to tell you.'

'What?'

He looked away, out to sea.

'Last night – your father, myself and Gianni ...'

'Yes?' she asked, gently, wondering whether he was going to elaborate on his indecent exposure. She hoped not.

'We talked about Bosnia,' he said. 'It disturbed me.'

It was her turn to look out to sea. She knew about Bosnia, about what it meant. It had been buried deep in her mind for four years.

'And your father,' continued Charles, 'told us about this friend of yours, Ciriaco.'

He pronounced the foreign name with care.

'Ciriaco,' she said, instinctively correcting his pronunciation.

'Did you know he was there?'

She did not answer. Had she known? No: it had been beyond her experience. But she had known that was where he had gone. Ciriaco himself had told her the last time she had seen him.

'You will think it strange,' she said at last. 'I know that he went there. But I only remember what I choose to remember. Certain things I have shut out of my mind. It was too painful to think that he could love all those nameless refugees more than myself. The

178

Ciriaco I created in my mind and the real man – they were two different things.'

There was another silence. In her mind, in the far reaches of deceptive memory, she could feel her Ciriaco beginning to crumble, and the real Ciriaco, the one she had never wanted to believe in, take his place.

Charles thought of altruism.

'There are better things to do in life than sailing yachts,' he said. 'Your Ciriaco is a better man than I am.'

'Don't say that,' she said, putting out a hand to touch him. 'I didn't want him to be a hero. I wanted him for myself. I thought that heroism had ruined my life.'

'I'll never be a hero,' said Charles. 'It would be quite safe for you to fall in love with me. That's why I suspect you won't. I mean, you must have loved Ciriaco because he was good.'

What had Ciriaco to recommend him, she wondered now, except goodness?

'Yes,' she said. 'I did. I can forgive everything except goodness. He was too good. I've not forgiven him.'

'Can anyone be too good?' asked Charles.

Her mind turned to Bosnia and the desolation of war. Perhaps she owed it to the refugees not to grudge them Ciriaco. Now that four years had passed, it was time to be generous, to let him go. He was a necessary sacrifice, if humanity were ever to be redeemed by love.

'At least I did not make the mistake of loving someone bad or indifferent,' she said. 'You know the Canon asked me to marry him when we were on Sombrero? I couldn't. Poor Canon. He is too ordinary. It would have been too happy an ending. And to think I wanted you to take on Artemis. None of these plans have come to anything.'

'Will you still come with me to Virgin Gorda?' he asked.

'Instead of marrying the Canon?'

She looked at his earnest face, waiting to be reassured.

'There are better things to do in life than sailing yachts,' she

179

reminded him. 'But until we find out what they are, we might as well sail on.'

He smiled.

'After the court case,' he said. 'I have to appear in court, say I am sorry and pay a fine.'

She smiled.

'You'd better tell me exactly what happened,' she said. 'Especially if we are going to share a yacht.'

'Yes. I shall row you over to Judy's and tell you on the way.'

Judy was waiting for them, when they landed, in a state of some excitement.

'She's here,' she said. 'The film actress. The one called Amelia Churchill. Surely you've seen it? Look.'

They looked out to sea, in the direction Judy was pointing. At about the distance of a mile, a floating gin-palace lay at anchor. Hollywood, or Pinewood, had arrived, taking them unawares. Miss Amelia Churchill had come, and with her, an enormous retinue, judging by the size of her yacht.

'She's come to pick up that ghastly man Peacock,' said Artemis knowledgeably. 'That's what he told me. They're making a sequel to that film in which she got eaten by a shark. This time she plays the twin sister of the victim, who seeks revenge. Peacock is technical adviser; it's his speciality – making himself agreeable in luxurious places.'

'What a way to travel,' said Charles. 'Taking all that with you.'

He could imagine it all: the secretaries, the assistants, the wardrobe staff, the hairdressers, the masseurs, the cooks; and somewhere, deep in the heart of the ship, turbanned and robed like an oriental sultana, restless except for the very few hours of sleep a day Mogadon could provide, lay the actress, bored to death.

'I don't suppose they'll come ashore,' said Judy. 'They don't need to. They are far too grand for the likes of us.'

'We saw Mr Demmer going out there on the police launch,'

180

said Artemis. 'About an hour ago. I bet his wife sent him to check the passports and suck up.'

'He ought to be back soon,' said Judy. 'Let's have a drink.'

They went into drinks. Soon, thought Caroline, this life would be over. The rhythm of existence was already broken. No more drinks and beach; there was no need now to stay here, chained by her past. She could go to Virgin Gorda with Charles, and, if she pleased, she could come back again.

Drinks continued, as drinks with Judy always did. For Caroline it was something of a wake. Artemis had confided in Judy about her father's intolerable behaviour. This topic and mention of Gianni, now renewed, made Charles a little uncomfortable. Perhaps to quarrel so violently was rather childish; and could one quarrel with Gianni for long?

'You know,' said Judy, looking at Charles and thinking that she was entirely to blame for the way things had turned out, as it had been her telephone call that had sparked the whole disaster off, 'I can't help wondering how it is that your family made all its money in beer, when you are an evangelical.'

'I'm not really evangelical,' he said. 'My family were in the last century. Perhaps I have just inherited their sense of disapproval.'

He did disapprove of things; principally himself. He wasn't a hero, but he knew he ought to have been one.

'Protestantism isn't coherent,' said Charles by way of self-defence. 'Like Catholicism,' he couldn't help adding.

'Oh, but Catholicism is,' said Judy, waving a cigarette around. 'It takes in everything. You should read St Thomas Aquinas.'

'But people don't read St Thomas Aquinas,' said Charles. 'I bet you don't.'

'I don't read at all,' said Judy. 'Apart from the *Catholic Herald*.'

'I can't think where you get the energy to discuss religion from,' said Artemis. 'No one really cares about it any more, do they? If they did they would still be burning people at the stake. But they simply can't be bothered. Who cares about …' she paused a moment, wondering what to cite. '… the Filioque clause or transubstantiation? All people care about are their bank balances.'

Caroline wondered whether Ciriaco cared about the Filioque clause or transubstantiation. She suspected that he did. Perhaps he thought about these things; perhaps he just thought. Thinking, and reflection in general, were such unusual activities in her experience. None of them ever thought; they had spent so long thinking about themselves instead, which was quite a different thing. But Ciriaco, now in some hospital worse than any Roman one, had discovered a secret: there was more to life than having a healthy bank balance; the important things in life were not material after all.

Did Judy know that? Beneath the haze of alcohol, under the clouds of cigarette smoke, did Judy know that love was the most important thing? She wondered.

'Judy,' she said suddenly. 'You never told us why you left England and came here. And you said you would.'

'I like to cultivate an air of mystery,' said Judy.

'You've done that pretty successfully,' said Caroline. 'But now, you ought to tell us. It may be none of our business, but perhaps you know something that all of us ought to know. You must know what I mean.'

'I know what you mean,' admitted Judy.

She did. She thought of her husband, a man forever suspended in time and space, just as she had left him. Poor Mr Blomberg: it hadn't been his fault. He was no duller than any other Kensington Man. He had made only one mistake – marrying Judy, a woman who, imprisoned in the luxury of London, had longed for the desert, the dark and stony places where the soul met God.

'I was meant to be a nun,' said Judy. 'My grandfather used to tell me that when I was a child. But he was such an ugly old man; he looked like a lizard. And prophets aren't accepted in their own countries. So I was determined that I would never be a nun. But despite everything, he was right.'

'But darling, you would have been a terrible nun,' said Artemis. 'Nuns don't smoke and drink. They aren't allowed to.'

'If I was a nun,' said Judy, picturing convent walls, 'I wouldn't need to smoke or drink. Smoking and drinking are for people who live uneventful lives.'

'Nuns live very quiet lives,' said Charles primly.

'No, they don't,' said Caroline. 'I don't mean they are occupied by activity all the time, though they are, I dare say. But they reflect; they look into things ...'

'They contemplate,' said Judy. 'The rest of us just gawp.'

'If I'd been brought up religiously I think I'd understand things more,' said Caroline. 'But when you are a rationalist, you don't understand a thing.'

She was thinking of Ciriaco, thought Charles. Naturally, she thought she understood nothing: how could you understand a man who deliberately took the narrower path?

Demmer entered.

'Ah,' he said. 'I thought somebody would be here. I am acting as postman today. I have just been on Miss Churchill's yacht and she's given me invitations to give out to people to come to drinks tomorrow night. It seems,' he added with evident distaste, 'that she wants everyone to come.'

He went around the company handing out the envelopes. As he did so, he wondered how he would explain this to his wife. Charles was, after all, charged with indecent exposure, and would have to appear in court soon. Mrs Demmer had been rather shocked to hear that. And as for Judy Blomberg, Mrs Demmer had never acknowledged her socially, and would doubt-less consider her own invitation to Miss Churchill's party somewhat lessened if it were to be shared with Judy.

'I'll take two for my father, if I may,' said Caroline, thinking of Gianni.

Gianni had been working hard all afternoon in the company of his new employer. Having got the word processor to work, he had typed out a letter to a London publisher of academic books, containing the news that *Ancient Latium*, the long-awaited sequel to *Ancient Attica*, was once more a real possibility. Then they had spent the rest of the afternoon sifting through boxes of notes, old articles and miscellaneous pieces of research, trying to determine the shape the long-neglected project would take.

Evening was approaching, and as their activities came to an end, a slight sense of disappointment crept over Gianni. The girls were not yet back. He imagined them sitting in Judy's bar without him, perhaps with the Canon and Charles. This was not what he had hoped for at all. Perhaps they were avoiding him. Even Caroline, whom he had thought to be well disposed towards him (he assumed all women were, before they were proved otherwise), even she had seemed aloof. And Charles, what had happened to Charles? He rather feared that Charles might take against him permanently. Resentment was not something he had ever felt against a fellow man – women were different – so it was hard to imagine that Charles might, in fact, bear him a grudge. The English were so strange. You could never tell whether they loved you or hated you – they never told you what they felt. Perhaps he had offended the whole lot of them: perhaps Charles and Caroline and Artemis and the Canon and Judy were all in the bar right now, united in racial solidarity against him, the foreigner.

On top of this was the strange case of Jamie Duxbury, *il professore*. He was just as mysterious. Gianni had the feeling that not all the cards were on the table. Over a cigarette and a glass of cold water earlier that afternoon, *il professore* had spoken of the Ptolemies. The twilight of Egyptian civilisation wasn't Gianni's speciality, but even he knew what the Ptolemies were famous for. However, it had still been confusing. Duxbury had approached the subject flirtatiously, drawing back from any actual clarity about what he had really meant. Nothing had been spelled out. There was only the suggestion that his daughters were somehow special, and that any ambitions Gianni might have in that quarter were affected by their status as his daughters.

Certainly, they were eccentric, these English. One felt adrift when dealing with them, he reflected, as he switched off the word processor. For what role had Duxbury chosen him? *Il professore* was pagan, his daughter Artemis a goddess in name and in fact. Only a specially chosen mortal could sleep with her. And though they lived in discomfort bordering on the squalid in Gianni's eyes, he knew they were rich. The rich English liked to live as if they weren't: that was another eccentricity of theirs, one he had noticed in Charles too.

'Why don't you go for a swim?' suggested Duxbury. 'You look tired.'

'Yes,' said Gianni obediently.

'I won't come,' said Duxbury. 'I don't swim.'

Gianni left for the beach. And when Caroline returned with Artemis, bearing the news of Miss Churchill's party, it was to find her father studying the view from the verandah with quiet intensity.

Even the Canon was feeling a mild sense of excitement at the prospect of Miss Churchill's party, and gave momentary thought to what he might wear for the occasion. Miss Churchill, after all, was no ordinary actress. Apart from enjoying the respect which is the natural consequence of having a great deal of money, she had supplemented her fame by regular appearances in illustrated magazines. Even a clergyman as obscure as the Canon, not given to looking at *Hello!* more than once a month, was still in possession of the salient facts of her life and career. Her country house in Gloucestershire, her elegant Chelsea *pied-à-terre*, perhaps some people knew these houses better than they knew their own. Where she went and what she wore – all these had been recorded with the loving attention to detail that journalists usually lavished on the Royal Family. For despite everything, her three marriages, her two facelifts, her daughter's well-publicised ingratitude and her son's equally famous sojourn in the Betty Ford clinic, despite all this, or perhaps because of it, Miss Churchill was a star. That was why her descent

185

on Anguilla, and her indiscriminate invitations, were causing such a flurry of excitement. Even Mrs Demmer had caught Churchill fever, and infected her impassive husband with it.

Demmer, cold, precise and dull, was being shaken out of his usual calm. His wife, blinded by stardom, possibly thinking of further invitations to those well-appointed residences catalogued in magazines, had categorically stated that it was Demmer's responsibility alone that Miss Churchill's visit to the island be a success. Demmer had protested that Miss Churchill was not visiting the island, and showed no sign of wanting to leave her yacht. But as a sop to his wife, the captain of the *Warspite* was posted at Road Bay, binoculars trained on the yacht, just in case she should show any sign of changing her mind, in which case, the entire machinery of Government might swing into action. Mrs Demmer had not been content with that. Shouldn't the police launch be guarding her, she suggested with a hysterical edge to her voice? (She felt a twinge of desperation that Miss Churchill might sail away without being made aware of the trouble being taken to ensure her comfort.) To guard her from what? asked Demmer. Pirates? Besides, there was only one police launch. If she thought that police launches were going to circle the yacht all night, that was simply out of the question. The launch would ferry people out there when it came to the party; although she would have liked to have had another police launch bought at short notice, Mrs Demmer knew that her husband would not budge further. How she hated him; he had as much life in him as a withered twig.

Apart from feeling furious with her husband, and running through her wardrobe at ever shorter intervals wondering what on earth she was going to wear, there was also Peacock to be entertained. The presence of the marine biologist in the house acted as something of a brake on the waves of frenzied activity she could feel welling up within her. She could hardly fly to St Martin in the hope of scouring dress shops on the off-chance of a find with him there. Neither could she quarrel with her husband or indulge in full-blown hysterics; there was no getting away

186

from the man, the Commissioner's house being open plan. Appearances had to be preserved at all costs: Peacock could, and she hoped would, be a passport to intimacy with Miss Churchill.

It was this, the realisation that his hostess valued him, not for himself, but for his friendship with the actress, which led Peacock to foster her illusions as to the depth of that friendship. Of course Peacock knew Miss Churchill, but so did thousands of people; he had met her on several occasions; he was a well-paid hanger-on of this latest production and he was sure that Miss Churchill would remember him from the last time. But Mrs Demmer, in thinking him intimate with the great woman, had assumed too much, and he had not had the heart or the courage to disillusion her. He had gleaned details of the star's disastrous third marriage from the newspapers, not from personal confidences, as Mrs Demmer seemed to assume. Though this made him uncomfortable as he sipped his rum and Coca Cola the evening before the party, he hoped that no harm would come of it. Mrs Demmer was surely too much in awe of Miss Churchill even to mention his name in her presence; and by tomorrow evening he would be aboard the yacht, safe from exposure.

'And who is Miss Churchill?' asked Duxbury at dinner that evening.

'She's an actress,' replied Caroline.

'What has she been in?'

Caroline told him.

'How well informed you are, my dear,' said her father. 'But I still don't see why she wants us to come out for drinks.'

'I don't suppose she wants us,' said Artemis. 'She doesn't know us for a start. She just wants numbers to swell the scene. The tribute of strangers.'

'I am looking forward to it,' said Gianni. 'I think it will be fun.'

Artemis ignored him, trying to do her best to seem as if pleasure was the last thing on her mind. But her performance was hardly convincing. Duxbury noticed it.

Caroline began to clear away the dishes. Dinner had been

singularly uninspiring: tinned mulligatawny soup, followed by anaemic chicken and lettuce, which, in their journey to Anguilla, had plainly not travelled first class. She wished she had been able to produce something better. How would they all manage if she went off to Virgin Gorda? Her father could perhaps make do with tins of corned beef from the Galaxy Supermarket, and be satisfied with that. But what about Gianni, who had been brought up to eat in the Italian style, what on earth would he think? What did he think already? He had played with his food at dinner – he had done everything except eat it with gusto. Perhaps he already despised them for eating such ghastly food. He had done Charles's cooking for him, in the narrow space of the yacht's galley, and she imagined that he had done it very well indeed. She pictured him being inventive with dried *funghi porcini*.

The plates were cleared away, and the four of them sat at the darkened table on the verandah, the empty hours before they could decently go to bed looming ahead of them. They seemed to Artemis to be like Agatha Christie characters: disparate people united in artificial circumstances – on a train, or a Nile steamship, or in a country house – just waiting to be stirred into life and action by the upstairs maid stumbling over the body in the library. Until that opportune discovery should come, they had no *raison d'être*, but were doomed to attempt false little conversations, and condemned to act according to type. This was what they were now doing. She was no longer a person, but merely a type – the frustrated female.

'Perhaps we should play bridge,' she said, remembering that was how the Queen of Crime kept her characters busy when they had nothing else to do.

'I'd like to,' said Gianni, maddeningly enthusiastic.

'Do you play?' she asked coldly, sure he couldn't.

'Yes. Carlo was very keen. I played with him when we were in Grenada.'

'Does Charles play bridge?' asked Caroline, with interest, realising how little she knew of him.

'Then let's play bridge,' said Artemis, the iron entering her soul.

She felt sure that whatever his pretensions, Gianni was bound to be a very bad player indeed. This was a weak point, and at bridge she would defeat him.

'Ordinary kitchen bridge,' said Duxbury, smiling, sensing blood.

Caroline obediently hunted for the cards.

'Shall we cut for partners?' she asked diplomatically, when she had found them.

'No,' said Artemis. 'I'll partner Gianni.'

She knew that one could never castigate a bad opponent, only a bad partner. 'Why didn't you bid your spades?' or 'Couldn't you see that I wanted you to lead a club?' lost much of their sting, if such mistakes had been made to your advantage; only when they had lost you the game did such taunts have the power to strike home.

Down they sat; they cut for dealer and Duxbury dealt. Gianni smiled while the cards were dealt, ever agreeable; Artemis was stony-faced; Caroline felt that she had been unwittingly re-cruited to witness a duel. Only her father seemed to be enjoying himself.

'No bid,' said Duxbury crisply, having considered his cards.

Artemis looked at her hand: did she have thirteen points? It was four for an ace, three for a king, two for a queen, and one for a jack. She did some mental arithmetic, looking at the smug little pictures. Not quite thirteen points. But it was such ages since she had played bridge; she felt that something very clever was ex-pected of her, without knowing quite what, and already sensing that whatever it was, the time for guessing it was fast running out.

'One heart,' she said, seeing that she did have at least four of them.

'No bid,' said Caroline.

Now it was Gianni's turn. He had a remarkably good hand, one of the best he had ever held. There were nineteen points in all.

His partner had to have at least thirteen. Their opponents had eight points between them. Perhaps it was worth taking the risk.

'Six hearts,' he said.

That meant twelve tricks and Artemis had to make them. He had, as the phrase went, left her in it. A look at her own hand was not reassuring. Her best heart was a jack. Her fate was rapidly sealed: the ace of trumps from her father and the king from her sister decided things at once.

'You opened on twelve points,' said Gianni accusingly, when it was all over.

She did not deign to reply. There was no logical defence to be made.

'A hundred above the line to us,' noted Duxbury. 'Your deal, Artemis.'

On they played for two more hours. The game soon became a nightmare for Artemis. The next hand was equally disastrous, as was the one after it. She even found herself feeling that her elementary knowledge of the game was slipping away from her. It was like one of those dreams one wakes from sweating, in which it seems one has forgotten some daily skill, like driving, and is hurtling down a motorway at eighty miles an hour. In just this manner did Artemis feel she was losing control of the game; sometimes bidding too high; sometimes bidding when she ought not to bid at all; and sometimes not bidding when she ought to have done so. And all the time, savouring her discomfort, Gianni sat opposite her like a sphinx, wrapped in an inscrutable smile, watching her discomfort, gently pointing out her mistakes, his very gentleness driving her to the edge of misery. He was doing to her what she had hoped to do to him. Her father, too, sat there, savouring her discomfort, watching the stranger in their midst humiliating his daughter.

By the time the rubber ended, and the post-mortem began, it seemed to Artemis that the adding up of the scores was pointless. She had lost. As for the post-mortem, the details the others were discussing were beyond her, flown from her mind; she could not remember who had had what card; all was swallowed up in the bitterness of defeat. Something had become clear to her now, the same fact that always dawned on struggling generals in their blackest hours. Even Napoleon had felt it: no matter how hard one strove, how stubbornly one endured, the battle was lost, and further resistance could not alter the result, but only delay it. Surrender was inevitable. He had beaten her. It was all the more galling because she knew she had wanted to be beaten. Her own nature had betrayed her. All that now remained was the when and the how of the suing for terms.

Her father went to bed. Caroline sat with them on the veran-dah, once again doing her social duty and attempting to be conversational, but with little success. Her words hung in the thick night air, struggled for a moment, and then drowned in the silence. Artemis felt beyond any effort. She sat on, weakly, feeling the blood circulate in her body, like some alien life-force.

'My dear,' said her sister, 'I think you must be ill.'

'Do I look ill?' she asked, without any real interest.

'Perhaps you have had too much sun.'

They were both so fair, that this seemed a possible explanation. Gianni was looking at her too.

'Why are you looking at me?' she asked.

He was beginning to feel sorry for her but had not the heart to say it.

The love-affair was ending, before it had begun. There was something pitiful about her defeat. He would never love her now as he had loved others. He was beginning to feel a new sensation, a guilty revulsion. He had done this to her, in conjunction with her father. They had taken away her freedom, deprived her of her humanity, and in the process taken the life out of her. What he had wanted was now losing its charm, now that it had become possible. It was depressing.

Caroline sensed something.

'Human relationships are so complicated,' she said. 'We need some expert to come and tell us how to live, what to do.'

'That's the sort of thing Judy says,' said Artemis. 'I want to go to bed.'

She limped away.

'Don't blame me,' said Gianni, when she had gone. 'It is all beyond our control.'

For he now knew that it was Duxbury who was in control.

XIII

The day of the party had arrived.

Demmer, sent down by his wife, was surveying Miss Churchill's yacht through binoculars from the jetty at Sandy Ground. The Canon and Judy stood either side of him.

'I can't see anything going on,' said Her Majesty's Commissioner at length. 'Want a look, Canon?'

'Perhaps they are all still asleep,' said the Canon, once he had had his look.

'Perhaps they are all dead,' suggested Judy. 'Perhaps they all took LSD last night and jumped overboard to be eaten by the sharks. I don't think they can have been wiped out by botulism or salmonella; that hardly ever happens to hedonists. It's the poor who generally die of eating the wrong things. Perhaps the simplest thing of all has happened; they suddenly realised how pointless their pleasure-seeking yacht life was, and committed mass suicide.'

'You're so morbid,' said the Canon admiringly. 'I wish I could be. It puts things in perspective.'

'It comes from reading the *Catholic Herald*,' she said.

'I'd like to know how many people are on board,' said Demmer, trying to steer the conversation away from despair and death, and back to the serious topic of the party.

'How many did you see?' asked the Canon.

'Two or three. I should have asked the captain who took me out in the launch to ask them to show their passports. That's what my wife said I ought to have done.'

'It is odd that they haven't been ashore,' said the Canon.

'Imagine just floating there, like a painted ship on a painted ocean.'

'Of course, we would go mad,' said Judy, generously including Demmer in her plural. 'But less sensitive people ...'

'Well,' said Demmer, with a note of finality, putting away his binoculars.

'Drink?' suggested Judy. 'It is past noon – just.'

Demmer considered.

'My wife will be waiting for me,' he said. He thought of her, and the ghastly Peacock. 'Yes,' he said. 'I think I will.'

They moved into the quiet darkness of the bar. Judy wrote their entries into her book; twenty dollars for Demmer, and five for the Canon. What a lot of drinking they all did on this island, she thought suddenly. And tonight there was a party.

'I hate parties,' she said.

'I am beginning to hate the idea of this one,' said Demmer candidly, thinking now how his wife and Peacock would fawn over Miss Churchill, who was only an actress; it seemed so demeaning.

'It is a thing for the young,' said the Canon, wondering what there would be to eat and drink, and whether people would be openly consuming LSD. Did one smoke LSD? Would they realise he was a clergyman?

'I can't think why we are going,' said Judy.

'But we are,' said Demmer. 'The police launch will be there to ferry us out from eight o'clock onwards.'

'The very idea of a police launch makes me feel like a criminal,' said Judy, remembering her denunciation that had got Charles into trouble with a guilty shiver.

'We owe so much to the police,' said Demmer in best official mode. 'The captain was very helpful when I spoke to him about it. I wouldn't trust anyone else to handle that boat. The yacht must be a good mile out from the jetty.'

'And then we'll have to get back again,' said the Canon. 'I hope no one will be sick over the side,' he added, remembering how, as a young curate fresh from Oxford, he had supervised

194

parish outings; and how the younger altar boys would always sneak off and drink cider, and throw up in the bus coming back.

'It's all arranged,' said Demmer, in a spirit of colonial efficiency, thinking that any embarrassing hitches would surely be caused by Duxbury, and no one else.

Bright, bright was the sun. Under its rays Caroline and Artemis had crept away towards the beach at Blowing Point, to sit by the sea, white figures disappearing into the heat of mid-morning.

Their father sat on the verandah, sipping a glass of iced water. Opposite was Gianni, shirtless.

'My daughters are very pale,' said Duxbury, watching them recede into the distance.

'Yes,' said Gianni, who, being Italian, associated paleness with ill health.

'Then you have noticed,' said Duxbury.

'Yes,' replied Gianni.

He had noticed. Duxbury was dark, and he never went into the sun. Their mother must have been a light-skinned woman, one of those faded Englishwomen, with flesh so translucent that you could see blue-grey veins underneath it. The pity of it, he thought. All the old racial prejudices that he had grown up with now assailed him: dark people – the Calabrians, the Sicilians – were violent and dishonest, akin to the Arabs; civilisation and kindness came from the North. Duxbury was darker than any Calabrian in this harsh morning light, even in the shade of the verandah. To whom had these pale northern women fallen? What had they suffered at his hands?

'You're tired,' said Duxbury.

'Yes,' said Gianni, wishing he could say something else. But Duxbury reduced you to helpless agreement. He thought of Charles – blond good Charles. He had really not treated Charles well. But it was too late for regrets now: he had thrown his lot in with Duxbury. Charles would never have him back, he thought, attributing to his English friend a sense of Italian honour.

195

'Did you sleep with my daughter last night?' asked Duxbury conversationally.

'No,' said Gianni.

'Any particular reason?'

Gianni felt a piercing sense of pity for her just then; but this was not something he could tell Duxbury; for he pitied her for having such a father. He shrugged, and looked away.

'Did you sleep with Charles?' asked Duxbury lightly.

'Of course not,' said Gianni. 'There was no need for that.'

'I want you to sleep with Artemis,' said Duxbury coldly, as if outlining some unpleasant duty.

'And if she doesn't want to?' he asked, fearing what the reply would be.

'You're not afraid of her, are you?'

'No. Of course not. But if she is unwilling …'

'What has choice got to do with it?' asked Duxbury.

Duxbury turned his attention to his glass of water, and took a delicate sip. Gianni realised that he was in the presence of evil.

'It's all arranged,' said Caroline, later that morning, a note of entreaty in her voice. 'You can't back out now; you're expected.'

'But this actress woman doesn't even know who I am,' said Duxbury reasonably. 'How on earth can she be expecting me? If I don't turn up she can hardly miss me.'

'But the Demmers, they'd notice.'

'The Demmers. Common little man, and what a ghastly wife.'

'And Peacock.'

'Another reason to stay at home. I've never liked Bryan Peacock. I don't think I'd even cross Norham Gardens to speak to him. Why on earth should I go out to a yacht to do so? And I don't have a thing to wear. Will Demmer be wearing a pith helmet, do you think?'

'Oh, honestly,' said Caroline. 'Judy will be there. You like her.'

'I've met her once. She's nuts.'

'Well, she likes you.'

196

'I told you she was nuts. Judy indeed. I can't be socialising with people called Judy at my time of life.'

'The police launch is perfectly safe, you know,' said Caroline, trying another tack, sensing this was the real problem. 'It's not a pleasure boat – it's dependable. The police use it all the time, and the captain will be handling it. I asked.'

'The captain? The one who arrested me and Gianni and Charles? I'd like to see him again,' said Duxbury. 'They used to have police launches in Trinidad. I don't suppose you have heard of the Floating Corpse Murder, have you? Have I ever told you about Boysie Singh?'

'Frequently.'

'I must be getting boring in my old age. I am far too old for drinks parties with people I've never met and will never see again.'

'If he doesn't want to go, leave him here,' said Artemis, coming into the room. 'Why force him?'

'Oh ...' said Caroline, wordlessly miserable. It was too bad of Artemis to take her father's part. She could have supported her. But when had Artemis ever done what was expected of her? She wanted her father to go to the party – quite why, she was not sure. But all those people were going to be there – Peacock, the old lecher; Mrs Demmer; the Canon; Charles. It might be awkward; they had all seen too much of each other recently; they all expected something of her. Some crisis lay ahead: and now her father, who ought to be there as some beneficent background presence, was refusing to go.

'I'll be fine here,' Duxbury was saying. 'Gianni and I can do a little work while you are off enjoying yourselves.'

Artemis pretended not to be listening.

'I am sure Gianni would rather come with us,' said Caroline, sensing an opening. 'Gianni!' she called.

The beautiful young man appeared.

'Yes?' he asked gravely, sensing he was stepping into a quarrel.

'You are coming tonight, aren't you?' asked Caroline, while Artemis idly picked up a book.

197

'Of course,' said Gianni. 'I am looking forward to it.'

'Oh, good,' said Caroline.

Gianni withdrew.

'I don't see why you had to ask him,' said Artemis bitterly, still remembering her defeat at bridge of the previous night.

Caroline looked hopeless. Now she had annoyed Artemis.

Duxbury was silent. He had lost his appetite for upsetting Caroline. It hardly seemed the moment to point out that Gianni was his research assistant, paid to work the word processor, and not to enjoy himself. Caroline had outflanked him for once. He remembered his deep-seated horror of the sea. He sighed. To stay away would be impossible. Free will and choice were illusions after all.

'I'll go,' he said. 'But don't expect me to dress.'

Having said that, he knew that to go with Artemis and Gianni in tow would present an unlooked-for opportunity. He gazed silently at his younger daughter. She was still pretending to read a book; but he had hurt her all the same.

Caroline felt she had won something of a victory. He would go, despite the fact that he hated boats, and crossing water. She knew he had an almost obsessive hatred of the sea – but this was not something she shared, and thus not something she could take seriously. It was merely a fact about her father that she carried in the back of her mind, something that she put down to his Trinidadian birth. He was a white West Indian, something most people did not realise. Even she was more used to thinking of him as an Oxford man; he had left the land of his birth long before she had been born.

She looked out to sea. She had never felt any curiosity about Trinidad, or the family he had left behind there.

'Why do people come to the Caribbean?' she asked idly.

'Because it is expensive,' said Artemis. 'And boring. Like Switzerland.'

'One can swim,' said Caroline. 'But only the tourists do that. You never see the Anguillians swimming, do you?'

'They're used to the heat,' said Artemis dully.

'There's something perverse in human nature,' said Caroline. 'Why spend so much money, as tourists do, going to places that only have advertisements to recommend them? Like Barbados.'

'Barbados is beautiful,' said Duxbury. 'Or was. Just like this place. When the tourists arrive here our little paradise will turn into hell. I think I will have to go back to Italy. I want to visit the museum at Tarquinia. And I want to see the tombs at Cerveteri again. Gianni will be a great help there.'

And what about me, thought Caroline. But she would go to Virgin Gorda with Charles. The coming of Gianni and Charles had changed everything – or was it simply that the old patterns were rearranging themselves? Would anything ever really change?

Artemis was looking glum, as she had done all the morning. She was oppressed by visions of her father rooting around in old tombs, accompanied by Gianni. Archaeology was the ideal ex-cuse for promiscuity. All sorts of things went on during field trips. Was this her father's last cruel joke, to pinch Gianni for himself after dangling him in front of her nose?

'Come on, dear,' she heard her sister saying. 'We really must think about what we can wear for this party tonight.'

Artemis had promised her the use of her blue silk dress, but in the event, Caroline did not wear it. Instead she wore a white one, which, when Judy saw her, made her think of ghosts, so thin and ethereal did she look in it, standing there on the darkened jetty, like a creature from another world. Judy felt a slight tingle of envy: for Caroline had achieved the effect seemingly without effort, while Judy had spent most of her life striving for something similar and had failed. A white frock in the tropical night air was just the thing, and she felt driven to say so.

'Don't,' replied Caroline. 'It's Artemis's anyway. She lent it to me.'

'Oh, clothes,' said Judy, looking at her with great sad eyes. 'The first thing that people did after the Fall was put on clothes and quarrel.'

'I wish we had quarrelled,' said Caroline, making sure that the others were out of hearing, confiding in Judy. 'But we haven't. We are merely eaten away with a feeling of impending doom. None of the others seemed to want to come.'

The darkness was too thick for Judy to be able to study their faces, to see if this were true. But she sensed that something was wrong. Demmer and his lady had already gone out to the yacht in the police launch. There was nothing to do but wait in the dark for the sound of the returning boat. Far out at sea, like Cleopatra's barge, Miss Churchill's yacht burned on the waters. The moon had not yet risen.

Presently the Canon arrived, large and jovial, intent on having a good time, dressed in a Hawaiian shirt.

'I rang Mrs Demmer and she told me it wasn't formal dress,' he said a little defensively, noticing Judy studying his shirt. 'Where is Charles?'

'Somewhere around,' said Caroline. 'In fact, that's him, over there, under the trees.'

At some distance she could make out a paler shadow.

'I'll go and talk to him,' she said.

'I am lurking in the shadows,' Charles said as she approached. 'I wanted to study the scene from a distance, to look at you as if through binoculars: the Canon's shirt, Judy's dress, your father ... they make me want to feel remote.'

'I wish to God I could be,' she said. 'I have the awful feeling that I can't go to Virgin Gorda with you after all.'

'Why not?' he asked.

'Artemis,' she replied. 'She was hysterical this afternoon, while we were getting ready for the party. She says something awful will happen to her if I leave her with Gianni and my father, alone. She's never been like that before. It's unnerving. And there is something wrong with Gianni too. I've felt a difference in him.'

'Gianni may have bitten off more than he can chew,' said Charles, a little sourly.

'You don't understand,' she said suddenly. 'My mother used to get like that – like Artemis is now. My father has this way of upsetting people. I used to think she was immune to it, but – '

She was interrupted by the sound of the motor boat.

'We'd better go,' said Charles. 'I suppose we've got to enjoy ourselves, even if we don't much feel like it.'

The police launch, complete with policeman, had drawn up at the jetty. It was their old friend the captain of the *Warspite*, who greeted them heartily. Caroline, forgetting earlier concerns, helped her father into the boat. They all got in, the Canon last, the boat lying low in the water under his weight.

'Aren't we a little low in the water?' asked Charles, who knew something about boats.

'You want to get out?' asked the captain a little brusquely, remembering this breaker of the law, the naked imperialist. In the captain's book there was something very arrogant about white men who strolled around with no clothes on.

'I think I will,' said Charles, noting the look of fear on Duxbury's face, and anxious the Canon shouldn't try to do so, lest he capsize them in the process.

'And I will too,' said Gianni, quickly following him.

The engine now stalled. The captain turned his attention to starting it, pulled cords and swore. Gradually the engine was coaxed back to life. A little uncertainly the frail craft began to pull away from the jetty, and they watched Duxbury, his daughters and the Canon being ferried away. Duxbury's eyes were closed.

'I wanted to talk to you,' said Gianni, putting a hand on to Charles's white sleeve.

'Well?' asked Charles.

'I feel foolish,' confessed Gianni.

Charles looked at him. Gianni was dressed in an expensive summer suit, the sort that Italians loved. His appearance was immaculate, smooth; his expression sheepish.

'You are foolish,' said Charles. 'What's made you realise it?'

'Duxbury is strange,' said Gianni.

'I thought that might happen,' said Charles. 'You mean he's told you that you're to be more than just a research assistant? It wouldn't surprise me in the least.'

'No, not that; it is worse than that. He has suggested that I rape Artemis.'

'That's illegal,' said Charles, remembering what Caroline had just said, but putting it out of his mind.

'Is that all you can say?' asked Gianni. 'It is much worse than illegal. He is her father; he's prostituting her. I don't want to stay in that house any longer.'

'Then don't,' said Charles, fearing what was coming.

'You'd take me to Virgin Gorda?'

'No. I wouldn't,' said Charles. 'I have other plans. I think you have got to get yourself out of this mess.'

'Oh, Carlo,' pleaded Gianni. 'If not for me, then for her.'

But Charles was thinking of the plans he had made, and how Gianni was fast becoming an incubus. He made no reply. Silence descended on them. Gianni lit a cigarette.

'Have one,' he said to Charles.

Silently, Charles took a cigarette, and let Gianni light it.

'If anything happens,' said Gianni, 'it won't be my fault. I tried to get away.'

'You are over-dramatising things,' said Charles, dismissively.

'You think that they are normal, those girls and their father,' said Gianni. 'But they are not.'

A distant sound came to them over the sea. It was the police launch. They waited in silence until it should arrive.

XIV

Duxbury's journey out to the yacht had been one of acute discomfort, passed with eyes tightly shut, wedged between Caroline and the Canon. It had brought back to him all the horrors of his youth, when he had been carried out on to rowing boats by his nurse, while his mother had stood by, watching. His mother had believed the old myth, that phobias could be exorcised only by being experienced. It hadn't worked at all. His hatred of the sea had remained with him all his life, and to it he had added another hatred, namely that of the woman who had so heartlessly condemned him to suffer the horror of boats. She had sat or stood on innumerable beaches, idly smoking an elegant cigarette, she who had had the power to rescue him from torment. But she had done nothing. She had looked upon his suffering as an uncaring God might have done, with distant and remote indifference.

The deck of the yacht was at least more solid, more like dry land; there, while the others went to meet their hostess, he paused and tried to regain his composure, watching the captain put out to sea again. Caroline stood with him. She had never known her grandmother. How could he explain to her what he now felt? But he had to explain.

'There's a reason for everything,' he said. 'My mother made a mistake when she married my father. She realised too late that she had married beneath her, and that he and I were beneath her. She couldn't forgive us for that.'

'But that wasn't true, surely?' said Caroline, who knew that her grandmother had only been a doctor's daughter from British Guiana, and that her grandfather had been quite rich, in an age where money had mattered.

'My dear, there are many types of snobbery. My father wasn't allowed to join the Union Club. There was too much of the tar brush in him. She thought she was doing well for herself, but when she got to Trinidad she realised that she hadn't done so well, and that she'd never get into the Union Club.'

'Is being a member of the Union Club so very important?' asked Caroline.

'Yes,' said Duxbury. 'The paler the better. That was why I married your mother, because she was so pale. I wanted beautiful white children. I was a snob; I inherited that from my mother.'

This was the truth, the only truth that mattered. There were other truths, but they seemed unimportant right now. It was true that he was dark, and that this more than anything else had given him his strange physical beauty, and preserved him from the ravages of ageing. It was true that few people apart from himself had ever thought of him as of mixed race, or that such a thing could matter. But these were truths that now made no sense, no matter how true they might be. He had been a snob. He had ruined his life for snobbery. All his life he had felt himself shut out of the magic circle, the Union Club, and all his efforts had been designed to get into it; and when it had not accepted him, as it had seemed, he had spent his efforts trying to destroy that same Union Club. But the effort had not been worth it. His mother might not have loved him; but he had hated himself more effectively than anyone else could have done. He had wasted his life.

Caroline, who did not understand the minutiae of race, did not understand him.

'We must go up to the party,' she said.

'Yes, the party,' he replied, hearing the sound of a piano from the upper deck. All his life he had felt excluded from the party. Now was his moment to go up to it; but he felt no enthusiasm. What did all these people have in common, apart from a love of alcohol? Why had they come all this way, to meet a stranger like Miss Churchill? Surely they could have sat comfortably at home and drunk rum and Coca Cola there, instead of making this uncomfortable journey through the hot night? It was as if they were afraid to be alone with themselves.

'You're not seasick, are you?' said Caroline.

'No. Not seasick. Just sick of the sea. Sick of life.'

'The party will cheer you up,' said Caroline, full of faith.

Obediently he followed her up to the upper deck, his heart wracked by despair, knowing that nothing would ever cheer him up again. The hollow emptiness of life was too much to be taken away by drinks or light conversation. There were no anaesthetics for such pains. All had been determined, even before his birth.

Within moments they were being presented to Miss Churchill. A severely beautiful secretary, in steel-framed spectacles and a chignon, was asking their names and making introductions. Miss Churchill was half sitting and half reclining on a deck chair. She had been asleep all day – the sun did strange things to her skin, she thought, and caused premature ageing, and for this reason she was a nocturnal animal; when she came out at night, she demanded entertainment. So far she had been disappointed: the Demmers, Peacock and Artemis, who was too young and too pretty, had all been introduced and found wanting. As for the Canon, she found that clergymen reminded her of death. Judy was preferable – being of a similar age, but older to look at. But now here was Duxbury: grave, thoughtful and darkly handsome. She had found her amusement.

'Is this everyone?' she asked her secretary, who was called Gibbon.

'No, Miss Churchill. There is another boat load.'

'Well, don't just stand there; see to the drinks, Gibbon.'

Gibbon saw to the drinks. Miss Churchill surveyed her guests with a fishy stare.

'I hate parties,' she said to Duxbury.

'So do I,' said Duxbury.

'And I,' added Judy.

'Then why did you come?' she asked.

'We were forced to,' said Duxbury, knowing now that he spoke for the whole of sad humanity, not just for Judy. 'Everyone else was coming, and we felt compelled to come too. You know what crowds are like, I am sure. They have no individual minds; same with us. Other people make our decisions; we can't think for ourselves.'

'God, I know what you mean,' said Miss Churchill with candour. 'I remember marrying my third husband thinking "I don't want to do this" all the time; but I did it all the same. There's something that carries you along. Somewhere you made a decision, and that is that; you have to go along with it. Just like that poor bitch Lady Macbeth. I did that play once in Brussels. God, what a place. Now who is this? Gibbon!'

'Mr Charles Broughton, and Giovanni Battista Colombo,' said Gibbon, with admirable self-control, perhaps understanding that her employer treated her like this out of habit rather than genuine dislike.

'Well, get them a drink. Leave Mr Broughton with me, and take Giovanni Battista What's-his-name to meet the blonde over there.'

Gianni was shepherded over to Artemis. Miss Churchill made Charles sit on a chair next to hers, and put a proprietorial hand on his arm. Duxbury studied the young man's arm, watching the actress stroke it gently. It was a pale fair arm, covered in blond hairs, bleached by the sun. He remembered the way Charles had undressed to swim from the jetty, and the sight of his white body in the silver light of the moon. The thought of it made him jealous even now. That had been miscalled indecent exposure. Artemis, too, was a white goddess, white as the marbles in the Vatican Museum. Whiteness was perfection: that was the opinion of the crowd. How different the world might have been, if one could have chosen one's colour.

'I knew some Broughtons once,' said Miss Churchill, and proceeded to get on with a series of anecdotes, confused fragments of forgotten histories about bearers of the name who had lived somewhere in Africa, and been made into the subject of some film. In this way she hoped to lift the hideous pall of boredom that constantly threatened her existence.

206

Miss Gibbon, meanwhile, was seeing to the other guests. The two young women, she noticed with steely compassion, were stuck with the clergyman, who was wearing the floral shirt. The young Italian was with the Demmers and Peacock, having shown some aversion to the blonde Miss Churchill had commanded her to introduce him to. Not that he seemed to find the Demmers and Peacock better company. His eyes were wandering around the deck, seeking an escape route. Noticing that her employer was at least for the moment amused, Miss Gibbon decided to join the group around Demmer.

A conversation was in progress. Peacock was talking about sharks. Demmer was listening with diplomatic politeness, while his wife gave the impression that she had not come to the party for such a purpose. Miss Gibbon came and stood amongst them, bestowing her attention on Peacock, joining his audience. But she could feel Gianni's eyes on her. Her attention seemed quite given to what Peacock was saying, but Gianni's experience told him that she was aware that she was being watched. Something about the curve of her cheek betrayed her; something about the way she held her glass told him that she knew she was an object of interest to him. While Peacock spoke about the remarkable sensory perceptions of the Great White Shark, Gianni sensed a message from the secretary assistant.

'Gibbon, Gibbon, see to the food,' shouted Miss Churchill from afar.

Gibbon made her excuses and went below, intent, it seemed, on her employment. Presently a waiter appeared on deck, with a tray of canapés. This created the necessary disturbance to break up the two standing groups and make them one. Caroline could not regret it, even if it did mean being brought into Peacock's orbit. Artemis still seemed miserable. It would need someone of Ciriaco's goodness to heal her sister.

Duxbury took a biscuit decorated with lobster meat and put it into his mouth.

'We can't get lobster on Anguilla,' said Judy sadly, watching him. 'It is all exported.'

'Darling, how wretched for you,' said Miss Churchill, brimming with sympathy.

'I can't think why anyone lives in the West Indies at all,' said Duxbury. 'No lobsters, no nothing. That is why all the West Indians have gone to places like London and Canada, places with supermarkets.'

Miss Churchill winced. She had spent forty years in the theatrical profession, four decades of intrigue and hysteria; her luxury yacht was her reward; and here she was, discussing supermarkets with strangers. Why did everything have to turn to the dust and ashes of boredom so quickly?

'Where is Gibbon?' she asked the waiter angrily.

'Seeing to the food, madam,' replied the man, giving the answer he had been primed to give in such an eventuality.

'Tell her to come up here,' said Miss Churchill. 'There's a chef to see to the food.'

'Where did you find Miss Gibbon?' asked Charles, wondering who this woman could be, who acted as assuager of that most deadly disease, terminal boredom.

'It sounds like a species,' observed Duxbury.

'I found her in a magazine,' said Miss Churchill grandly. 'She came with the most excellent testimonials.'

'But what does she do?' asked Charles.

'I can imagine it all,' said Judy, before the actress had time to reply. 'She's a cross between a James Bond girl and a highly efficient dentist. What I can't imagine is what it must be like to have everything under such perfect control. I can't grasp order: I could never even work the pressure cooker my husband gave me. I was always afraid it would blow up. I am not equipped for modern life; Miss Gibbon is.'

'It's her job,' said Amelia Churchill. 'Ah, there she is!'

Miss Gibbon appeared as if from nowhere, looking icy in the night air.

'What have you been doing?' she was asked.

'I have been examining sausage rolls below,' said Gibbon.

'Sausage rolls! This isn't a bloody garden fête. Go and throw them overboard at once. And then come back immediately.'

Miss Gibbon went to do as she was told.

'Do you hate modern life too, dear?' Miss Churchill asked Charles, now turning her attention to him.

'You must excuse me,' said Duxbury, getting up, noticing that Miss Gibbon had come back, but that Gianni had unaccountably disappeared. He got up and made for the lower decks, as if intent on looking for a lavatory.

Gianni was in a cabin below, a cabin that belonged to Miss Gibbon. He had followed her to the kitchens, and then into her cabin, where a few passionate kisses and no words had been exchanged. Then she had been called away. Now he stood in her cabin, idly examining its contents, waiting for her to come back. His eyes took in the well-appointed luxury, his fingers examined the texture of the sheets on the bed; he opened her wardrobe and looked at her clothes; he scanned the very few books the room contained; and finally he paid close attention to what was on her dressing table. He was like a careful visitor to a museum, intent on missing nothing, examining even the smallest exhibits with painstaking scrutiny. It was odd the way his mind could do this. He hardly thought now of what he was there for, as he examined the little bottles of nail varnish and the various skin creams. Even his sexual desires had gone into suspended animation.

Eventually, having looked at everything, he was curious to know what had happened to Miss Gibbon. He did not want to be missed from the party for no reason. Perhaps he should go back up, and take some other opportunity, should it present itself, to rendezvous with Miss Gibbon. Already Miss Gibbon seemed a rather remote prospect. He stuck his head out into the corridor, to see if she were coming; there Duxbury saw him.

'What are you doing down here?' asked Duxbury.

'Just exploring,' lied Gianni.

'All alone?' asked Duxbury.

'Yes,' said Gianni, feeling Duxbury's eyes look past him into the room, at the crumpled counterpane on the bed, becoming aware that he might have lipstick on his cheek, very much fearing that he had been detected in his lie, wishing he had thought before he had spoken.

Duxbury was silent. So Gianni was lying, that was clear. One expected Italians to lie; all those nasty villains in Shakespeare and Webster made careers out of lying. But what was one lie, after a lifetime of untruth? How could he be offended?

'You're awful,' he said, suddenly feeling a wave of revulsion, more against himself than Gianni.

'What have I done?' asked Gianni angrily, guiltily. 'I haven't done what you have done.'

'And what have I done?' replied Duxbury. 'Am I so very bad?'

'You've ruined Artemis's life,' said Gianni. 'And you want to ruin mine.'

'A fair estimate,' said Duxbury, imagining how it would have turned out, had Gianni slept with Artemis, how he would have to live with the burden of her broken life, and carry the weight of her unhappiness in his stead. 'But you are too kind,' he said, with sudden self-lacerating savagery. 'I killed my wife.'

'Nonsense. She was run over crossing the road.'

'I killed the love that was in her first; and then I killed her happiness. But she only realised she had to leave me, when she caught me with Artemis. That was what I had to do to show her that there was no such thing as love.'

Gianni felt in his pockets for a packet of Marlborough. He was too shocked to reply. Was there such a thing as love? Was this love, this furtive encounter with Miss Gibbon, amidst so much floating luxury? Why did he feel the need for these dismal pleasures?

Steps came down the corridor. It was Miss Gibbon.

'Oh,' she said, realising she was interrupting something.

'I have to go,' said Gianni, knowing he had to get away.

Miss Gibbon followed him down the corridor, realising, with vagueness yet certainty, that there would be no pleasures for her that evening, and that she had better get back to work.

Duxbury was left alone, standing in the door of the cabin,

looking at the feminine impedimenta that cluttered the room, contemplating the lives he had ruined. His wife's, Artemis's, Caroline's perhaps, but chiefly his own. And once again he found himself being dragged on to the pleasure boat that had terrified him as a child, and saw his mother, a distant figure, in white, smoking a nonchalant cigarette on the beach, she who could speak a word that would save him, but who was forever silent, deaf to his cries. The only way to exorcise a fear was to experience it. He wondered. Nothing could save him now except oblivion.

Gianni stumbled out on to the upper deck once more. He was aware that Miss Gibbon was following him, somewhat puzzled, but nevertheless sure that something had changed. And something had changed. He knew now of the injustice that he had done to Artemis. He approached her. She was there, glass in hand, talking to the Canon, her vigilant sister next to her.

'I've decided not to be your father's research assistant after all,' he said to them, forcing out the truth, in case someone, who but Duxbury, should by some demonic power force him to change his mind.

Caroline looked too surprised to speak.

Artemis was confused.

'I will go somewhere else,' said Gianni. 'Back to Italy perhaps. I don't know.'

It was a clear indication that he had given up the struggle, that he was sparing her.

'Did my father tell you you could?' asked Artemis cautiously.

'No. I told him.'

'Good,' she said quietly. Then she turned to the Canon.

'We were just saying,' said the Canon, 'that travel doesn't broaden the mind. I think you are lucky to have Italy to go back to. Some people travel the earth but they never progress because wherever they go they take the same experiences with them. They are always confined.'

'Is escape possible?' asked Artemis, looking out into the black sea and sky, the horizonless distance.

'I bought a yacht to tour the Antilles with just that in mind,' said Charles. 'Hoping for some new life.'

'And isn't there one?' asked Judy.

They were now all gathered in a circle, the six of them who had kept each other company all summer long, and who now that they were at a party with strangers still wanted to talk only to each other.

Was there a new life, wondered Gianni? Could one escape from the ruinous influence of Duxbury? That man was the devil, a ruiner of souls.

'A friend of mine went and found a new life,' said Caroline suddenly. 'But he had the new life in him all the time, I think. He was other-worldly.'

'Who?' asked Artemis, suddenly curious about someone else for once.

'He was called Ciriaco. Silvia's brother. He was a doctor. He used to help refugees. And one day he went to Bosnia.'

'Without telling anyone?' asked Judy, thinking of the saints fleeing their parental homes to seek a better life in the harsh terrain of the religious life.

'Actually, he told me,' said Caroline slowly. 'We were close for a time. He told me he was going to Bosnia, but I didn't understand him, though he did try and say why. I suppose because I didn't understand it at the time, I blotted the memory of it out of my mind.'

'I'd love to go to Bosnia,' said Gianni, 'but I haven't the courage. All those wounded people, and no medical supplies, and the constant threat of renewed war, and the hunger ...'

'It sounds awful,' said Charles.

'It is awful,' said the Canon.

'Is this any better?' asked Judy. 'We've got caviar and champagne, but have we got love and sacrifice and hope and charity?'

Demmer entered the circle, a little apologetically.

212

'Miss Churchill thinks that your father may be locked in the lavatory,' he said to Caroline.

'A case for the fire brigade,' said Charles.

Caroline went slightly pale. It would be just like her father to do this at a party, to create some scandal. She looked around: Miss Gibbon was still in evidence, and of course, so was Miss Churchill. But where was Mrs Demmer?

'Have you asked the staff?' she asked, remembering that there had been a waiter in attendance. Staff tended to help on these occasions, being used to seeing their betters behave appallingly.

Demmer, who was a diplomat, read her mind. It really was too bad. People like Duxbury gave small islands a bad name. In a place like Trinidad or Barbados, it would not have mattered, but here, where everyone knew everyone else, it was shocking. What would everyone think if it got about that Duxbury had committed immoral acts in the middle of a cocktail party at which he and his wife had been present? It would be hard to overlook; and of course that gossip Peacock would be sure to make sure everyone heard about it. But where was his wife? He couldn't see her anywhere.

'Found him yet?' Miss Churchill was asking loudly.

'We can hardly search the boat,' said Demmer under his breath, now realising what his wife's absence could mean. 'Besides, God only knows what we would find.'

Then Mrs Demmer appeared on deck, and nonchalantly joined them, unaware of what they had been thinking. It was one of those moments, in which many minds begin to work in synchrony, along similar lines.

'We think Duxbury may be locked in the lavatory,' Demmer said to his wife.

'He can't be,' she said. 'That's where I've been. Of course, I suppose Miss Churchill has more than one …'

'Where has he got to?' asked Miss Churchill, ignoring this compliment. 'Gibbon, go and look.'

'I saw him below only quarter of an hour ago,' said Gibbon.

'Then look below,' said Miss Churchill.

Demmer, with a premonition of evil, went with her, instructing the others to stay behind. Down they went.

'He was here,' said Miss Gibbon, looking into her cabin. 'At least he was in this corridor. Perhaps he went into the galley to talk to the cooks.'

They went into the galley. But there were no cooks there; the cooks were in a room further on, listening to an evangelical radio station. The kitchen was calm and peaceful, the large table arrayed with food. Only one thing was out of place: on the table, in the midst of the cold plates and the chopping boards and the various sharp knives, was a large droplet of drying blood.

'Call the cooks, and ask them if all their knives are here,' said Demmer, knowing what the answer would be. 'And whoever you've got who sails this boat had better call the police out.'

It had been a very sharp knife. He had tested it on his thumb. Now, far out in the dark deserted sea, blanketed in tropical darkness, comforted by the warmth of the water, he could feel the blood trickling through his veins. Physical sensation, soon to end forever, was heightened. Thus Seneca had died, bleeding slowly to death in his bath-tub. That was the way philosophers went. What was so strange was that he was floating. It was like lying in some huge downy bed, drifting off to sleep, floating away from them all, away from the yacht, into the freedom of death. And his life blood, mingling with the warm Caribbean, would summon the sharks, those ancient monsters of the deep that never slept.

He would not have long to wait now.

The cooks had been listening to Radio Paradise, and had heard nothing. The man who sailed the yacht had been in his cabin, and admitted he had heard a gentle splash, as if someone had been lowering himself into the water from the steps. All the guests had been making too much noise to hear anything. Now, they were plunged into silence.

Gianni was pale and trembling: he could see what had happened, but was unable to speak, in case Demmer formed the wrong conclusions. Thus the last person to have seen Duxbury remained Miss Gibbon.

Demmer approached Caroline.

'We think your father has fallen overboard,' he said.

'He can't swim,' she replied, too shocked to say anything else.

'It's so dark, we can't see anything,' said Demmer, hopelessly. 'I mean the police launch ...'

'I want the Canon to take me home,' said Artemis, who up to now had been silent. 'If the police launch is here, we can go home.'

'Yes, yes, of course,' said Demmer, gesturing to his wife to make herself useful.

Caroline felt she ought to accompany Artemis. The two sisters, assisted by the Canon and Mrs Demmer, made their way down the steps and into the police launch, rather in the manner of women leaving a sinking ship, walking away from tragedy. They were silent, numbed, and moved with uncertainty; and soon they were gone.

'This is the worst party I have ever held,' said Miss Churchill. 'A guest killing himself. He must have been bored.'

'It could have been an accident,' said Charles. 'He had been known to get drunk before this.'

'An accident,' said Demmer gravely, remembering the drop of blood on the kitchen table. 'Yes.' Then he added: 'We will have to search for the body – how, I don't know.'

'You'll have to wait until light,' said Peacock. 'By that time there won't be any body left; not in these waters.'

Demmer looked uncomfortable. Even in death, Duxbury was an embarrassment. A drowning; a corpse eaten by sharks – these were hardly the things to encourage the nascent tourist industry. Perhaps he would be blamed.

Judy felt glum. Everyone was assuming that Duxbury was gone forever, that he had committed suicide. That would be just like a man. Suicides always left complications behind them. This was the final enigma of Duxbury's life; he had preserved his air of mystery to the end. It was the last act of self-indulgence. What on earth had she ever seen in the man? Now, stronger than ever before, she felt the desire for the barren and stony places.

Miss Gibbon was bringing round brandy, with professional solicitude. Gianni wept into his cognac, filling it with large silent tears.

'What on earth is the matter?' asked Charles gently.

'I'm thinking what a waste my life has been up to now,' said Gianni. 'That if Duxbury has killed himself, perhaps I should too.'

This was hardly comforting, thought Charles.

Soon they were ashore again, and, with nowhere else to go, they went and sat in Judy's bar. Demmer had rushed off, with Peacock in attendance, to try to do something – quite what, was not clear. There was a floating corpse to be found – but there was nothing to be done before light. True, the solitary police launch, commanded by the captain of the *Warspite*, could search the waters – but what good would this do? Yet there was no possibility of sleep while the search went on. So they sat in the bar and talked, until it grew light. And as dawn arose, they fell asleep on the benches.

Artemis too was asleep. Mrs Demmer had put her in one of the guest bedrooms and watched her take a tranquilliser; Caroline had refused the pill, but had lain down on the double bed next to her sister. Artemis had been remarkably calm, but Mrs Demmer had assumed that she was the one most affected by what had happened. People always did fuss over Artemis; that had always been the rule – and why should Caroline find the energy to resent it even now?

She didn't sleep, but through the night lay in the dark room, alert, staring at the ceiling, reliving the life she had lived up to now. It came back to her in all its clarity – all the things she had suppressed, all the memories she had deleted. She remembered in particular the day of her mother's death, and how Artemis had reacted then, and how her father had reacted. On that day,

Artemis had not been shocked, or grief-stricken, but merely guilty. She and Duxbury between them had killed her mother. She saw that now. And now Duxbury was dead. She was sure of it. Liberation was at hand.

She was sure; what he had told her on the steps of the yacht as they were going up to the party now made sense. To live without love was the slowest form of suicide. To die by water when you had lived hating the sea was the worst of self-inflicted punishments. Duxbury in death had admitted that he had been wrong. Love was worthwhile after all; it was more than that – it was essential. Now he was gone, they would discover love. Ciriaco had shown the way. Not the love that took you to desolate mountains to work in field hospitals – they weren't brave enough for that – but something quieter and more domestic. A new life was beginning, she felt, watching the shadows lighten, realising dawn was near, comforted by the calm and regular breathing of her sister lying next to her. Not even the knock on the door that would surely come, to announce that no body had been found, that there was no hope, not even that could frighten her now.